THE MEMORY BRACELET

PAMELA RALEIGH

Black Rose Writing | Texas

ISBN: 978-1-68513-639-0
LIBRARY OF CONGRESS CONTROL NUMBER: 2025932011
PUBLISHED BY BLACK ROSE WRITING
www.blackrosewriting.com

Printed in the United States of America
Suggested Retail Price (SRP) $21.95

The Memory Bracelet is printed in Minion Pro

*As a planet-friendly publisher, Black Rose Writing does its best to eliminate unnecessary waste to reduce paper usage and energy costs, while never compromising the reading experience. As a result, the final word count vs. page count may not meet common expectations.

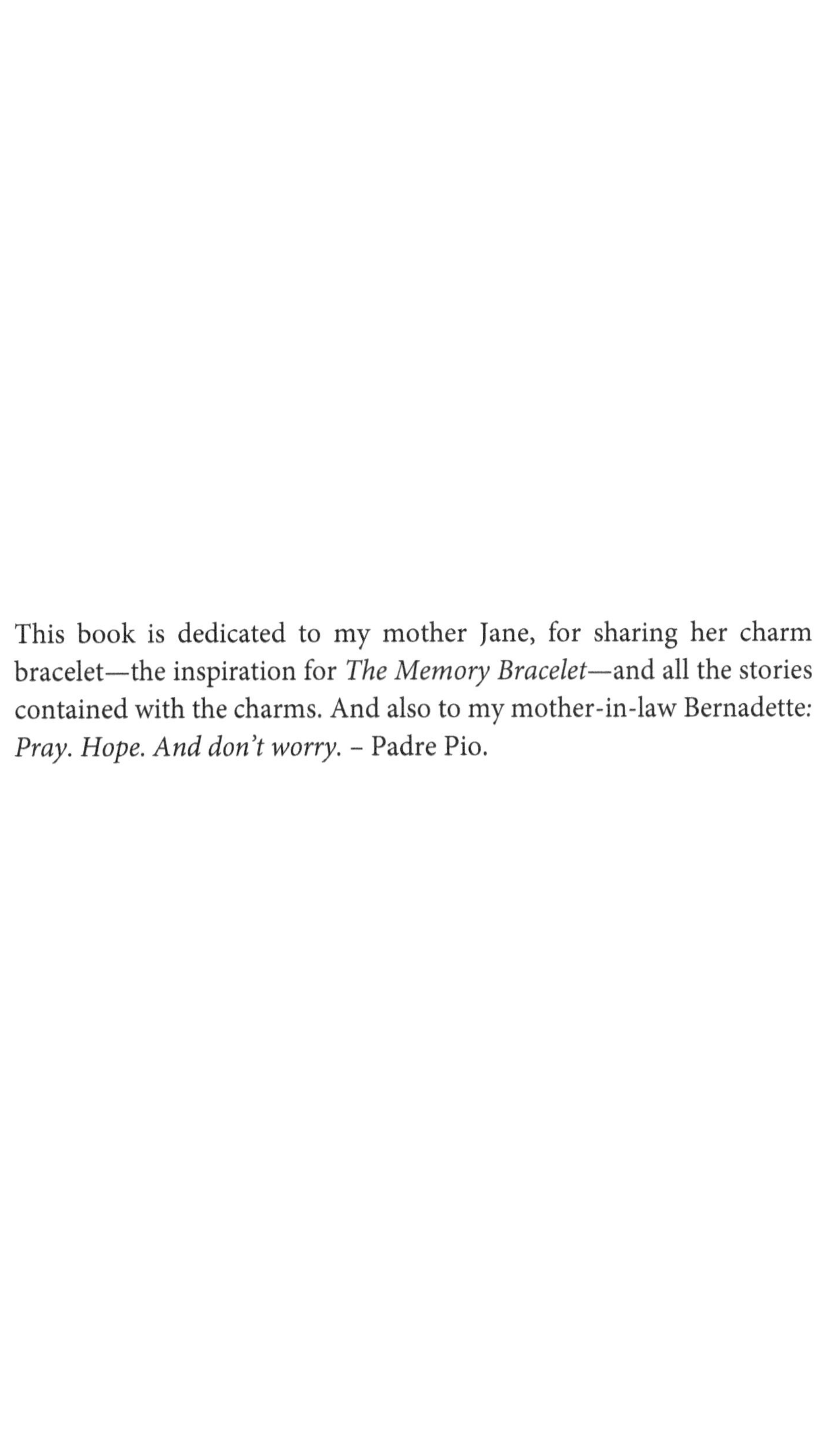

This book is dedicated to my mother Jane, for sharing her charm bracelet—the inspiration for *The Memory Bracelet*—and all the stories contained with the charms. And also to my mother-in-law Bernadette: *Pray. Hope. And don't worry.* – Padre Pio.

THE MEMORY BRACELET

CHAPTER ONE

Tessa

Tessa Wilde stood poised to knock on the door of her grandmother's room at Sunset Shadows Assisted Living Facility. Hand raised, fist closed, she was ready. *Knock,* she told herself. Unclenching her fist, she used her hands to prop herself against the door frame and breathed deeply instead. She didn't want to see the grandmother who'd criticized, judged, and insulted her most of her life. But her sweet mother, Debra, had asked that she check on her grandmother who'd recently moved near Tessa, and she couldn't say no to her mom. Besides, at twenty years old, Tessa should be able to handle an Alzheimer's-ridden woman she hadn't seen in two years. *You've moved on; you've forged a new life in college; you've put the past behind you.*

Her bracelets clanged against one another as they slipped from her wrist to her elbow, silver bangles she wore like a tattoo. She closed her eyes, recentering her courage and tossed her long, blonde—well, currently blue-streaked—hair with a shake of her head. Esther Wilde couldn't hurt Tessa anymore.

She pulled herself as tall as her five feet two inches allowed and adjusted her backpack on her shoulders. As Tessa raised her hand once again to knock, her phone chirped from her back pocket.

Oh, sweet reprieve.

The name on the screen showed Kendra, Tessa's free-spirited, outspoken, currently-purple-haired friend.

"Girl. Where are you?" Kendra asked before Tessa could complete the standard *Hello.*

"Out. Why?" Tessa hadn't shared that her grandmother lived there. Their relationship was not a good one.

"In honor of Valentine's Day coming up, school's showing some old, sappy, love story movie tonight in the student union. Since you like that old-timey stuff, I figured I'd be Tessa Wilde's #1 Friend and suffer through it with you."

"What movie is it?"

Kendra sighed loudly enough for Tessa to hear. "Does it matter? Honestly. You're such a hermit. You need to get out more."

"Kendra, you're not fooling me. Who's running the movie?"

"What do you mean?" she asked, feigning innocence. When Tessa remained silent, Kendra added, "Okay, fine. Jed. He is so hot."

Tessa rolled her eyes despite Kendra's inability to see it, but she smiled inwardly. Kendra might have ulterior motives for accompanying Tessa to see *Love Story* (yes, she knew that movie was showing tonight), but Tessa didn't really care. Kendra was the first friend to encourage Tessa to conform to no one's standards except her own and to choose her own path forward, not someone else's. A nagging worry reminded Tessa that she hadn't done that. She needed to pick a major. And she had to answer her advisor's repeated badgering about it tomorrow.

Tessa touched her nose ring, a tribute to rediscovering her adventurous spirit which had been buried long ago, thanks to her grandmother. "All right, I'll go. But you're gonna bawl when you see Ali MacGraw's got a terminal illness."

"What?" Kendra groaned. After a few seconds, she added, "That just gives Jed reason to comfort me. See you at the Student Union at 6:45 sharp," and she disconnected.

Just then, someone pushing a medical cart started down the hallway toward Tessa. To avoid conversation, Tessa rapped on her grandmother's door, ready to get this one-and-done well check over.

She waited for sounds of movement or that raspy voice she tried to forget. The one that could cut into Tessa's heart. She didn't hear anything. Maybe her grandmother was napping, or at Bingo, or making a craft. *More like directing everyone else how to do it. And telling them how they'd messed it all up,* Tessa added silently.

"Hello!" A tall, brown-skinned woman in a teal uniform waved at Tessa from down the hall where the medical cart sat. Her hair was cut close to her head, gelled in waves against her scalp. She strode toward Tessa. "I'm Mayra, one of Ms. Esther's CNAs." She pointed to Grandmother's room. "She's in there, honey. Just go on in."

"I don't want to disturb her—" Tessa began backing away from the door, her resolve wavering. She could just come back another day.

Mayra gave a hearty laugh and shook her head. "Oh, honey. She's probably dozing. That's what she does most afternoons. Here, I'll go in with you and wake Ms. Esther up. You her granddaughter or something?" The woman didn't wait for Tessa's reply but rapped loudly and cracked the door open. "Ms. Esther, you decent?" She chuckled. "You got a visitor," she added in a singsong voice. Mayra held the door open wide, grinning like she'd given Tessa the winning lottery ticket. "Go on in," she prodded as Tessa hesitated in the doorway.

Inside, Tessa was aware of the quiet and crossed her fingers that Grandmother was at some old people activity. She peered around. A small bathroom was on her left, the open door revealing a toilet with grab bars on each side, a shower, and a small sink. On Tessa's right was a short hallway that led to another door, one Mayra walked through. Ahead of Tessa was the living area, but she barely noticed it before Mayra called for Tessa. "Come on in, sugar!"

Tessa peered toward the bed where Grandmother lay. She did not resemble the woman Tessa remembered. She looked frail, not forceful. Docile not domineering. But she was dressed as nicely as always: slacks with a blouse tucked in, conservative but stylish. And her silvery gray hair lay against the pillow in her signature bob.

While Tessa told her stomach to stop churning and shook her arms to loosen her tense muscles, Mayra approached her grandmother's bedside. "Hi, Ms. Esther," she said quietly but firmly. She gently rubbed Grandmother's hand. "Wake up. You've got company."

"Huh?" she said groggily.

Tessa saw her grandmother's legs wiggle. Gnarly fingers with perfectly polished nails batted the lady's hand away. "Who are you and what are you doing in my house?" Grandmother demanded, all tiredness gone, and her eyes narrowing Tessa's way.

Those childhood insults flashed before her.

Tessa, how do you expect a boy to like you if you refuse to look pretty?

Your hair hangs like straw and you wear boy clothes.

Clean up.

Wear a dress.

This was a bad idea.

"Hush now. This beautiful girl came to see you." It's . . ." Mayra turned to beckon Tessa forward and raised her eyebrows questioningly.

Tessa inhaled deeply and stepped forward.

"Tessa."

"Who's that?" Grandmother snarled as she struggled to a sitting position.

"Let me get a wheelchair and take you out to your recliner. Then you can have a nice chat with Tessa," Mayra answered. "I'll be right back," and she left.

Grandmother propped herself on an elbow. Even lying in bed, petite and tiny as she was, she commanded the room. "Now who did that woman say you are?"

Tessa wanted to cringe but fought it. "Grandmother, it's Tessa." She enunciated and declared, two qualities her grandmother had always harped about.

Grandmother set her mouth in a firm line. "That's impossible. My granddaughter is a child. You're a teenager. And you certainly aren't as pretty as Tessa even if you have long, thick hair like she does. She wears pretty dresses that I bought, and little Mary Janes, and beautiful patterned bows in her hair. I'd never allow denim pants ripped all over the place or ragged shirts with writing on them. And for heaven's sake, why do you have all those loud, noisy bracelets? Every time you move, they set my teeth on edge. Now who are you and what do you want?" Grandmother's voice was loud.

Here was the grandmother Tessa remembered. Alzheimer's had done nothing to soften the hard-nosed woman. Tessa's silent promise to remain composed and not allow Grandmother to get under her skin vanished. "*My* bracelets are noisy? How about that clunky charm bracelet you used to wear? It was loud and banged into everything."

Grandmother furrowed her brows together and looked at her wrist. She lifted her left hand and stared at her empty arm. Her eyes widened and her gaze darted to her lap, her nightstand, and around the room.

"Where is it?" Grandmother hissed at Tessa. "Did you take it? Give it back!"

Tessa took a few steps back while holding her hands up in defense. "I don't have anything, Grandmother."

"Who are you? What did you do with it?!" Grandmother yelled.

Mayra returned pushing a wheelchair. "What are you going on about?"

Grandmother pointed a crooked finger at Tessa. "That girl took my bracelet."

"No, Ms. Esther. I put your bracelet away when you took a rest." Then she opened a nightstand drawer and pulled up the old, silver bracelet laden with charms. Instead of fastening it on Grandmother's wrist, Mayra handed it to her, and Grandmother clasped it in her left hand like a beloved treasure.

Tessa couldn't help but notice how calmly and soothingly Mayra spoke. Grandmother settled immediately.

Mayra helped Grandmother into the wheelchair and whispered over her shoulder to Tessa. "Esther gets confused with the past and the present, typical for Alzheimer's patients. Especially those in the middle to later stages, like she is. She confuses people, too. But that bracelet always calms her down." Louder, she said to Grandmother, "I'll help you into the recliner and you can have a nice visit with Tessa."

Tessa followed behind Mayra and the wheelchair and watched as her grandmother shuffled, with Mayra's help, to the recliner. Such a difference from the assertive stride Grandmother once had.

"We're happy to have family visit," Mayra said to Tessa. "Ms. Esther's only been here a couple weeks. It's nice to know she's got someone in the area. Visits are important."

Yeah, well, there wouldn't be any more visits from me, Tessa thought. *Mom can visit her mother-in-law—**ex** mother-in-law—herself.*

Grandmother swatted Mayra's attempts to settle her in the chair. "I can do it myself, whoever you are," she grumbled.

The main living area of Grandmother's room was cozy and demure, nothing like Grandmother. The walls were a soft, powder blue with framed movie posters. Those Tessa remembered from Grandmother's old house. *Breakfast at Tiffany's* and *Some Like It Hot* hung side-by-side, her grandmother's favorite romantic comedies. Tessa remembered when she showed her grandmother *White Chicks.* Grandmother had said it wasn't nearly as funny as *Some Like It Hot.* But Tessa had caught her stifling laughter when the Wayans brothers pranced around the screen dressed like Brittany and Tiffany Wilson.

Tessa's eyes roamed the place, taking in a small kitchenette. No stove. A tiny refrigerator, sink, and no coffee pot. But it was wiped down, dust-free, and smelled like Pine Sol. She could report to her mother that Grandmother was in a clean place.

Mayra put a quilt over Grandmother's legs. Tessa recognized that, too. She used to snuggle under it with her grandmother and watch old, scary movies. Alfred Hitchcock films were their favorites. Tessa banished the sentiment of long ago. Grandmother had ruined the sweet memories, replacing them with edgy criticisms and passive aggressive overtures that grew harsher as Tessa aged.

"I'm gonna get Ms. Esther her afternoon coffee she loves so much. You want one too, Tessa?" Mayra asked.

Tessa shook her head.

"Young lady, speak up. You have a voice. State 'yes' or 'no' firmly and decisively," Grandmother admonished.

Some things hadn't changed. "Thank you, but no. I won't be here long," Tessa said to Mayra, ignoring her grandmother.

Mayra slipped out of the room leaving the two women with the same laser sharp blue eyes to stare at one another.

Her grandmother grumbled, "What is it with you young women today? Can't you assert yourselves? In my day, a girl knew how to be proud, confident, and respectful. I don't know who you are, but you'll never get a nice boy with your mousy demeanor and your torn clothes and that ridiculous thing in your nose. And is that *blue* in your hair?" she sneered. "Now who are you and what do you want?"

Tessa clenched her jaw and her fists. It was all she could do not to storm out of the room. But she wanted to prove to herself that she could handle Grandmother. "It's Tessa, and I only came to see that you're doing okay." Tessa heard the defensiveness in her tone, a slip into the past. She tucked one side of her hair behind her ear and crossed her arms protectively across her chest. Her bracelets jangled.

Her grandmother's face softened. Her eyes grew wider, and she leaned forward anxiously. "Tessa? *Junior's* Tessa?" she said gawking. She peered past Tessa. "Where's your father?" she demanded.

Tessa stood confounded, her mouth opened in surprise. Her father had been dead four years.

Grandmother's door opened and Mayra strode in. *Thank God.* Tessa didn't know how to answer that question.

"Oh, Sally, thank you. Please put the tray—" Grandmother started. Then she stopped and glared at Mayra who bustled about setting up cups and getting cream and sugar placed on the little eating table. "Who are you?" Grandmother demanded.

"Oh, Ms. Esther. It's me Mayra, your CNA. I brought some coffee for you to share. I'm sure you'll have a lovely chat." She turned to Tessa. "I brought an extra cup in case you change your mind. I gotta tell you we do make a mean cup of coffee here," she chuckled.

Tessa hadn't moved, standing across from her grandmother's recliner, her backpack hitched on her shoulders. Sally was Grandmother's housekeeper from years past and hadn't been in her house for at least ten years. Just how much had Grandmother forgotten?

"This is Tessa," Mayra said again as she placed a coffee cup next to Grandmother. "She's come to visit you for a spell," she said cheerfully.

Grandmother muttered and rolled her eyes. "I'm not an invalid. I don't need anyone spying on me."

"No one's 'spying' on you, Grandmother. I'm here as a favor to Mom. You could be a little more appreciative." Tessa's eyes flashed while tears built up. Grandmother might have forgotten that Sally was gone but she hadn't forgotten how to be unpleasant.

Grandmother's gaze hardened and her eyes narrowed as she stared at Tessa.

I will not let her get to me.

"I know what you're here for, Lou Ann. I'm not giving you another penny. Neither is Junior. You're trash and you're not welcome in my house. Don't come back here again." Grandmother had leaned forward in her recliner, practically hoisting herself off the seat.

Tessa's jaw dropped. *Who was Lou Ann?*

"I'm not Lou Ann, whoever that is," Tessa said coldly, regaining her stature. She held her back straight and her arms by her side.

"Oh, you'd like me to forget, wouldn't you?" Grandmother shook her head, her shiny gray hair bobbing as she did. She pointed an arthritic but manicured finger at Tessa. "I told you that you'd amount to nothing. Just look at you, dressed like a street urchin. You deserve whatever life has given you." And she sat back, her mouth curling in a sneer.

Tessa couldn't be certain if those words were aimed at Lou Ann or herself. Either way, Tessa felt the insult in her bones. This was the grandmother she'd pledged to cut out of her life. And had. Two years ago. And Alzheimer's or not, she was a nasty woman. "I see you're well taken care of and in a clean, safe environment. My job here is done."

And with that, Tessa spun on her heel and strode to the door, ignoring Mayra whose mouth was open and whose hand was raised in protest.

As she flung open the door and made her way down the hall, Tessa's muscles unclenched, and her pulse returned to normal. Nothing was going to bring her back here.

CHAPTER TWO

Esther

Esther watched the door close, vague stirrings of familiarity dinging in her head. That girl. . . those piercing blue eyes. Why did they feel familiar? She clutched her bracelet, aware that she was clasping it so tightly that she had indentations in her palm. She sat back in her recliner. Her heart was pounding, and she felt out-of-sorts. There was no other way to describe it. This happened often. A sudden misplace of time, like she blinked and her world shifted.

She looked at the walls and saw her favorite movie posters. On her lap was her comfortable quilt. They settled her.

"Ms. Esther, don't you worry. You watch the birds you love so much and have a cup of coffee." A brown-skinned woman hovered over Esther, fussing and fixing. Esther didn't know who she was, but her words were kind and her hands were soft. She exuded gentleness.

Esther accepted the coffee while the woman pulled open the covering on the window. Blinds, that's what they were. As she sipped, she looked at the trees that seemed so far away. They didn't look like the trees of home. Her Georgia childhood home. Where was she?

She was about to ask, when the woman said, "I'm going to catch Tessa right quick. You sit here and I'll be back." Then she bustled out of the room.

Esther's gaze caught on the bookcase which sat under the window. On top was a photo. She recognized Junior, his wife Debra, and baby Tessa.

A memory of little Tessa at Christmastime flashed by. Was it last Christmas? Esther couldn't be sure. Names tumbled through her head. *Junior. Debra. Tessa.* Pictures flickered in front of her vision, like flashcards. *A smiling child. A surly teenager.* Thoughts dropped in her brain with no discernable meanings. *Lost opportunities. Unredeemable mistakes. Last chances.* Esther struggled to make sense of them, willing her synapses to fire correctly.

"Tessa," Esther said the name quietly. The word felt familiar in her heart but not altogether comfortable.

The teenage girl who had just been here couldn't have been her Tessa. She closed her eyes. and conjured up the image of the girl who'd just left. Dishwater blonde hair, thick and long. Esther unconsciously brought her hand to her own hair. The chin-length bob—Esther's signature cut—was just as thick as that girl's. The blue eyes that flashed at Esther were the same bright blue as her own. But didn't plenty of people have blue eyes and boring, blonde hair? And her sweet Tessa wouldn't have had streaks of blue throughout. Esther wouldn't have stood for that.

Esther didn't remember Tessa having grown up yet sometimes she saw scenes in her mind that featured a teenage Tessa. Were they memories or dreams? She brought her hand to her mouth. She just couldn't be sure. People spoke to her all day as if Esther was supposed to know them, but she didn't. Surely if that girl were Junior's child, Esther would have felt something. A tugging on her heart, a surge of love for Junior's daughter. She'd felt nothing.

Esther gently shook the bracelet. It always brought her comfort. Every charm represented something from her life, and she often closed her eyes and allowed herself to be whisked away to happy moments. But her thoughts followed no pattern. Sometimes a memory would become foggy, the crisp edges of a story washing away, like a sand sculpture fading as water rushed over it. She pictured Tessa as clearly as she could. She remembered a young child following closely behind Debra's feet, watching Esther and Debra's interactions. The snapshot changed and there stood a brooding teenager, sitting as far from her grandmother as possible.

Her fingers encircled a round charm. A pearl. Tessa's birthstone. Esther laid her head back, remembering when she first met Tessa.

•   •   •

Peering out from the sheer curtains of her formal living room, new grandmother Esther peered up and down her street for the familiar blue Honda. Today, Junior was bringing over the week-old baby to meet Esther. No matter that she couldn't visit in the hospital. Esther was about to see her granddaughter for the first time. The humidity of June wouldn't dampen the joy of holding Junior's child. Turning her head right and left, she conjured up the nonexistent car, anxious to see baby Tessa and fearful that Junior would forget.

Finally, the hood of a blue sedan appeared in her peripheral vision. As the car made its way down her lane, she exhaled. Esther threw open the door and took the four porch steps quickly. She arrived on her cobblestone sidewalk just as Junior turned into her driveway. The passenger seat was empty. Only Junior, and the baby in the backseat. Thank God.

She itched to retrieve the baby from the car, but she knew Junior would want to present her, like a princess. Esther clasped her hands in front of her and rooted herself to the spot. Finally Junior walked toward her, carrying a pink cushioned car seat snuggling a beautiful baby girl. Oh, she was even prettier than Esther thought she'd be. Petite with blonde fuzz on her head that almost sparkled when the sun hit.

"Oh, Junior. Let's get her inside before the sun burns her. She's much too delicate to be out here on this hot summer day."

He said nothing, but he did hand her the carrier. Surprised, she took it and climbed the steps, assuming Junior was behind her. "I just made some lemon pound cake. Fresh coffee is waiting for us, too. I thought I could show you the baby's room that I—" Esther stopped at the screen door, aware that Junior wasn't behind her.

She set the baby carrier just outside the door and turned. Junior stood in the driveway, raking his fingers through his hair.

"Something wrong, son?" she asked carefully. His distress might cause him to become angry or frustrated. She could never predict which.

He toed the ground, his eyes downcast. Then he shoved his hands in his pockets and stood straight. "I'm meeting the guys at the club for a quick drink. They just want to congratulate me. No big deal. I'll be back in an hour."

Esther felt herself stiffen. "Do you really think that's a good idea? What time does Tessa—"

"Mom!" He held his hand up to thwart her words, backing up and opening the car door. "I'm twenty-two years old! Don't lecture me."

He would leave despite Esther's protestations, suggestions, or reminders, but she tried anyway. "Why don't you spend some time with me and tell me about the baby. I don't even know her! You can show me how she likes to be held. . ." her voice trailed off. She'd lost this battle.

"Geez, Mom. Elliot and the guys just want to buy me one round. You'll have much more fun with Tessa without me. I trust you to figure it out. Look what a great job you did with me!" And he grinned broadly, shouting the last sentence out the window. Without even saying goodbye to his daughter, Junior backed out of the driveway and headed to Sutton Country Club.

Esther brought the carrier inside, little Tessa stirring. The ticking of the grandfather clock and her own worries fed the silence. Junior would be longer than one hour. How much longer was anyone's guess. As she bent over to pick up the baby who wiggled, starting to wake, she noticed a can of formula, a bottle, and a few diapers stuffed in the side between the pink cushion and the plastic car seat. At least she could take care of Tessa's basic needs.

She picked the now mewling infant up carefully, cradling her like the precious commodity she was. As she hummed and rocked her in her arms, Esther whispered to the baby, "Don't you worry, little Tessa.

Grandmother will teach you what's important in life. You'll be safe, secure, and completely loved. And Daddy will be back in no time. You'll see." And Esther kissed the downy hair, praying she would be right.

•   •   •

Esther shook herself out of that memory. While the birth of Tessa was one of the best days of her life, the hours she'd spent waiting for Junior to return were not. When she'd spotted the headlights of Junior's car, she was relieved and angry. He had stumbled into the house and passed out in his old childhood bedroom. Esther had driven Tessa home.

She looked at the little pearl now. It was her beginning. Where Junior might fail, Esther would succeed. Her brain flipped through a book of memories. Esther knew Tessa wasn't that baby anymore. Was she nine? Thirteen? She sighed. Junior would come over and tell her. She lay the bracelet in her lap and closed her eyes. She'd wait for his visit.

CHAPTER THREE

Tessa

"Tessa! Wait!" she heard a voice call behind her.

She considered walking faster but that would be childish. She turned to see Mayra hurrying toward her. "I'm not going back," Tessa declared.

The woman nodded. "I understand. Let me walk you to the front desk to sign out." Mayra said.

Tessa didn't need an escort; she needed a fast lane to the door. "I know where to go."

Mayra joined her anyway.

They walked the halls of cool beach tones and calming waters. Sand-colored walls provided a background for beach landscape pictures blending pale turquoises, sea-greens, and creamy blondes. The colors of Florida. Tessa supposed the photos and color choices might settle fraying nerves, jumbled minds, and unpredictable outbursts, but they did nothing for her own anger. How could her grandmother spew such venom against someone? Even if it wasn't directly intended for Tessa.

"It's a shame your first visit was during one of Ms. Esther's bad moments. She can be lucid sometimes, you know."

Lucidity might be even worse. "Do you know who Lou Ann is?"

"No. Like I said, she gets confused. Alzheimer's patients can't control which memories pop up and sometimes the past blends together."

Tessa didn't know anyone from Grandmother's past with that name.

They reached the lobby area and Tessa reached for the visitor's log to sign out, Mayra at her heels. "Alzheimer's can take away the ability to bury frustrations. They come out in unexpected, uncontrollable ways."

And Tessa was probably a trigger for any frustrations. Her grandmother was always irritated with her hair, her friends, and her choices.

She turned to Mayra. "Be honest. You don't actually *like* my grandmother, do you?"

"Oh, she's a spitfire of a woman but I like a little sass. Plus, she doesn't mean it. She's just trying to be the woman she never got to be. She gave up her dreams in order to become a wife and mother, but those were the times back then. I'm sure if she had pursued her travels, she could have been a renowned anything-she-wanted." Mayra grinned and opened her arms.

Tessa couldn't help but raise her eyebrows in disbelief. None of those descriptions sounded like the grandmother she knew. The only dream Grandmother ever had was to be a wife and mother, which she'd fulfilled, as she told Tessa constantly. The same ideal she tried to force upon Tessa for as long as Tessa could remember. And travels? Grandmother never went anywhere. What ideas had she filled Mayra's head with?

Mayra slowed her pace. "Alzheimer's is unpredictable. It doesn't follow a routine or a schedule. Sometimes Ms. Esther calls me by my name and even follows conversations. But she doesn't usually remember them for long. Other days she forgets questions I've just asked and of course, forgets me, and gets irritated easily. Like today. One thing I'll say, though, is she loves her showers. Whereas some Alzheimer's residents refuse to bathe, not Ms. Esther." She chuckled.

"She seems to appreciate fine clothes and having her hair styled. Is that how she's always been?"

Tessa remembered the woman who loved for Tessa to wear her shoes and clothes. Loved braiding, curling, and even brushing Tessa's hair. But that tenderness ended and was replaced with scurrilous comments and outright insults as Tessa got older and chose her own clothes and hairstyles.

"She always liked to look good," Tessa admitted with a tight smile.

"You know, visiting is a good way to learn what she enjoys talking about. What made her tick, back in the day. It's like working a jigsaw. I gotta put the puzzle of her life together with the pieces she gives me. Sometimes, she doesn't start with the edges, know what I mean?"

No, Tessa didn't. Grandmother only gave her the same pieces, over and over.

Mayra said quietly, "I know she's a tough cookie, but it would do her a world of good to have company besides me. She's not always salt and vinegar. There's some sugar in there, too." And she smiled. "The more she sees you, the more those lovely memories might come forward."

Tessa smiled politely. Her presence would do little to spur any lovely memories, but she kept that thought to herself. She said goodbye to Mayra without a promise to return.

As she walked back to her car, her grandmother's words reverberated in her head.

Not as pretty.

Mousy demeanor.

Self-conscious of her ripped jeans, bangles, and *Grateful Dead* t-shirt, Tessa felt herself shrink a little. And that made her mad. She should never have come. She unlocked the door of her Volkswagen Bug and slid into the front seat.

Her mood lightened as the distance lengthened between herself and Sunset Shadows. Fiddling with the radio station, her silver bracelets clattered against one another. Grandmother had no room to criticize them. That old, clunky one Grandmother wore knocked into everything when her arm moved. Loaded with charms, it made much more noise than Tessa's did. She could almost feel the weight on her small wrist now, remembering how she'd shake her arm and jingle the charms. She loved wearing it as a kid, liking how it slid it up and down her arm while she pretended to host dinners and bridge parties. Just like Grandmother did.

She shook the memories away. Those good ones ended at about the same time pretending did.

Mayra had described Grandmother as sassy. Tessa would never use that word. Overbearing and controlling, yes, but sassy implied kind of fun. Grandmother was never fun.

Tessa turned into Florida Coastal University and pulled into the student parking lot. She grabbed her backpack and headed to her dorm. She pulled out her key card and let herself into the building. She was one of the few sophomores who had landed a private room. When her freshman roommate bailed at the end of last year, the Resident Assistant offered her this tiny room. Even though it meant living across from a busy elevator, she'd grabbed it. It afforded her privacy for studying. Not that she had a potential career to study for. Yet.

Tessa unlocked her door and stepped into her personal space. It was more closet than room, but she liked the cozy vibe it gave. The soft pastel walls not only provided an appearance of larger space, according to Debra the Designer mom, but also gave Tessa a sense of peace and comfort. Although she wasn't feeling too peaceful right now. Ms. Madden would grill her tomorrow in an effort to find Tessa's major. And Tessa didn't have one. But with only a four-year scholarship paying for her school, she couldn't afford to wait.

Tessa plopped her backpack near the desk that overlooked the only window and sat down. Her room faced a marsh. She liked seeing the egrets and blue herons that picked their way through the grasses. During rains, she watched them hide behind tall reeds and cattails, using palms fronds as their covers. That afternoon, she didn't see any birds. She put her elbows on the desk, her bracelets sliding down her forearms. She'd beg Ms. Madden for another week. And by then, she'd have figured it out. Procrastination was Tessa's superpower.

Her phone trilled with *I Got You, Babe.* Her mom's personal ringtone, compliments of Sonny and Cher. "Hey Mom. How's the design conference?"

"Wonderful. I'm learning so much. How are you, honey?"

"Okay." She tapped her fingers on her desk. "I saw Grandmother. You owe me a big one."

"Oh, thank you. Does she look okay? What's the place like?"

"She looks fine. Smaller than I remember but the same." Tessa recalled the vacuumed halls and the disinfectant smell. "The place is clean." She leaned back in the chair. "I don't know why you take it upon yourself to look after her." Tessa remembered the comments Grandmother used to lob Debra's way:

Debra, the house is a mess.

Debra, why do you let Tessa dress like a slob?

Debra, Junior's hard-earned money should be plenty to support you and Tessa; I shouldn't have to help you. Be thriftier.

"Oh no. What happened?"

Her mother's voice pulled Tessa out of the past. "At first she sort of recognized me. Of course, she insulted my clothes and hair. Then she said I couldn't possibly be her granddaughter because I wasn't as pretty."

"Oh, honey. I'm sorry. You won't—"

Tessa cut in. "That's not even the worst part." When her mom remained silent, Tessa plowed on. "She thought I was someone named Lou Ann and told me I was trash, and I wasn't getting money from her or Dad."

When her mother said nothing, Tessa looked at the phone to see if the call had been dropped. "Mom, you there?"

A short intake of breath and her mom's voice wavered. "Um. . . yes, I'm here."

Tessa knew something was up. She sat up straight, looking at the phone as if to conjure her mother's face. "Do you know who this Lou Ann person is?"

"A girl from your father's past."

"Nuh-uh. Really? Oooh. . . she must have been awful. Grandmother was so angry. I've never heard her so hateful. What did this Lou Ann do to her?"

Silence grew and again Tessa wondered if the connection was poor. "Hello?"

"Sorry. Still here, honey."

Tessa noticed her voice was shaky and lacked confidence. Very un-Debra like.

An uncomfortable feeling pricked at Tessa's neck. "So who is she?"

"Was," her mother corrected. "Lou Ann passed away many years ago. I don't know why your grandmother would call you that."

The answer was slow and deliberate. When nothing more came from her mom, Tessa asked, "No reason at all?"

"Nuh-uh," her mom answered. But the casualness of her answer sounded forced. Tessa let it go for now. She stood up and moved to her bed. "I'm going to watch *Love Story* tonight."

"Oh, that's nice," her mother answered distractedly.

"Kendra likes some guy that runs the film room." She waited for her mother to pepper her with questions about other guys on campus, grilling Tessa to find out if she'd met anyone. She was rewarded with silence. "The movie is rated X."

"Uh-huh, sounds good."

"Mom! You aren't even listening!" She jumped up from the bed.

"Oh, gosh. I'm sorry. So, you're going to the mall with Kendra tonight?"

"Not at all. Mom, you're being weird." Tessa paced.

Her mother coughed lightly. "It's nothing. Don't you have a meeting with your advisor tomorrow? Did you decide on a major? You'd be a great teacher, you know."

Tessa knew where her deflection skills came from, but she followed her mother's change of subject anyway. "Definitely not teaching, Mom. I hate being on display, you know that. The last thing I'd want to do is stand in front of a bunch of people, kids especially, all day."

"Okay, okay. I'm sure you'll figure it out. Gotta go. The next session is about to start. I'll see you in a couple of weeks when I visit. Okay?"

"Fine," Tessa huffed, still miffed at her mother's evasiveness and unhelpfulness.

They hung up. It didn't really matter who Lou Ann was. Life was full of people who came and went.

•   •   •

Tessa yawned and stretched, the morning's brightness blocked by her dormitory-provided shades. She retrieved her phone. Eight o'clock. "Practically dawn," Tessa mumbled as she crawled out of bed. Her appointment with Ms. Madden was at nine. She hadn't gotten any closer to a decision of what to study. No epiphanies dropped from the skies; no sudden realizations dawned with the day. She really *would* have to beg for another week.

After a shower, she styled her hair in a long ponytail, taking more care than usual. Digging through her closet for something to wear, she thought of last night. The movie was as expected. A tear-jerker. But the epitome of true love. At least Tessa appreciated the romance of it. Kendra was too busy peeking at Jed. Peeking might not be the right word. More like gawking. Tessa wished she had Kendra's confidence. She'd dated briefly in high school; flings only, short-term. Almost like speed dating. She wasn't looking for anything serious, much to her grandmother's disapproval. Tessa had fielded Grandmother's *When will you find a boyfriend and think about getting married?* at least a dozen times. And Tessa's answer had remained the same: *I'm only in high school. And I'm following my dreams, not some guy.* The answer was a dig at her grandmother who had married straight out of high school. And it never failed to cause Grandmother to jut out her chin and counter with, "Your grandfather was a wonderful man. You'd do well to find someone like Arthur Wilde."

The conversation was a lesson in circles. They always came back to where they started: Grandmother advising Tessa to find a nice boy and get married; and Tessa proclaiming her determination to build a career first.

And now that conversation bit her squarely on her butt: she had no idea what she wanted to do in life.

After rummaging through her closet, Tessa chose khaki pants instead of her favorite jeans, a solid color shirt instead of one of her band tees, and black ballet flats. Maybe looking the part of a serious college student would inspire a decision. She shoved her usual assortment of bangles onto her arms. After grabbing her phone and backpack she left her room, locking the door and taking the stairs down. She was too anxious to wait for the elevator this morning.

Florida Coastal University was a small school by college standards. Tessa could navigate it on foot, but it still required a bit of hustle to get to the Janssen building for her meeting. Taking the building steps two at a time, she opened the door to the Student Advisory offices, breathless as she spoke to the student receptionist.

"Hi, I'm Tessa Wilde. I'm a little late for my app—"

"Tessa! Come on in," Ms. Madden called from an inner office behind the reception area.

The girl at the desk pointed casually behind her in the direction of a hallway. Unfortunately, Tessa had been here enough times that she knew exactly which office was her faculty advisor's. Enroute, she passed posters and flyers advertising career fairs. They were useless to her until she had a direction. Three labeled doors invited in students whose last names matched the nameplate. Tessa Wilde bet Ms. Madden rued the day she'd received last names P – Z.

She poked her head in the doorway where Ms. Madden sat behind her desk. The woman waved her in, her bright pink nails calling attention to the clasped hands resting on her desk. A pinched smile told Tessa she would not welcome any more procrastination on Tessa's part.

Tessa placed her backpack on the floor beside her as she sat across from her advisor.

Ms. Madden wasted no time or words. "Hello, Tessa. I hope you're here with some good news for me." She raised her eyebrows expectantly.

Tessa opened her mouth, but no words came out. Ms. Madden leaned back and sighed, the chair squeaking under her heavy frame. "Tessa, you're a college sophomore and it's February. You need to declare a major. Your scholarship only goes so far."

Tessa listened to the words she'd heard before. She was as frustrated with herself as Ms. Madden seemed to be. Tessa had never thought she'd be in this position. A good student, she'd secured the necessary funds for college, assuming her life's calling would find her, not vice versa. High school was pretty easy, and Tessa never thought much farther ahead than the next test. Upon graduation, college appeared as the beginning of adulthood, the route to conquering the world. She never considered how or in what way.

Had she spent so much time declaring what she didn't want, everything her grandmother pushed, that she hadn't discovered her own dreams?

Pie-in-the-sky dreams of being a woman of independent means are just impractical, Tessa. Work, if you must, but do it as a means to an end—to find a husband and raise a family.

Those were the words Tessa had heard all her teenage years.

"What do *you* think I should do?" she asked Ms. Madden. She immediately wanted to take back the question. She was asking a practical stranger for life-changing advice.

Ms. Madden leaned forward over her desk and tilted her head much like a parent does to the child who just doesn't get it. "Tessa, you know it doesn't work that way. Your future is yours and yours only." She hesitated long enough to suggest she was choosing her words carefully. "Think about what you enjoy in your classes and the hobbies you take pride in. Take one of those online aptitude assessments. Then put it all together." She straightened her posture and her tone. "You're a smart girl. You have two weeks to decide." She turned toward her computer and typed. "Same time two weeks from today. That's the last available date to declare your major and remain a sophomore." Her voice softened. "Don't be afraid to define yourself, Tessa. No more 'exploring avenues' and 'testing the waters.' You need to choose a path."

Her words were everything Tessa expected and nothing she wanted.

CHAPTER FOUR

Esther

"C'mon, Ms. Esther. You've got to eat something." The brown-skinned not-Sally was trying to coax Esther to eat spaghetti. She didn't particularly care for Italian food, and this was like a heap of white shoelaces with red gravy swirling through. And she didn't know why she wasn't dining at her own table. Pot roast or pork chops or fried chicken. Delicious meals that Sally made. Or did Esther make them? She'd forgotten. Darn that Junior for moving them here. Wherever *here* was.

And where was Junior? It seemed like he never came when she called out for him. He must be on yet another business trip. How long had it been since he'd left? Left her alone in this strange place, this new apartment or condominium. Yet, she wasn't really alone. People popped in and out of her place day and night. People wearing uniforms and bringing medicine. Others who cleaned quickly, and never faces she recognized. Like this one.

Who is this woman who keeps trying to feed me? It wasn't Sally—this woman had mocha eyes, smooth skin, and gentle hands. Sally was white and brisk and efficient.

"Ms. Esther," the voice pleaded. "Please eat a little. You'll lose your strength. We don't want to see you bedridden. You've hardly touched a thing all day." The arm waggled a forkful of noodles near Esther's nose, but the smell was not enticing.

Esther turned her head away, wrinkling her nose. She thought about the strange woman's words, though. She didn't want to be a burden to Junior when he returned home. She'd eat a little something. He'd be angry with her if she got sick from not eating enough.

Oh, how she worried about him. Of course, she'd never voice her concerns. Her son hated being coddled, but with Junior's weakness for the drink, she wanted to keep tabs on him. It was increasingly difficult to find the notepad where she kept his hotel numbers. Items disappeared like names on her tongue.

She turned back around and accepted the food. It wasn't bad.

"See, Ms. Esther? Pretty good stuff," the lady beamed. "After lunch, I can take you out to the patio you like so much. The bougainvillea is blooming like crazy. Even the roses are out. And the butterflies! My, my…they're everywhere. That's good. Eat all this lunch. I'll bring your coffee out there if you like."

Didn't this one ever stop talking? Didn't she know that a lady should speak selectively? No man wanted a chatterbox. And this one wore no ring. No wonder.

Later, Esther sat on the lanai. Not-Sally was right. The flowers were spectacular in color, the bold fuchsia and bright pink attracting butterflies and bees to pollinate and spread their beauty. Wherever this was didn't compare to her beloved Georgia hills and pecan trees, but it was pretty in its own way.

This new apartment complex didn't even look like normal apartment buildings. One long hallway led to the lobby, numbered doors and small hallways jetted off the main one. It seemed more like a hotel. And the old people! Everywhere she looked there were wrinkly, old codgers—men hunched over and women pushing walkers. The staff in this building were lovely, though. They called her "Mrs. Wilde" or "Ms. Esther" and dressed in the same color teal uniform. The bellhops, or whatever they were, pushed the wheelchair people around; others pushed medicine carts and food trays. And housecleaners. What a gift—people in all white sashayed in, dusted, vacuumed, and mopped. Then they sidled out without asking for payment. She could appreciate that. She supposed Junior had put her in this apartment complex so she would be waited on, hand and foot. That part was lovely. The times when they hovered were irritating. *Take a pill. Take a walk. Take an art class.* Ridiculous.

Junior had been gone, traveling she-forgot-where, and no one seemed to know him. When Esther asked the housekeeper lady when to expect Junior, she murmured incoherently and changed the subject.

Whatever happened to Sally?

Esther got confused so often now; it frustrated her to the core. And at night, she just couldn't get her bearings. An unfamiliar noise would awaken her, sometimes voices outside her door. Eventually the sounds faded, but anxiety kept her awake. The shadows in her bedroom were in the wrong places. Where was her favorite dresser that hugged the wall by the bedroom door? Or her Queen Anne make-up table? Why did the bathroom light shine from the wrong side?

Tears sprang to her eyes like sprinklers. She rarely stopped them anymore. What was the point? This apartment would never be home. Esther supposed their old house had gotten too big for her and Junior, but this new place seemed too small.

She closed her eyes and grasped one of the charms on her bracelet. The miniature swing. She rubbed the contours of it and let memories take her away to a yesteryear of joy, a place that made sense and had order. Her beloved Georgia childhood home.

•   •   •

"Esther Mae," Essie heard her mother call. "Where are you?"

Essie tilted her head back and pushed just a little higher in the tire swing. She could tell Mother wasn't too desperate for her yet; she could get a couple more minutes of swing time. Essie loved her swing, even though Mother tsk-tsked that she was getting too old for childish joy. But at fifteen, Essie used that swing as much now as she did when Daddy put it there ten years ago. Several ropes later, the swing was still strong. Daddy told her he'd never be able to grow grass on the spot where she rubbed her feet when the swing was still. He always smiled when he said it, though. He was proud that Essie loved her swing. She could tell by the way his eyes crinkled when he talked about it.

And she loved her father. Whenever she heard the thwat of the screen door and the stamping of his bootclad feet before dinner, her heart would swell with happiness. He always took his hat off and placed it on the coat hook before entering the kitchen. And his hair always had a dent the diameter of the brown rim, even on Sundays when he rested.

The late September days were slowly turning cooler, and Essie basked in the last of the sun shining valiantly through the oak trees, turning her face up to catch the rays. The swirling, feather-like red, yellow, and orange leaves floated down. They held her spellbound, and she let her head hang back, giggling when the leaves landed on her as if they were saying hello.

"Essie! Now, please," she heard her mother call in her I'm-serious voice. With a small sigh of pleasure, Essie let the swing slow its momentum naturally, and she hopped off with a silent good-bye to her favorite pastime. "I'll be back tomorrow after school, Swing," she whispered. With a skip, Essie headed to the back porch and opened the screen door. Carefully, she wiped her shoes on the doormat. One of Mother's pet peeves was tracking dirt on her kitchen floors. Just in case, Essie took off her white tennis shoes and placed them in the mudroom. "Mother, I'm here," she called, looking around for her mother.

"Up here, in your room, dear," she heard.

Essie hopscotched up the stairs jumping from side to side.

Her mother peeked out of Essie's bedroom. "For heaven's sake, Esther, you're a girl not a puppy. Please walk up the stairs instead of stomping and bouncing."

Essie slowed her pace and did as she was told. Entering her room, she saw Mother rummaging through Essie's closet. "Where is that pretty yellow dress you wore Sunday to church?" she asked, poking through the hangers.

"Why?" Essie asked, taking a seat on her bed.

"We're having dinner company in an hour. I thought the yellow dress with the ribbon would look nice," she said, her words muffled as she was partially hidden in the clothes.

Essie's radar went up. "Why?" she asked again.

"Good gracious, Esther. You sound like a broken record." Mother had straightened up from the closet, hands on hips, looking exasperated.

Essie straightened her own back and planted her feet firmly in front of her, the demeanor of a proper young lady, as Mother preferred. "Who is coming for dinner, and why do I have to look so nice for them?"

Mother found the dress and brought it to Essie, then proceeded to sort through shoes while answering. "Well, the widower Wilde and his son are coming. I'd like to look as if I'm raising a daughter, not a tomboy," she said as she regarded Essie's old dungarees.

Self-conscious of her clothes, Essie felt her face grow hot and probably red. Mother and she had had more than one argument about appropriate clothing. Essie couldn't think about that. All she could focus on was the impending dinner guests. "Awful Art was one of the snobbiest boys at school," she blurted, giving no thought to manners or politeness.

"Now, Esther. You be nice. Mr. Wilde is lonely and I'm sure he and his son could use a dose of good cooking. Besides, Art is four years older than you. He has been out of school for a year and has a good job as a salesman. He's probably a charming young man." Mother shook her finger gently at Esther. "You're confusing snobby with selective. He knows who the nice young ladies and gentlemen are. I'm sure he chooses his friends wisely. You should do the same, young lady."

It was no secret that her mother cared little for Essie's best friend. Millie spoke her feelings and asked questions, apparently the behavior of an "upstart" as Mother called her. But Millie didn't give off airs or pretend to know things just to be admired. Awful Art was known for that very thing she hated. What a travesty to spend time with him.

"Mother," Essie whined, giving up all semblance of maturity. "He turned his nose up at anyone who had fun." She remembered the boy who was all seriousness and frowns. "Why are they coming over, anyway?"

Mother wouldn't look Essie in the eye. "You know Mr. Wilde owns that big bank downtown. Your father and I have been talking to him about a loan for the farm."

"So you're bribing him with dinner?" Essie cringed as the words flew out without restraint.

Mother turned on her heel and put her hands on her hips, fire in her eyes. "Esther Mae Overton, we don't do anything of the sort. Watch your mouth or I'll wash it out with soap! We are simply doing a kind thing for someone in need. Imogene has been gone three months and I'm sure that poor man and his son haven't had a decent home-cooked meal since." She smoothed her dress and blinked a few times. "It's simply a neighborly act of kindness."

Essie bit back her words instead of reminding her mother that the Wildes lived clear on the other side of town, not neighbors at all. She knew she'd get a tongue-lashing and maybe a mouth-washing if she mentioned it. Instead, she resigned herself to pleasing Mother and getting gussied up for company she didn't want.

"I'll wear the yellow dress but don't bother finding my flats. Teenagers wear high heels with dresses. I'll wear the black kitten heels and a headband, not a ribbon." Mother couldn't dictate everything she wore.

"What a ridiculous word, 'teenager,'" her mother mumbled. "That word will be out of style faster than that awful new music you listen to." But she pulled Essie's requested shoes out of the closet and placed them on her bed. It was her way of giving in.

"Mother, Elvis Presley is here to stay. He's not awful—. He's . . . he's . . . cool."

Mother threw her hands up and tsked-tsked her way out of Essie's room, still shaking her head as Essie hummed a few lines of "Jailhouse Rock" and tossed her dungarees on the bed.

She held the dress in front of her, twirling to watch it swish. The A-line cut jutted out just above the knees, its bouffant petticoat splaying as she turned. The dress hugged her small waist and she felt very grown up in it. It was all the rage for dances, and Essie loved feeling older than her age. Mother might have old-fashioned ideas about how a girl was supposed to behave, but she did buy Essie pretty clothes.

The thought made her stand still. If Mother and Daddy couldn't get a loan for the pecan farm, they might have to sell it. What would they do? Pecans were all her father really knew, and Daddy always said pecans in Georgia were better than pecans anywhere else. Essie wouldn't know; she hadn't left Georgia . . . yet.

The excitement of wearing her dress was tempered with the reality of why she was wearing it. Mother and Daddy wanted to impress Mr. Wilde. A bank loan was their only option to save the farm, and the Wildes owned the biggest bank in town. The Overton family needed their approval. And their money. With a reluctant sigh, Essie resolved to try to impress old Mr. Wilde. She didn't care one hoot, however, about impressing Awful Art.

•   •   •

Esther was startled out of her dreaming by someone gently tapping her shoulder. For a moment she searched for the familiar pecan trees in the distance and reached up to grasp the well-worn ropes of her childhood swing. But instead of rows of trees, she spotted manicured grass and flowers, not the sights of her Georgia farmland. A cool hand gently lowered her raised arms to her lap. The peach-infused air of her memories was replaced by a spicy perfume. A woman stood in front of her, teal filling Esther's sight. The woman placed Esther's legs on the pedals of a chair in which she sat. Then after the woman fiddled with a knob, the chair began to move.

"Where are you taking me?" Esther demanded.

The chair stopped moving and a kindly-faced woman came into view. "Ms. Esther, it's me, Mayra."

Who was Mayra?

As the chair moved Esther thought, *Oh, how I miss Sally.* She had been with them since the birth of little Arthur… Junior, as they called him. She was a treasure—housekeeper, cook, and nanny all rolled into one. She could calm the colicky baby and prepare the house for Esther's bridge luncheon like nobody's business. And her roast turkey! Esther's mouth watered just to think of it. Art loved Sally's cooking, too. The smile left Esther's face as she remembered that Art was gone. Died too soon. A heart attack that came on as suddenly as a summer storm, leaving her to raise a confused adolescent boy by herself.

As she was wheeled into a building she didn't know, Esther was becoming more familiar with feeling unfamiliar. She'd wake up in the morning and not recognize where she was. She was alone, and the strangeness was isolating. The only place she felt like herself was in her memories.

"Ms. Esther, can I get you anything?" Not-Sally asked once they returned to a sort-of familiar room.

Esther recognized a recliner and its blanket—a quilt she had made years ago when she was busying herself and waiting to get pregnant. An aroma of cloves and orange hung in the air. Esther closed her eyes, letting the smells replace the discomfort of loneliness. "Where is my bracelet?"

"Oh, I know the answer to that one, Ms. Esther." The lady chuckled and handed it to her. She placed it in Esther's open palm. The cool silver tickling her hand made Esther feel better. Her favorite possession in its proper place.

Her memory keeper.

Esther hugged the bracelet to her chest, willing sweet memories of childhood to infiltrate her heart and replace the anxiety of the present.

CHAPTER FIVE

Tessa

Tessa acknowledged Ms. Madden's instructions with a nod as her stomach dropped to the floor. She had two weeks and Tessa could tell that would be the extent of Ms. Madden's flexibility.

After she left her advisor's office, Tessa strolled the campus pathways, hoping inspiration could be found outdoors. The palmetto-bordered walkways transported students everywhere. Blacktop trails wound from the academic to the residential buildings and into the main artery of campus life—the cafeteria, student union, and library. This place was her second home; she had been connected to it like a charger to its phone. The bright sun usually inspired her good mood, but the swaying palm fronds and live oaks with their dripping mosses failed to lift her spirits.

How hard can it be to find a stupid major?

Kendra was a business major, but numbers and figures and marketing strategies were not Tessa's thing. She hated blood and wounds, so medical careers were out. Teaching was out.

She thought of Ms. Madden's words. *Hobbies.* She loved old music and old movies but there was no career in that. She liked her art classes but didn't want to paint or draw or design. She wasn't sports-oriented or debate team worthy. So, nothing there. Her mother used to tell her to find something she was passionate about, but she never did. Her grandmother used to tell her to be passionate about finding love. Also something she never did.

Lost in thought—part self-recriminations, part half-hearted reflection—Tessa bumped into something or someone, stopping her momentum, and meeting the sidewalk butt first. A tripod clattered to the ground, and a camera landed next to Tessa. She scrambled up, searching for her backpack which fell near a boy. Man. Whoever he was.

"What are you doing?" she yelled.

"Me? Can't you watch where you're walking, Sorority Girl?" A guy stood up brushing off dirt from his knees and scowling at her. He looked older than the typical college student, late twenties, Tessa would guess. His longish brown hair was tied back in a short ponytail. With his slim, buff build, she'd have pegged him for a surfer not a photographer.

"What are you doing standing in the middle of a pathway, Camera Boy?" She could give as well as he could.

He scoffed and righted his tripod stand. "You're all alike," he murmured. "Elite, self-centered pretty girls who think they don't have to be accountable for what they do."

Pretty?

Tessa reached down and plucked his fallen camera off the ground.

"Hey, be careful with that!" Camera Boy's eyes widened with panic, and he practically lunged towards her.

Tessa jumped back, holding it in front of her like a shield, her heart racing with panic. She'd heard about ploys to get girls in the woods at colleges all around the country. Had she played into a predator's hands? She gripped the strap in her palm so she could hurl the camera at him if necessary. "I'll scream louder than any giggling coed you've ever heard if you don't take five giant steps away from me."

"Whoa, whoa," he said, holding his hands up in surrender. Then he chuckled, turning it into a full-bodied laugh. But he did back up. "Five giant steps? Like that old timey children's game *Mother, May I?*" he sputtered.

Her heart rate decreased to a normal level. She unwound the camera and let it dangle harmlessly from her hand. Okay, so maybe he wasn't a predator. Maybe he was just a guy taking some pictures. Still.

"Hey, don't make fun of me," Tessa said. *Most people sit under the trees, not photograph them,* she could have said.

Too late for a snappy comeback now.

Camera Boy stopped laughing and concentrated on her hands still holding his camera. "Look, I'm sorry," he said. "Could you just give me my camera?"

He didn't look sorry; he looked like he was patronizing Tessa and that just made her madder. "Oh, this?" she asked sweetly, swinging the camera from its strap dangerously close to the ground.

His eyes opened wide, and he held his hands out, bargaining a deal. "Seriously. It's expensive and hard to replace. Just hand it to me, please."

This was stupid. What did she hope to accomplish holding a camera ransom?

Before she could hand it over, Camera Boy tried one last tactic. "Look, if you'll just give it back, I'll come to your sorority dance or whatever and take pictures. For free," he added. "I just really need that camera." Pleading replaced mocking. And desperation reflected in his eyes.

Tessa felt a pang of shame. Who was she to hold someone's camera captive? She sighed loudly. "I'm offended on behalf of all non-sorority girls. You shouldn't have to bribe me or anyone else to give you back your own property. "Here!" She thrust it at him.

Camera Boy closed the gap between them. "Look, I'm sorry, Sorority Girl—"

She prepared to interrupt him, but he corrected himself. "Non-Sorority Girl," he stressed. Then he took a deep breath. "I apologize if my photography work was in the middle of your path. I'll be more careful, so other pretty girls don't get tripped up." He smiled.

Pretty . . . again.

In spite of her attempts to be cool, Tessa warmed inside. This handsome guy called her pretty. Twice. What was he doing on a college campus taking pictures anyway? Was he a graduate student?

Instead of asking him, she shook her head. She had her own studies to worry about.

Tessa couldn't resist some final, parting words. "Another thing. Don't assume all female college students are flighty and selfish or belong to sororities. It's very narrow-minded and judgmental." With that she flung her backpack on her shoulder, lifted her chin, and stalked away.

"Yes, ma'am, Non-Sorority Girl," he called after her.

Safely back in her room, Tessa dumped her backpack on the floor and paced. She shoved thoughts of the handsome Camera Boy out of her mind and worked on an English essay due by midnight. A few hours later, she sat back, pleased with herself. Her essay was done with hours to spare.

She twirled the silver bracelets. Ms. Madden had said something about online aptitude assessments. Tessa remembered those in high school. Weird tests that guidance counselors proctored. Tessa had never taken those seriously. Getting through high school was the hard part; everything after that was supposed to fall in line like marching ants.

"Might as well give it a shot," she said aloud to no one but herself. She opened her laptop, searched for career aptitude tests, and sat down to figure out her life.

She clicked through the questions, this time answering them honestly. She had no real hope that it would spur a decision, but effort counted. She sat back to watch the rainbow-colored wheel spin while the computer magically assessed her life. *Who designed these things?* she wondered. *How did they know what to ask to figure out a person's future?*

Just when she began to think the whole process was bunk, the wheel stopped.

Art Conservator. Art Restorer.

What the hell were those?

She didn't know anyone with those titles; she didn't even know what they meant. A few clicks later Tessa sat at attention. Being an art restorer or an art conservationist was a totally savage career. And it related to her childhood *hobby*! One she'd totally forgotten. As a kid, she and her mother had spent Saturday mornings at flea markets. They'd have contests—who could make up the best story about an item they'd found, or they'd race to find the most unique object. Tessa liked that part best.

She stared at the information in front of her now. Were there really people who got paid to learn about old objects—their origins, purposes, and owners? Another hour of Internet surfing told her yes. Tessa sat back and exhaled with relief. She had an answer for Ms. Madden. Not to mention newfound respect for career aptitude tests.

Her rumbling stomach told Tessa she had a new urgent need. Dinner. Grabbing her backpack, which often felt like another limb, Tessa left her little haven of privacy still absorbing the good news. Art restoration was her future. *Take that, Grandmother.*

The cafeteria was busy, and she scanned the room for familiar faces. She could use the mindless, easygoing chatter of other college kids. She caught the eye of a girl in her history class who waved her over. Tessa made her way through the buffet line. In her haste to leave the room, she had stuffed her lanyard that held her Student ID in her backpack instead of draping it around her neck like usual. Now, she had to rummage through the catch-all bag to find it. Once she found the golden ticket, Tessa swiped her card then put the lanyard around her neck. She carried her tray toward her classmate.

"Hey, Non-Sorority Girl," a voice called out, stopping her.

The rich voice resonated next to her. The voice that had teased her on the pathway. Her stomach quivered when they locked eyes. He grinned.

"Camera Boy," she said by way of greeting, trying to inject just the right amount of confidence and graciousness to disguise her sudden nervousness.

"Get here without running into anyone?" He sat lazily at a round table with a few others, a Cheshire-cat grin on his face.

She searched for a clever retort, something suave and playful. Nothing came. She wasn't a game-playing kind of girl. The others passed a few looks of confusion between themselves until Tessa finally said, "I have a real name. Tessa."

"Ah, so she does," he mused. He explained to his tablemates, "Tessa stumbled into me on a pathway earlier. Literally ran right over me," he added with a grin.

"The path for *walkers*," she stressed, "is a good one for thinkers, too." She put one hand on her hip, balancing her tray with the other. She held her head up high. "One doesn't expect to find a random guy setting up a tripod and taking pictures of leaves."

Camera Boy gave Tessa a small nod. "Touché. And the name is Chip, if you care to use it." He then lowered his head in a mock bow.

"Sure. Well, nice to see you again, *Chip*. I'm going to eat my dinner now." She lifted her tray towards her sort-of friends. Wanting to keep her composure and hide the fluttery feeling inside, she smiled charmingly at his tablemates. Then she made her way to the girls.

"Hey, Tessa," Charmaine said. "Haven't seen you around for a while. What's up?" She nodded to the empty seat next to her.

"Not much," Tessa answered. She set her tray on the table, put her backpack on the floor beside her, and scooted in the chair.

"So, who's the cute guy?" Charmaine teased as Tessa unwrapped her chicken sandwich.

Tessa shrugged, aiming for nonchalance. "Some photographer I met on the path." No one could hear her heart pound or feel the magnetic pull to glance his way. She opened her sandwich, squirted some special sauce on it, and kept her eyes averted.

"Well, he seems interested in you. He keeps checking you out. And he's hot. Why don't you ask him out?" Charmaine poked her side.

"Ugh, no," she answered digging into her chicken sandwich like she was starved. Mostly she hoped to hide the blush.

It was perfectly acceptable to ask out a guy, but Grandmother's constant recriminations about Tessa's lack of femininity and how girls were supposed to be lady-like and wait to be asked, had left an imprint. Besides, she had no time for a relationship. Especially since she'd just found her footing in life. Like an hour ago.

She couldn't very well explain all that to Charmaine, so she didn't. She opted for something vague and socially acceptable. "I'm not interested. Too busy with classes." Tessa absorbed herself in opening ketchup packets for her French fries.

"I hear that. What's your major?" Dani, the girl on the other side of Charmaine, piped in.

Tessa took another big bite of sandwich to buy herself time while she ran through the possibilities. If she confessed to her indecision, they'd give her the standard line of how she was running out of time and had to choose *something*. She didn't want to hear again what she already knew.

She took a leap. "Art History. But only as a steppingstone to art restoration." The words felt fake. Like she was a child pretending to be a grown-up.

"What's that?" Dani asked.

Tessa had only about an hours' worth of knowledge, but she tried. Effort and all that. She finished with "It's not a degree here. That's why I have to major in Art History. Then I'd get a graduate degree in Art Conservation and study under an art restorer. I can look for internships in museums while I do the conservation classes."

Nervousness had made her chatty. But the chattiness gave her something else. Confidence.

Charmaine asked, "How did you get into that?"

"Um ..." So much for confidence. Tessa sat slack jawed for a few moments trying to think of a mature way to say she rolled the proverbial dice on a career assessment test, and this was what came out.

Thankfully, Dani filled in the beats of silence. "Hey, that museum downtown had a big display of Timucuan pottery last year. Did you see that? It was pretty cool."

Tessa shook her head. She thought she'd left her interest in ancient pottery at the flea market trips of her childhood. Now, though, she'd jump at the chance to look at artifacts through new eyes.

The conversation segued into upcoming downtown events, and Tessa breathed easier once the focus shifted. After what felt like an appropriate amount of time, she said her goodbyes.

She put in her earbuds, letting the Eagles' "Take It Easy" play. She would try.

With a brisk pace she set off toward the dorms. The setting sun left a pink and coral hue in the sky, and Tessa took it as a sign of approval for her major. A few faint stars seemed to wink at her. She smiled, metaphorically patting herself on the back.

Ahead of her, she spotted Chip the Camera Boy and his friends. She'd pass them quietly, quickly, and hopefully unnoticed.

No such luck.

"Hey, Tessa," he called as she passed the group, head down, earbuds in.

She looked back and smiled. She pulled one earbud out to be polite, intending to wave quickly and keep moving.

"Thanks for not running us over," he said in mock gratitude.

"Very funny," Tessa returned, still moving, and holding the lone earbud in her hand. She'd resume her listening and get back to the dorms.

He jogged up to her.

Reluctantly, she stopped and took out the other earbud. He was interrupting Glenn Frey's encouragement—telling her to loosen up and take a stand. Tessa looked up to meet Chip's eyes, pools of chocolate. They were beautiful eyes.

"Hey, you look quite pleased with yourself." He rocked back on his heels. "Catch another camera?" He grinned and smiled.

She broke eye contact and shook her head, ignoring the melting feeling that rushed over her. "No. Hopefully I just found my major. I had two weeks left to do that before losing my scholarship, and I think I have."

Whoa. Where did *that* come from? She'd just unloaded her biggest decision to an almost stranger.

"It's not easy being asked to commit to your life's work at what, nineteen or twenty years of age?" said Chip.

"Twenty. But I should have had some idea of what I wanted to do with my life *before* I came to college." Self-conscious of oversharing, she mumbled a quick goodbye and hurried away before he had the chance to respond. She could almost hear Grandmother *tsk-tsking* in her ear.

Something about Chip made her want to pour her worries out, and that just wouldn't do. Growing up with a grandmother who reminded Tessa to put image first and feelings last, she was immensely uncomfortable sharing. *Never let them see you hurt.* Or in this case, *indecisive.*

"Happy to talk things over if you—" he called, but the rest of his words were lost as she resumed her private Eagles concert. She didn't know Chip. Even if he seemed kind, he was an unknown entity. And she'd learned from her grandmother that smiles could be masks. She slid her key card in the outside doors of the dorm and took the elevator to her room.

As she sat in front of the computer again, she read more about art conservation vs. art restoration and realized they went hand-in-hand. Conservation implied preservation. Once she restored the splendor of an item, she'd have to ensure it stayed that way. And she wasn't so much interested in paintings and art as she was artifacts and antiques. A spark of excitement filled her. Sifting through estate sale items and garage-kept knickknacks would be right up her alley. Maybe she'd finally found her future. And it wasn't as Esther Wilde's doppelgänger.

CHAPTER SIX

Esther

Esther slept more than she stayed awake. People came and went, tidying up, straightening the bed, or bathing her. Some days she followed their conversations; most days she didn't. Today she sat in her chair by the window and watched the wildlife through the open blinds. Squirrels scrambled and lizards slinked on the porch. Esther missed the scampering chipmunks and free-flying butterflies outside her old kitchen window. This place didn't even have a kitchen window. In fact, it was hardly a kitchen at all. There was no stove. How was she supposed to prepare a meal for Junior when he came back? And where was he supposed to sleep? There was only one bedroom in this apartment.

Whatever happened to her beautiful cottage near the beach? The one she and Art raised Junior in when they left Georgia? No, wait. They left that one when Junior was a teenager and moved into the bigger house with the pool. She sighed. The days ran together. The years ran together. Separate memories blended into one, and time was vague. And now, Art was gone. And she hadn't seen Junior in quite some time. He was all that was left of her family. Except . . . except Junior's child. What was her name? Tessa!

Esther's mind captured a snippet of memory. She saw herself sitting in a strange living room, Christmas tree lights blinking. Junior was not there, but his wife was. Now, what was her name? Donna . . . Debbie . .

. Debra. That was it. Esther almost patted herself on the back. Debra. Esther closed her eyes and remembered.

.   .   .

"Grandmother, did you bring me a dolly?" Tessa asked.

"Tessa, dear. We don't ask guests if they brought us presents," Esther chastised.

Tessa's face scrunched in bewilderment. "You aren't a guest, Grandmother."

"Of course, I am. I don't live here, so I'm a guest," she corrected the four-year-old. Esther straightened her shoulders and crossed her legs at the ankles. "See how I'm sitting, dear? This is how a young lady sits on a chair," she told the watchful child.

Tessa copied her actions on the sofa, her little legs dangling in the air in front of the couch.

Esther could tell her granddaughter's heart wasn't in a lesson. It was natural, being Christmas, and Esther decided not to correct the girl's unfocused attention. Instead, she glanced towards the doorway. Still no Junior. Surely, he would show up on Christmas Day. For his only daughter. Debra had said he'd left the day before and hadn't returned. Oh, how Esther hoped he wasn't lying in a gutter full of the drink.

"Grandmother?"

She refocused on the child.

"I won't ask for a present, but did you bring anything at all?" Tessa blurted out. Her eyes lit up expectantly, and she checked the area around her grandmother for a wrapped box.

Debra had told Esther that Tessa was desperate for some kind of doll. American Girl. Esther had begged her son to buy it for his daughter. It would be wonderful if Junior brought something that Tessa really wanted. He had disappointed Tessa before—birthdays forgotten, promises of park dates broken. Today was Christmas. He wouldn't forget today.

"Now, Tessa. Remember what I told you. Nice, little girls are patient and understated." She saw the smile dim and the light go out of her granddaughter's eyes. If only Tessa understood how good this advice was. Esther wanted this little girl to have the best life, free from mistakes.

Tessa had too much of her father inside. A wild streak of stubborn independence was forming. Debra wasn't doing enough to correct it.

To make up for her earlier admonishment, Esther lifted a red-ribboned box from her pocketbook. "Here you go, sweetie," she said grandly.

Tessa hesitated for a moment, probably sizing up the fact that a doll couldn't be stored in that small of a box.

"Thank you, Grandmother," Tessa said politely but subdued. She opened the box which contained a locket and listened as Esther explained the purpose of a locket and how the wearer could store anything she wanted in it. Except, of course, a doll.

Hurry up boy, Esther thought, peeking towards the doorway again, wanting to conjure a father and a doll with mere wishes.

Two hours later, dinner was done, and Junior was still missing. No one mentioned the elephant NOT in the room. Tessa's eyes grew heavy, and Esther escorted her up the stairs to bed. Esther slipped the satin nightgown over little Tessa's head in between yawns and eye rubs.

"Grandmother?"

Esther glanced around for Tessa's hairbrush. Her golden locks were a tribute to her mother, but the thickness was all Esther's doing. She smiled a little, happy to see herself reflected in Tessa's hair texture as well as saucer-round blue eyes. Finding the brush, Esther nudged Tessa who scrunched forward, hunching herself over several piled-up pillows, her back towards her grandmother.

"Hmm?"

"Doesn't Daddy like me?" Tessa asked, her eyes struggling to stay open.

Esther just about dropped the brush. What in heaven's name propelled Tessa to say that?

"He loves you, dear. He had business that took longer than he anticipated." The lie tripped smoothly off Esther's tongue.

"Mommy says no one does business on Christmas."

Damn that Debra. Why couldn't she just let Tessa believe in the goodness of her daddy? Why plant the idea in her little head that her father wasn't her hero?

Before Esther could find an excuse, Tessa's shoulders relaxed; she'd drifted off. Settling her on the pillows, Esther pulled the unicorn comforter to Tessa's chin. Esther remembered when Debra bought this bedding. A proper young lady should have pink and white, or lace eyelet coverings. Not some silly, trendy, make-believe animal. Oh, what did it even matter now?

Junior weighed on Esther's mind, as usual. A tear leaked. This was not how she'd envisioned her grandchild's Christmas.

"Do you think Daddy is trying to find me a Lindsey Bergman?"

Esther startled.

Tessa continued sleepily, "Lindsey's the doll I want, and she wants to make the world a happy place." Tessa's voice quieted as she drifted off. "She wants to do the right thing, but sometimes she just can't help but get in trouble." Her tired eyes gave up and she fell asleep before Esther could answer.

"Lindsey sounds like all of us," Esther murmured. Then she tiptoed out of Tessa's room, vowing to find a little doll with a big heart to give to a little girl with big hope.

It took two days of hustle and bustle to find that doll, but Esther did and presented it to Tessa on behalf of the still missing father. They all pretended he bought it. Tessa slept with it, gave it a chair at the dinner table, and talked to that Lindsey doll like they were best friends.

•   •   •

Whatever happened to Lindsey? Whatever happened to Tessa?

The sounds of cackling laughter outside her door jolted Esther from her dream. Or memory. She looked around the room and spotted her favorite photos and movie posters. Her lovely quilt was on her lap. She missed Junior. When would he come home?

A knock on her door claimed her attention. Before she could find Sally to answer it, someone barged right in. The sort-of-familiar lady in the teal uniform. The Not-Sally lady.

"Hi, Ms. Esther. I've brought your medicines for the afternoon. Would you like water or juice with them?" Not-Sally pushed a cart.

The top of the silver cart held a tray with a little paper cup. Esther had a vague recollection of that cart. "What are these pills for?" she asked suspiciously as Not-Sally picked up the paper cup and brought it over.

"You take these every day. They help when you feel anxious or sad."

"Are you sure Junior knows about these?" she demanded. Not-Sally nodded, and Esther reluctantly accepted them.

She swallowed the pills and leaned her head back, patting the bracelet on her lap. Every charm represented a memory that transported her back in time. Her favorite moments lived within the charms, each bauble linked to a piece of her life. Holding them helped her hold on to her world.

"Would you like to sit outside for a spell, Ms. Esther?" Not-Sally asked.

Esther shook her head and resumed her watch outside the window. The squirrels darted around, and the small, black birds sat casually in the trees. *They've got no worries about the future. They don't know how lucky they are.*

There was a time when Esther felt the same way. When she and Millie believed they'd tackle a man's world, and when the future beckoned them with hope and anticipation. Then, reality intervened. She caressed the small cap and tassel charm that signified a successful end of high school. The turning point for Essie Overton.

•　　•　　•

When the Pomp and Circumstance song began, Essie followed the others towards the rows of metal chairs set up in the gymnasium. With each footstep, her childhood ended and adulthood began. Anxiety and excitement vied for a spot in her chest. She was dating Art Wilde now, much to the surprise of her friends. She had once claimed feminism and independence would influence her marks on the world, concepts still largely unheard of. Millie reminded her of that claim every chance she could.

Essie was a little ashamed that she so willingly gave up her dreams to accept an engagement ring just a few short months ago. Art was a good man, though, and her parents were overjoyed to welcome him to the family. He had brought relief and, surprisingly, fun to their small trio. Essie was surprised that Awful Art really wasn't awful.

When his father had agreed to loan the Overtons money to rehab the farm, you'd think they'd won a million dollars. To hear her father's hearty laugh, and watch her mother throw her head back giggling had made Essie's heart swell. Sacrifice was worth security.

Her ideas of writing and traveling about the countryside were pipe dreams anyway. Mother was right. Women simply didn't have a place in a man's world. Essie would have struggled, been turned down at every door she knocked upon, said Mother. No, the world needed women who could lead from behind the scenes. Fundraiser presidents and Parent /Teacher volunteers. Essie would embrace that world and make her name there.

As Essie claimed her seat in the row between MaryBeth Nubak and Billy Owatcher, she put sentimental longings to rest. Millie had only thrown Essie's words back because she was jealous; any other reason was too difficult to entertain. Essie knew what she had was coveted by many high school girls. She was engaged to a twenty-one-year-old. Even if it was Art Wilde. She clamped down the pestering voice. The one that taunted her how she would never slay the writing world once the "I do's" were said.

The speaker's voice faded as Essie recalled her own doubts, and the nights she woke sweating and fearful, as if someone had imprisoned her. She'd shaken off the fear, reminding herself that she was following her destiny, and that her childhood fantasies had been just that. But she'd lie awake unable to return to restful sleep.

She told herself she was losing her independence but gaining so much more—a steadfast, solid, secure life.

After all the speeches, the distribution of diplomas finally began. Essie stole a few peeks trying to spot her parents in the audience. Her eyes were drawn to a cluster of boys and girls cheering for their girlfriends and boyfriends. Their applause drowned out polite family handclapping. She half-hoped she'd hear whistling and Art would shout her name, but he wasn't that kind of guy.

She stood with her row of classmates to begin the procession towards the stage. This was it. The moment she'd waited for. The biggest accomplishment of her eighteen years. She stood at the base of the stage steps while MaryBeth made her way up. After the smattering of applause, Essie finally heard "Esther Mae Overton." She climbed the stairs and extended her hand for the predictable handshake with the principal. Then she took the padded cardboard holder that would contain her high school diploma.

It was over so quickly. She walked back to her seat and stood with the others. Before she knew it, she moved her tassel on her cap to the left and tossed it in the air. That was it. Essie Overton was a graduate. It was a bit of a letdown after all the hullabaloo leading up to that moment.

Essie didn't have time to think about it as her parents found her in the sea of other graduates on the gym floor. Art followed behind. She spotted Millie and a group of kids laughing and posing for pictures. That was exactly how she'd always pictured her graduation day. Instead, she waited alone as her fiancé and parents approached. Watching Millie from the corner of her eye, Essie felt the stab of remorse. They'd grown apart that year. Art took space and time that once was Millie's. Essie shook her sadness away, choosing to concentrate on what lay ahead of her. The future was wide open with possibilities and a long, fulfilling life with Art.

•　　•　　•

Esther allowed herself a moment of self-pity. What if she'd become famous or won a Pulitzer Prize? Where might she have gone as a successful writer? Instead, she'd had the security and steadfastness of a traditional life. Even that hadn't turned out how she'd thought. She'd only had one child, and not until she was thirty-five years old. She'd expected to raise more than one. And she certainly couldn't have foreseen that the child she'd so desired would be prone to drink, or that her husband would die so soon.

Young Essie Overton had pictured herself hobnobbing with photojournalists and big travel names. She'd assumed she'd draft fantastic articles inspiring people everywhere to travel to cities near and far, exploring their great country. Never once in her childhood had she imagined herself engaged at seventeen years old.

Life has been fair to you, Esther Overton Wilde. Quit your bellyaching and count your blessings.

Esther was startled out of her trip down Memory Lane by a buzzing. An alarm echoed in her room, but the source was somewhere outside. It was a shrill, ear-piercing sound like what a smoke detector made, but she didn't smell fire. Craning her neck to peer out the window, she spotted uniformed men and women scurry by on the patio. She heard the *thud-thud* of running feet. Her apartment door flung open, and Not-Sally peered in, brows furrowed, eyes darting around.

Breathlessly she said, "I'm just checking that you're here, Ms. Esther."

Before Esther could react to this intrusion and ask where else she'd be, Not-Sally ducked out with a vague, "I'll be back shortly."

The staccato buzzing that could wake the dead finally stopped.

Esther turned her head back to the window. People everywhere scattered about. My goodness, but they were old! Decrepit, some of them. She looked down at her own fingers gripping her bracelet and almost gasped. Gnarled, old lady fingers. Her breath quickened. Where were the pieces of life that had transpired between high school and now? Where, oh where, was Junior?

CHAPTER SEVEN

Tessa

Tessa had shared her newfound revelations about her career with Kendra who'd immediately inundated Tessa with related trivia.

"Hey, did you know Lomekwi stone tools discovered in Kenya are the oldest artifacts, dating back 3.3 million years?" she'd asked, flopped on Tessa's bed and scrolling through her phone. "Or the first flute, made of bone, was found about 33,000 years ago in Germany?"

The trivia was interesting but not helpful. What was helpful was Kendra's badgering that Tessa request an earlier appointment with Ms. Madden.

She headed there now, more than a week before Ms. Madden's deadline. As Tessa crossed the wide quad area toward her advisor's office, she tried to steady her jumpy nerves. A dose of "Crocodile Rock" from her playlist put a jaunty bounce in her step. But instead of relieving her anxiety, the song only masked it. Her nerves were still hopping and bopping. Would Ms. Madden agree with Tessa's choice?

Stopping at the bottom stair of the building, Tessa pulled out her earbuds, put her phone in her pocket, and inhaled deeply. She mentally reviewed her plan as she climbed. Step one was to procure an undergraduate degree in art history. Step two involved getting her master's degree in art restoration or even conservation, and if she could find a job near home, she could live there, save her salary, and pay for that master's degree. The plan, though vague, was a plan. Something she'd never had before.

While pride had her crossing the quad with her back straight and her stride strong, she faltered as she climbed the steps. *Once you've made a decision, stick with it.* One of Grandmother's mantras might be worth listening to now.

She strode into the building, stopping at the familiar reception desk. The receptionist, talking on the phone, held up one finger and Tessa waited. She shifted from one foot to the next in anticipation.

Restless, she wandered over to a poster: *Picture Your Future and Make It Happen!* She pictured it: Tessa the Art Restorer dusting artifacts and cleaning intricate niches and making them shine like new. Researching who used that snuff box and why, and how did it get away. No piece of jewelry would escape a story; no tool would be left to rust; no relic would remain undiscovered. Her services would be in demand, her name synonymous with *expert!* . . .

"Tessa? You can go back now," the student receptionist said, disturbing Tessa's fantasy.

She nodded and headed to her advisor's office.

Ms. Madden was filing papers in a large cabinet. Apparently not all paper died with the advent of paperless technology. "Good morning, Tessa." The woman turned her large frame towards Tessa. "Should we sit?"

Tessa heard the hopeful anticipation in her advisor's question. The certainty Tessa felt wavered, and she took her usual seat, tucking her fidgety hands under her thighs again. Once Ms. Madden had settled into her creaky office chair, Tessa untucked her hands and clamped them on her knees.

"Ms. Madden, I did it," she declared, releasing an exhale that left her breathless.

The advisor raised her eyebrows but seemed to withhold her own excitement. "Okay, I'm ready."

"Art restoration," Tessa said assertively as if that had been her choice all along.

Ms. Madden didn't suppress her surprise. "Huh." Not the seal of approval Tessa had hoped for.

"You've never expressed interest in art."

Tessa admitted, "Not so much art as art objects. I took a few of those aptitude tests, and they kept leading me to this." She felt the need to explain. "When I was a kid my mom and I would go to flea markets and look for objects we'd never seen before. We'd make up stories about what they were, how they were used, and who used them. I always wanted to know what each one *really* was, why someone was selling it, and how its history played out." She thought a minute and added, "I think I was made for this career."

With this speech over, she waited, and the butterflies danced. Would her childhood antics sound frivolous?

Ms. Madden seemed to choose her words carefully, tapping a pen on her desk a few moments before speaking. "Tessa, I think you've done a good job mining your interests to find a suitable career."

Tessa heard the unspoken *but*.

Ms. Madden said, "But art restoration is not an undergraduate degree here."

Tessa explained her plan to major in art history and follow through with a graduate degree in art conservation.

Ms. Madden's face remained stoic, neutral.

For all her supposed independence and maturity, the child in Tessa wanted someone to affirm her decision.

Ms. Madden inhaled deeply. "Okay, then. You need to meet with the art history department head since it's midway through the semester." She consulted her computer. "Looks like you've already taken some of the prerequisite courses so you're in pretty good shape to go forward, but you might have some catching up to do," she warned. "That means summer school."

Tessa nodded. "I understand."

Ms. Madden took a post-It note and wrote something down, then handed it to Tessa. "Here. Email Professor James and set up an appointment. We'll go from there. Let me know when you've arranged the meeting."

Ms. Madden's reaction was not the proud congratulations Tessa had hoped for. Was Grandmother right all along when she'd told Tessa she was full of "fancy dreams and silly notions"?

The woman's tone softened. "I think you've made a fine choice. Good work, Tessa."

Tessa allowed her body to relax. She stood and held up the post-It. "I'll contact him right away. Thanks for your patience," she added with a rueful smile, earning a sort-of chuckle and a headshake.

Tessa eased out the door, down the stairs, and into the grassy quad. Birds and butterflies danced in front of her as if to tell Tessa she'd done the right thing. Her usual stroll was a hop as she practically bounced toward her dorm along a familiar pathway. This time she didn't need "Crocodile Rock" to put energy into her step.

Lost in dreams of the future, she almost missed the familiar tripod. An orange cone sat in front of it, alerting pedestrians to its presence. How humiliating if she'd knocked it over again! Her heart sped up as she looked around cautiously for Camera Boy. No, Chip. Not seeing anyone, Tessa spotted a camera bag on the path's edge.

"Hello?" she called out. What could Chip be photographing now? Swampy, marshy water and sawgrass hugged one side of the walkway. Surely nothing noteworthy about that.

A rustling in the shrubs to her left caught her attention. She peeked through the thick foliage and saw Chip squatting in the middle of a clearing, camera in front of his face, clicking away. Trees. He was taking more pictures of trees.

"Are they growing right before your eyes?" Tessa called. "Or moving? Or talking?" There was something about him that brought out her sarcastic side. She peered around the palmetto fronds.

Chip sat back on his heels, his camera hanging on his neck like a giant pendant. "Well, well, well. If it isn't Tessa, the non-sorority girl." He crawled out until he stood in front of her, several inches taller. "I see my tripod is still standing so you must've remembered to open your eyes while walking."

Though his words teased, his eyes smiled.

"Very funny. Are you actually taking pictures of trees and leaves?"

"I'm a photographer. I want my viewers to feel the blade of grass or sliver of sun or smell the damp earth."

Tessa had never met a guy who spoke so unashamedly about beauty or nature. It left her speechless.

Chip gave her his full attention. "And how about you? The last time I saw you, you'd just found a major. What is it?"

His gaze magnetized her, and she felt her heart quicken. She tried to remain nonchalant. "Art history for now. Art conservation after that." The words felt awkward. Like trying on new shoes.

"Cool," he said. "You want to restore old paintings?" His eyes focused on her completely, like no one else mattered.

Tessa shook her head both in response to his question and to ground herself. For the second time that day, she outlined her plan.

Chip nodded in reply. And seemingly, approval. "I've always loved history. All kinds of history. People today are so anxious to get over the next hurdle or conquer a new piece of technology that they forget to appreciate what they already have. Or had." He shook his head, one hand under his camera and the other relaxed at his side. He exuded confidence.

She, on the other hand, felt as awkward as a schoolgirl standing in front of her high school crush. She didn't know where to put her arms, so she grabbed the straps of her backpack. And she planted her feet, straight legged and robotic. She said, "I'm not a big technology user. I prefer books over e-versions, paper over a screen, and shopping in person over Internet scrolling. I think I've been called 'old-fashioned' or 'behind the times' more than once." Her high school classmates had thought they were insulting her, but she didn't see it that way at all. Her love of old movies and old music made her sort of a curiosity in school. One she hadn't minded.

She told herself to stop talking so much.

"If you want to go to a photography show with actual photos that aren't digitally enhanced or computer-generated graphics, I'd be glad to take you. Some of my friends have an exhibition coming up downtown in a couple weeks." He stopped talking, fumbling to remove the camera from his neck, breaking eye contact.

Was he asking her out?

Her face grew warm as she considered the possibility. And truthfully, if she were going to be an art restorer, she needed exposure to the art world. Agreeing to a "date" with Chip Whatever-His-Last-Name was an opportunity to learn more about this world. Not that she was even certain it was a date. Maybe he was simply offering to help out a fellow art student.

The silence between them grew to an awkward length.

Tessa finally answered, playing it cool. "Sure. I've never been to a photography show." She was a big girl; she could handle a day with Chip. All she had to do was ignore his possible flirtations. And his eyes. And his smile.

"I can pick you up, or you can come to the exhibition yourself. There will be some sculptors and artists in addition to us photographers. People usually look around and ask questions." He grinned. "If we're lucky, we might sell something."

Tessa smiled back. It sounded uncomplicated and harmless. She offered to drive herself. She wanted control of when she arrived and when she left. Not to mention, she'd watched enough *Dateline* episodes to be cautious. Just in case his suave demeanor was a coverup for something more sinister.

After exchanging numbers, they parted. Tessa peeked at her newest contact in her phone: Chip Foster. *Nice name.*

Back in her dorm room, Tessa made good on her promise to contact Professor James. She read and re-read her email and finally pressed *Send.* And willed a response in her favor. If he didn't let her join mid semester. . . well, she just couldn't go there.

Later that night, Tessa sat at her desk working on a paper for English class when *I've Got You, Babe* rang from her phone. "Hey, Mom."

"Sorry I missed your call earlier. Everything okay?"

"All's good." She closed her laptop and plunked on her bed, snuggling into the pillows. "Remember how I told you about that aptitude test and how I could be an art restorer? Well, I just asked to be admitted into the art history program." Tessa's chest filled with unaccustomed pride.

"Oh, I'm so proud of you! And you're right—art restoration sounds just right for you. Oh, it's all so exciting! My daughter, the art restorer!" she gushed.

Debra's mother-ness was a little overboard. But Tessa drank it in anyway. Her mother had always accepted Tessa's choices, whether she put ketchup on scrambled eggs or proclaimed her independence from Grandmother's pushiness.

She and her mom had always been a united front. Tessa's dad Arthur Wilde, nicknamed Junior, had mood and behavior changes as early as Tessa could remember, and she'd clung to her mother for steadfastness.

When Tessa was old enough to understand these changes were a result of his alcoholism, her mother had stopped sugarcoating them. She'd answered Tessa's questions while reminding Tessa her father had an illness.

Debra had always known how to soften a blow but keep it real.

Now Tessa explained how their flea market runs inspired her choice.

"Oh, remember the stories we made up about the things we'd find? The crazier the story, the better. I don't remember a time when your eyes shone more brightly, or you looked more forward to a Saturday." She sighed. "Maybe you've found your passion."

Tessa laughed, sloughing off the weight of the past few weeks. "How about the time I opened the old-timey cabinet and the door fell off? I thought we'd have to pay a fortune when those owners accused me of damaging an antique."

"Right? Until you found the 'Made in China' label they forgot to remove."

They shared a quiet laugh.

"Maybe your old mom played a part in shaping your desires." Then her mother added, "And I'd be thrilled to have you home while you work toward that graduate degree. There are quite a few museums near us, you know. At least within a thirty-minute drive."

Tessa smiled. She appreciated that her mother wanted her around, and she knew that was her way of telling her. "I know. And hopefully one of them will take me on."

"They'd be lucky to have you."

Spoken like a true mom. Tessa's heart filled with love. She had the best mom in the world.

"Are you going to start spending your weekends at museums and art showings?"

Although her mom was teasing her, Tessa thought about Chip's offer to see an art show in person. She also knew that Mom would pick up on Tessa's attraction if she told her about him. She was intuitive that way. Even just dropping the information casually. "I might," was all she said.

After a brief pause her mother said, "I called to let you know I'm coming down this Saturday."

"I remember. I cleared my day completely for you." Tessa smiled even though her mom couldn't see it. She did love that her mom made the two-hour trip to Tessa's college every so often.

"I'm coming Friday, instead of Saturday, to visit your grandmother. I'll stay over so we'll still have our day together."

Tessa had just been to see Grandmother. And she'd reported on her condition. It was all her mom had badgered her about for days. Why was Mom coming now?

"Why? I just went there," Tessa asked. Was her mother trying to push Tessa back in her grandmother's life? Surely not. Even her mom knew how stressful being around Grandmother was.

"It turns out I have to see a client in your area."

Plausible but weak.

When her mom continued, the excuse seemed even weaker. "As long as I'm coming on Friday and you don't have classes, maybe you could come with me."

Tessa jumped up. Yes, her mom was definitely up to something. But Tessa was not going to reestablish any relationship with the grandmother she'd distanced herself from.

When Tessa didn't answer, her mother added, "I just wondered if you might want to find common ground before it's too late."

"'Common ground?' Tessa's voice rose. "We don't have any. And I am not trying to win the approval of a grandmother who doesn't even like me, Mom. And before you say anything—" Tessa could feel the tears prick behind her eyelids. "She *doesn't* like me, and we both know it." She exhaled slowly and shook her arm as if to steady herself. The silver bangles jingled, somehow soothing her. It was time Tessa preserved her feelings. And that meant no more interactions with Grandmother.

"Your last visit here was at our house for your graduation lunch. Remember she'd bought you something but you two had that tiff and you didn't open it?"

Of course Tessa remembered. "It was more than a 'tiff,' Mom." She had no desire to relive that bad scene. "It doesn't matter now. And that gift disappeared anyway."

Her mother couldn't think she actually wanted it, could she? The thought was ridiculous.

"I'm not demanding an old graduation gift from Grandmother. She probably forgot she ever bought me anything, and she certainly wouldn't still have it." Tessa began to pace. Anytime the topic of her grandmother came up, Tessa's anxiety levels rose.

She heard her mom sigh. "I suppose not. Still, you never know."

Tessa knew. "No." She would not visit her grandmother again. Not after the awful words Grandmother had said. Even if she'd thought Tessa was someone else.

Now she wanted to get off the phone before the argument escalated. Her mother had ruined Tessa's good vibe. "Gotta go, Mom. I'll see you Saturday. Text me when you're on your way, and I'll be in the lobby."

"Okay, fine."

They disconnected. Tessa grabbed her earbuds and brought up some favorite music on her phone. She needed a walk. In her ears Tom Petty sang "I Won't Back Down." Good advice. Tessa tucked Grandmother into a compartment marked Messy Family Stuff and left it there alongside the graduation day fiasco.

CHAPTER EIGHT

Esther

"Now Mayra, I know I put that little box somewhere," Esther said as she directed Mayra to search through her closet. Esther resumed looking through her shoe boxes, which she'd piled on her bed while Mayra rifled through pockets of clothes on hangers. "Check the red coat. I used to wear that all the time. Look for a jewelry box, one that rattles when you shake it. There's a bracelet inside."

For all her frenetic searching, today was a good day for Esther Wilde. She remembered Tessa and knew the girl had visited recently. And she remembered to call the lady "Mayra." When the pockets turned up empty, Esther fretted. "Do you remember seeing me put it anywhere else? It's a white box with a pink ribbon," she added.

On lucid days like this, Esther refused to let self-pity dictate the day. She had known for several years that her brain was misfiring. What began as misplacing keys morphed into forgetting daily tasks like turning off the stove and operating the washing machine. Her independent skills had waned beyond living alone. For a while, a crew of caretakers from Angels Wings had come in during waking hours. Esther was humiliated to have someone present while she bathed, cooked, or rested. Eventually, frequent falls stripped her of that final mask of self-sufficiency. Her horrors were realized, and Esther had to live in a "home" as she called it.

Nonetheless, Tessa's high school graduation gift, one Esther had never given her, stayed in Esther's possession while she waited for another opportunity. The charm bracelet lay in pale pink tissue, wrapped carefully and tied with a matching ribbon. Even during her foggy episodes, a term Esther coined, she didn't forget about the gift.

"I simply must find that box. We have to get it to Tessa," she implored Mayra.

"Ms. Esther, what's so special about that box?" Mayra paused, moving over to Esther and placing her hand on the old woman's arm. "Slow down a moment and let's talk."

"You don't understand, Mayra. The bracelet is the key to getting through to Tessa."

At Mayra's puzzled expression, Esther explained. "I once had dreams of a career. I wanted to carve my name into literary history. That unrealistic notion hurt plenty when life's demands brought me back to Earth. But," she held up one arthritic finger, "my bracelet was my treasure chest of good memories. They reminded me that life could be wonderful, even if it wasn't so exciting. Now, where could Tessa's gift possibly be?" Esther's voice shook and tears threatened to appear.

"Ms. Esther, how about we check your end table by the bed?" Mayra said. "I know you keep special items there."

The drawer was a catch-all for everything Esther considered important, whether it be a TV remote, Chapstick, or diamond earrings. It was one place Esther was sure to find whatever she needed at any given time. Her own charm bracelet sat there, in its original satin bag of forty years.

She allowed Mayra to wheel her over. While Mayra reached through the drawer, sorting the ordinary from the unusual, Esther watched as each object was brought out, holding her breath in anticipation, then exhaling in frustration when the box didn't materialize.

Finally, Mayra held up a little white jewelry-sized box with a frayed pink ribbon. "Look what I found, Ms. Esther."

"Oh, heavens," Esther exclaimed, her hand over her heart. She let her head fall back in relief then popped it up and remarked, "I don't know why I didn't think to look there first."

Mayra handed it over, and Esther clasped the box to her chest, a little smile growing on her face.

The good day was fading fast, and Esther's brain felt fuzzy around the edges, like it was bordered with cotton. This box belonged to Tessa. Why did Esther still have it?

Tessa.

Tess—.

A lady next to her asked, "Will you give this to Tessa on her next visit?"

Esther Wilde stared at her unblinking. "Who?" The cloud was back, obliterating any connections of past to present.

"Tessa," the lady said.

Memories of a little golden-haired girl flashed in Esther's mind. "You know Tessa?"

The lady said Tessa came to visit last week, but Esther just stared at her and rolled the name in her foggy brain a few times. She tried to grasp why it sounded familiar and sad at the same time.

Esther looked at the woman next to her. "Are you Sally's replacement?"

When the lady just smiled, somewhat sadly, Esther's eyes traveled to the little box she held onto fiercely. Esther couldn't remember what was in it, but she knew it was important. She brought a shaky hand to her mouth patting it mindlessly, as if she could tap the answer out. What was in this box? When no answer came, she shook it. The box rattled like something small and jingly was inside. Jewelry? Recognition remained a foreign, unclaimed asset.

Not-Sally patted Esther's hand. "You can give it to Tessa next time she comes. Why don't you hold on to it a bit. I'll be back shortly," she said and left.

Esther closed her eyes, keeping a grip on the box and remembered a time when she had her own little box to open.

•   •   •

"Yoo hoo, Essie girl! Where are ya?" Art's voice boomed from the front entry.

Essie scurried from the kitchen untying her apron and fluffing her hair. "Oh, my. You're home early, dear. I've only just begun prepping the roast—" Her voice faltered as she took in Arthur's exuberance.

His eyes danced in merriment, and he held his hands behind his back, as if hiding a treasure.

She only wished she could absorb his excitement. Art was a solid provider and an honest man. But this was not the life she had foreseen fifteen years ago. Although she was pleasantly surprised that he wasn't the ogre she remembered from school, she hadn't intended to date him, let alone marry him. She was a modern woman. Essie Overton had intended to become a travel writer, to break ground as one of the few women journalists in Georgia.

Fate had different plans.

She had done what she'd needed to do for her family. With the bank loan, her parents had kept the pecan farm running, adding machines to speed shelling and picking, offering bundles of pecans to the new chains of grocery stores that were sprouting up. Without the help of Art's father, who knows what would have become of it? Of them?

When Art had asked her to marry him, she'd hesitated only a moment, allowing the wisps of the dying dream to flow around her. Then she had put her feet on solid ground and took the common road. Maybe sparks didn't fly for her, but she loved Art's values and sacrifices. He worked hard to make something for himself— for them—and she appreciated that work ethic. Now, at the age of thirty-four, she was an accomplished bridge player, a savvy dinner hostess, and a reliable volunteer. But she hadn't made him a father. If only she could get pregnant. She had such hopes that a quick and growing family would bury the ache of her dashed dreams.

Rarely did she allow herself to imagine a life different from what she had; those days of big dreams belonged to the past. But in a moment like this when she stood before her excited husband, a wave of something unsettled washed over her. She'd done the right thing, made the tough choice; why was motherhood denied her?

She faced her eager husband with hands on hips, a smile playing on her lips. "What did you do, Arthur Wilde?"

Better to play along than allow her runaway thoughts to focus on the fact that her husband often "surprised" her with things she didn't really want—a membership to the local country club, dinner party invitations for political bigwigs that she didn't give a whit about, etc.

"Close your eyes, my dear, and hold out your hand," he teased.

Essie closed her eyes, hoping he hadn't bought tickets to some fundraiser where she'd have to play hostess first. She extended her hand, palm open.

"Ta-da!" He presented a small square box.

She found herself holding a tiny box, a ring-sized box. She didn't wear a lot of jewelry and Art wasn't usually a jewelry-giving kind of man.

When she turned her curious gaze to her husband, he was practically bouncing with anticipation. "Go ahead, open it!" he said.

She did. Curiosity turned to incomprehension as she held a small— only a half inch in length and width—gold typewriter. A charm. "Art, I don't have a charm bracelet," she said.

He whipped a longer jewelry box from the inside pocket of his suit jacket. "You do now!" Art rocked on his heels, puffing like a peacock with his double surprise.

Art presented the gift to Essie with such flair and pride that she didn't have the heart to say she found charm bracelets cumbersome. She avoided most jewelry unless it was the simple strand of pearls which she wore daily. That gift from her father on her fourteenth birthday still held dear sentiments.

"Oh, my!" was all she could exclaim. She fought furiously to find the words to express gratitude while her husband's face began to wither. "Oh,

really, Art, you shouldn't have," she whimpered, trying to buy time to show the joy he expected her to feel.

"Oh, well, if you don't like it," he started, the hurt obvious. Art was not a man to hide his emotions, not like Essie could.

"No, no, that's not it at all," she started. Then she found something to cling to that made it all better. The charm. She looked fondly at her husband. "You got me a typewriter as my first charm."

He understood. He knew how important writing was.

It meant the world to Essie, and she threw her arms around him.

It didn't take long for his disappointment to turn to relief. "You like it?"

She had tears in her eyes. Tears of gratitude. He had accepted the part of her she'd quelled years ago. "I'll wear it, Art. Proudly," she gushed, happy to be genuinely excited by this surprise.

She vowed never to pity her lot in life again.

•   •   •

"You want me to put Tessa's gift away, Ms. Esther?" Not-Sally flitted about stirring up dust and odd feelings. "I left you an hour ago, and here you are in the same position as before." She chuckled.

Hazy recognition and half-remembered words. Tessa. Gift. That was as close as the memory came. She looked at the box, still sitting in her lap. Esther unfastened the bow. The pink ribbon fell away, and shaky hands lifted the lid. A charm bracelet, different from her own, lay nestled inside tissue paper. When she pulled it out, a lone charm hung from it. A graduation hat. Her mind's eye, though dimming, saw herself handing this very box to her granddaughter, and Tessa setting it down and stomping upstairs, never opening it. The memory brought sadness. That was the last day she saw her granddaughter.

Something etched itself vaguely at the edges of her brain. She had a vision of an older Tessa, more mature and confident. Now where would Esther have seen her? She examined the cap and its tassel. The first symbolic gesture of Tessa's adult life. Esther remembered how she had hoped to impart her wisdom. How Tessa could use the charm bracelet the same way Esther did, as a talisman for significant events. How each charm Tessa chose or received would symbolize her life's journey. More than that even. A tiny trinket could shape or validate her worth. As the ones on Esther's bracelet did. Esther planned to teach her willful granddaughter how to start her own memory bank of charms. Tessa would see value in experiences and learn to appreciate small events instead of searching for risky, untested adventures.

Not-Sally stood in front of her. "Do you want me to put it back in the drawer for you?

That way, we both know where it is. You can give it to her next time she comes, hmm?"

Esther handed her the box. "Make sure you tuck it safely back there," she said, unsure why it mattered. The Not-Sally lady said she'd be back in a few minutes to take Esther to dinner. Dinner? Esther peered outside at the sunny sky. Who ate dinner in broad daylight?

Her gaze traveled to the patio where old people sat in chaise lounges and uniformed workers lingered about. She saw an iron fence across the way, partially hidden behind some shrubbery. With a sharp intake of breath, panic overcame her. She'd been imprisoned. Or hospitalized. Against her will.

She tried to stand but fell back in her chair, stifling a whimper. She couldn't alert the guards—the uniformed people. A knock at her door startled her. When it opened and a man in a teal uniform strode over, she jerked the chair toward the back door. It didn't move, and the man in the silent black sneakers crept closer

No, no, no, she silently screamed. She would not be taken God knew where. She tried to stop him, shaking her head and swatting at him with her arms, but the man didn't leave. In fact he messed with the chair and it began to move. Her scrawny arms couldn't stop the large wheels from turning although she tried.

"Ms. Esther," the strange man's voice said over Esther's shoulder, "just relax. I'm taking you for dinner." He pushed the chair toward that front door.

She didn't believe him and cried out.

Instantly, the chair stopped moving and the man stopped pushing. "Are you okay, Ms. Esther?" he asked.

He sounded genuine, but Esther knew better. He was trying to trick her. She mustered all the assertion she could. "No, sir. You are not taking me out of this room. You leave me right here until Junior arrives. He and I will be leaving this place immediately. I will not stand for you people holding me against my will." Her voice had escalated, but she didn't mind. Maybe someone would come to her rescue. She channeled her most intimidating voice but all she heard was a trembly, weak sound.

The man stood quietly next to her. He wasn't unnerved or taken aback by her words. To her surprise, he knelt beside her. His eyes were kind and compassionate.

"Ms. Esther, I'd like to take you to the dining room. Would that be all right?"

His gentle voice calmed her. She still didn't know where she was, but if it had a dining room and people who spoke kindly, it couldn't be prison. And it might even be nice. She nodded.

CHAPTER NINE

Tessa

Tessa wandered toward the college track. She figured there she could walk freely, letting her mind wander without the worry of walking into people. Or tripods.

Why would her mother urge Tessa to re-engage with Grandmother? She knew how their last face-to-face encounter had ended.

•   •   •

After commencement, Tessa, just barely eighteen years old, drove home. The summer morning progressed smoothly. She and her three hundred fellow seniors clapped and applauded in the right places and behaved themselves. Now they were free. Humming one of her favorite tunes, Tessa pulled in the driveway, lost in thought about upcoming graduation parties. She carried her diploma, cap, and gown as she walked through her door. "Hey, Mom! I'm home. Can you believe I'm a—" She stopped as a powdery floral scent hit her nostrils. She knew that smell.

"Hello, Tessa."

She spotted her grandmother sitting primly in the wing chair by the bay window. Her ankles were crossed, and her purse stood at attention on her lap. Tessa's smile and light-heartedness faded. Lunch with Grandmother. Tessa had forgotten. She moved into the room, eyeing her grandmother while tossing her cap and gown on the back of the couch. As expected, Grandmother's pursed lips converted to a grimace.

"Grandmother," Tessa said by way of greeting. She plunked unceremoniously on the sofa and twirled the padded diploma in her hands. "I'd forgotten you were coming."

"Well, it is a big, if not expected occasion. Of course, I'd be here," Grandmother sniffed.

Tessa mentally rolled her eyes, hating that she was too timid to physically do it.

"What took you so long, dear? The high school is just a few miles away."

Tessa couldn't contain her snarkiness. "I do have friends, Grandmother. We took pictures." She stopped fiddling with the diploma. She placed it on the end table and looked at her grandmother.

"No need for rudeness, Missy," Grandmother said.

Tessa tightened her mouth into a thin line. She didn't want to have an argument on the day of her high school graduation.

She was saved by her mother walking in. "Hi, honey. Lunch is ready."

Tessa pushed off the couch, heading for the stairs and the safety of her little loft room. "Jordy is coming at five o'clock to pick me up, Mom. Dinner and grad parties later, okay? I'm gonna change, and I'll be right down." She didn't wait for her mother's reply. Or Grandmother's.

"Just a minute, Tessa Catherine," her grandmother commanded. Her voice, strong and cold, wafted across the room as heavily as her signature cologne.

Tessa stiffened at the foot of the staircase and turned, fixing a smile on her face. "Yes?" She used her saccharine sweet voice, the one that made her want to scream. The fake one.

Grandmother's blue eyes blinked a few times, and her brows came together as if she had forgotten what she wanted to say.

Tessa waited impatiently. After a moment of continued silence, she asked again, "Yes?"

"What?" Grandmother stared blankly.

With eyebrows raised, Tessa watched her. Curiosity replaced impatience. Senior moment? Brain fart?

Grandmother cleared her throat and shook her head almost imperceptibly, seeming to regain her ground. "Here's your graduation gift." She stood up and held her arm straight out to Tessa, her fingers gripping a small jewelry-sized box.

Tessa stared at it, wondering what her grandmother could have bought. Most of her gifts were practical, not sentimental like a piece of jewelry would be.

Grandmother shook the package a little, a cue for Tessa to take the box.

Tessa reluctantly crossed the room and took the proffered gift. "Thank you," Tessa offered tentatively, more of a question than a statement.

Her grandmother rolled her eyes.

A shot of anger coursed through Tessa. Eye-rolling was okay for a seventy-something-year-old, but not for a teenager? Tessa reminded herself she was eighteen and technically an adult.

"Be firm with your words, Tessa. A young man wants a young lady who is not a weakling." Before Tessa could respond that she wasn't looking for a man and she wasn't a weakling, Grandmother gave a cluck of her tongue and moved toward the dining room. "Now, shall we sit for lunch?"

Tessa watched her grandmother. Her outfit, sleek and crisp and elegant, belied the humidity of June. How did she keep her slacks perfectly pressed and her blouses unwrinkled in the Southern heat? Perhaps her cold heart seeped onto her clothes. Tessa smiled to herself.

With a glance at her mother, Tessa placed the unopened box on a table near the stairs and followed her grandmother into the dining room. She'd change her clothes after lunch. Normally, she and her mother ate their meals at the kitchen table, but Grandmother would expect a fine dining experience. Mom always obliged. Sure enough, the table was set with good dishes, cloth napkins, and the fancy serving platters—for the carryout food Tessa knew her mother had purchased and placed in her own dishes. She smiled knowingly and her mother provided a small wink. The three of them sat down for a delicious restaurant-cooked meal.

"Thank you for the graduation gift," Tessa said, trying to be polite and making sure she declared it. She hated admitting Grandmother's disapproval still got under her skin, but she felt herself consciously strengthening her tone and voice.

Grandmother shook her napkin and placed it carefully on her lap. "It is your high school graduation. It's what family does, dear."

"Family" was not a term Tessa would use to describe the three of them unless you were speaking strictly DNA. Even that, Grandmother and Debra didn't share.

They passed around the mojo chicken, yellow rice, black beans, and sweet plantains. As traditional as Grandmother was, at least she enjoyed Cuban food, one of Tessa's favorites.

"So, you're cool with me staying over at Jordy's house tonight after the party, right?" Tessa addressed her mother.

Debra nodded and began to respond when Grandmother butted in. "Honestly Tessa, a young lady does not need to be hooting and hollering through town like a crazed animal just because she's reached an expected milestone in her life. Why in heaven's name do you need an all-night party? Shouldn't you celebrate with an elegant dinner somewhere? I'd be glad to pay if that's the issue. In fact, you could invite a few of your friends to Mauricio's tonight."

Mauricio's was the hoity-toity restaurant old people went to. It was the last place Tessa wanted to go. And she sure wasn't going to invite her friends to that stuffy place where everyone looked down their noses at each other.

Her mom saved Tessa from answering. "Esther, these kids want to shed the stress of final exams and let their hair down. Celebrate this accomplishment." Mom always tried to use the lingo Grandmother would understand. She was good about being the bridge.

"Fine, but don't say I didn't warn you if she gets branded a hoodlum or a tramp. She traipses around with a bunch of wild-natured girls she calls friends," Grandmother said, shaking her fork in warning.

Tessa's blood shot up a thousand degrees as Grandmother denounced her lifestyle and friends. For the hundredth time.

She jumped up from the table, threw her napkin on her chair, and faced her grandmother. Years of listening without speaking or swallowing retorts instead of spitting them out ended. She'd watched Grandmother belittle her mother while praising the father who'd walked out on them years ago. It was time to declare her independence from her grandmother's wrath. "I'm eighteen years old, Grandmother. You've criticized me all my life, judging everything I did as not up to your standards. You've hated my clothes, my hairstyles, my choice of friends, and even the way I walked. I've had it."

"Now, Tessa." Her mother rose slowly from her chair, and Tessa knew her mom intended to diffuse the situation. "Let's just sit down and discuss this."

Tessa faced the two women who had influenced her the most. The one whose love made up for not having a father around, and the one whose love was only for him. Tessa pointed to her grandmother. "Most of my childhood was spent trying to please you and all you did was criticize me. You can take back your . . ." She looked towards the staircase where the gift was stashed, realizing she'd never opened it, "—whatever is in that box. I don't even want it. You only gave me a gift because 'it's what family does.'" Tessa used air quotes and a condescending tone. She didn't care if Grandmother was offended, angered, or disgusted. With that diatribe, Tessa stormed up the stairs to her room. Ruined. Her graduation was ruined. No, she wouldn't let it. Grandmother was not taking that away from her.

She heard her mother talking to her grandmother, but Tessa put in her ear buds, covered the noise, and turned off her feelings.

•   •   •

Tessa pushed the memory from her mind. She'd moved on. It had been two years since that lunch. She wasn't walking back into another Grandmother-infused disaster. Uh-uh. No way.

She thought about the momentary lapse of attention when her grandmother had handed Tessa the gift. At the time Tessa had written it off as old age but now she wondered if it was a sign of Alzheimer's. Not that it changed anything. She would not reconnect with her grandmother.

"Hey girl!"

Tessa pulled her ear buds out to hear Kendra calling her name and jogging up toward her.

"I thought that was you," she said huffing heavily. She put one hand on her waist and tried to catch her breath. "What are you doing on the track?"

"I thought you had study group or something," Tessa answered, ignoring the question.

Kendra waved her hand dismissively. "Nah, we got it covered. Too nice a day to waste in front of a tablet or computer screen."

"Little early for St. Patrick's Day, isn't it?" Tessa teased, nodding at Kendra's green-streaked hair.

"This is what you'd call an experiment that won't be repeated," she said, touching the curly, pea-green locks.

When Tessa snickered Kendra added, "No judging, friend. Can't learn what doesn't work if you don't try, ya know. Speaking of learning, are you going to class or what? You don't have a backpack, and you're walking around the track, so I'm going out on a limb and saying no."

Tessa gave a short laugh but stopped walking. "Just thinking." She turned to Kendra and took a leap of trust, so to speak. "My grandmother just moved into Sunset Shadows Assisted Living about twenty minutes from here. She has Alzheimer's. I went to see her a couple of weeks ago, and it didn't go well."

"Ouch. I didn't know you had a grandmother around here."

"I didn't until a few weeks ago."

Kendra gestured to a bench off the track, and they went over there and sat down.

"Are you close?" Kendra asked.

Tessa refrained from snorting. "Absolutely not." When Kendra seemed to be taken aback, Tessa explained. "We don't get along. Never really have. In fact, I hadn't seen her in two years until the day Mom asked me to check on her. The day you and I went to see *Love Story*."

"And you never said a word." She seemed a little hurt.

Tessa scooted back on the bench, letting her head fall back. "I don't like talking about it much, Kendra. My grandmother has never really liked me."

"You want to talk about it now?" Kendra asked.

Tessa sat up straight. "Not really. My mom asked me to check that Grandmother was taken care of so I went over. The place is clean and safe, and she looks fine. I did my duty and that's the end of it."

"You're not going back?" Kendra asked slowly. "Ever?"

Tessa crossed her arms. "Why would I? When she didn't recognize me, she told me I wasn't nearly as pretty as her granddaughter. And when she did recognize me, she only cared where my father was." She turned her head away. "He's been dead for four years."

Kendra linked her arm into Tessa's. "I'm sorry. Family's tough." Leaning close, she whispered, "You want I should go to that place and dye her hair purple?"

Tessa imagined her composed, straitlaced grandmother parading around with magenta hair and laughed out loud. She was grateful for Kendra's humor.

"You want to grab a coffee?" her friend asked.

Tessa didn't want to think about Grandmother anymore. She nodded and stood. Together, they blended with the other college students at Florida Coastal University. The ones who laughed away their worries.

CHAPTER TEN

Esther

Soft rains tinkled outside Esther's bedroom window. The slats of her blinds filtered in a grayish light. Esther lay in bed. Her eyes roamed the length of the room settling on her bedside table where the light from her digital clock cast an eerie glow. It was 7:17 a.m. and Esther rolled to her side to grasp her charm bracelet. She let the charms filter through her fingers, feeling the weight of them. The weight of her memories. Most days the memories filled her with contentment, occasionally with regret. This morning she wasn't sure how they'd make her feel. She chose one charm, and in the semi-darkness felt the contours until she could identify it. The graduation cap. Instead of relishing the memory of her own high school graduation, Esther's mind recalled Tessa's.

The day she set out to buy Tessa a charm bracelet Esther did so with determination. She bought a silver rope bracelet and tiny graduation cap charm. Tessa's adult life would start upon her high school graduation, just like Esther's did. If the girl could see how life could build memories, and charms could capture them, Esther knew Tessa would ground herself and make practical plans. She wouldn't traipse all over knocking down walls or breaking glass ceilings or whatever she planned.

Esther had recognized the wanderlust in Tessa's eyes years ago. The girl had ignored Esther's sage advice to find a steady beau in high school. In fact, she'd insisted on more schooling. She wanted to "be somebody."

Phooey. Tessa's misguided beliefs didn't stop Esther, though. She'd ignored Tessa's desires, the frivolous, unrestrained dreams that danced in her eyes, and determined to set her on a proper course. Esther couldn't bear the thought of Tessa getting highfalutin' ideas about independence. It only bred regret. She knew Tessa would have her heart broken—not by some boy but by her own dreams. Like Esther's dreams were. She wouldn't let that happen.

The gently falling rains gained speed. Esther turned her attention to the water cascading out her window, falling from the outside gutters like giant faucets on full blast. The sound was loud enough to wake anyone who might still be sleeping.

Someone knocked on her door outside the bedroom. Esther set down the bracelet and pulled her covers up to her chin.

A lady with the teal uniform and wavy, slick hair sailed in like she knew exactly where to go. But for heaven's sake, Esther didn't know who she was, even if the woman carried an air of familiarity about her. "What are you doing in my bedroom?" Esther demanded, gripping the edge of the comforter.

"Mayra, ma'am," the lady said as she poured a cup of water and encouraged Esther to sit up in bed. "It's time for your medicine," she urged.

"I don't take medicine. Now, you get my son right now," Esther demanded.

The brisk woman who reminded Esther of her beloved Sally, stood next to her bed. "Now, Ms. Esther. I've got your medications. You take these, and I'll go get the wheelchair. You can have your coffee in the living room." Not-Sally said this while propping pillows behind Esther to raise her to a sitting position.

Wheelchair?

Esther held a little paper cup in one hand, two pills inside it, and a glass of water in the other. As she watched Not-Sally move about, that aura of familiarity drifted along with her. Like an aroma that triggered comfort. But she did not know this woman, this room. And for goodness' sake, Esther Wilde didn't need a wheelchair. She'd been walking on her two legs for—. She paused. *How old was she?* Didn't matter. She was capable of walking from point A to point B on her own. She put the pills and the water on the side table and threw off the bed covers.

Esther gasped when she saw the bird-like legs that stuck out from under her flannel nightgown. They were dotted with brown spots and as skinny as a chicken's. She wiggled them just to make sure they were hers. Good God in heaven, how did she get so old? She brought her hand to her mouth in surprise and received another shock. Arthritic, knobby knuckles covered her mouth. She was an old person. Was this a dream? She squeezed her wrist with her other hand. No, not a dream.

"Let's go out by the window and enjoy the beautiful day." Not-Sally chuckled. At Esther's frown, she added, "Just kidding, Ms. Esther. It's a nasty morning. Raining like God's watering the whole earth." As Not-Sally transferred Esther into the wheelchair, Esther pointed to her bracelet.

Not-Sally handed it to her, along with the paper cup. "Ms. Esther, you gotta take this medicine. It helps you. You take it every day."

Something Sally would have said. Like her, this Not-Sally was bossy. Esther swallowed them down.

Meanwhile, Not-Sally continued. "I kinda like rainy days. We get so much sunshine in this lovely state that a rainy day reminds me to appreciate it."

Esther caressed her bracelet as they moved through the little apartment. Movie posters, knickknacks—she remembered these adorning the walls and shelves of a different home. And Tessa. The name still echoed in her heart, love and regret beating simultaneously.

Esther took the coffee Not-Sally offered. Sitting in her recliner with her special quilt over her lap, Esther watched the droplets of rain on the windowpane, trickling one minute and fading away the next. Like memories. Sometimes images ran rampant in her head, vivid and life-like. The next minute they vanished.

A phone rang, breaking into her thoughts. Esther searched for the kitchen wall phone, but it wasn't there.

"Sally, my phone's ringing. Can you please answer it? Maybe Junior's calling."

"It's my phone, Ms. Esther." She reached into a pocket of her teal shirt. "Hello? Mayra here."

A few uh-huhs and "Oh, reallys?" later, Sally turned to Esther. No, not Sally. *Not-Sally.*

"Was that Junior?" Esther heard the hope in her voice even as sadness filled her heart. She didn't know why.

"No, ma'am," Not-Sally said. "That was the front desk. You'll be having a visitor later today. A Debra. Said she's your daughter-in-law. That Tessa's mom?"

DebraTessaJunior. The names ran together like one. Esther linked them in her mind, or rather they did it themselves. Debra. An uncomfortable part of the word. She was good to little Tessa and good for Junior, but she'd upended Esther's world when she'd divorced Arthur Junior.

•   •   •

"Esther," Debra said, "you know how hard it is to shield Tessa from her father's drinking. He comes and goes with no phone call. I worry day and night if he's in a ditch or in the hospital or worse. I knew he was a drinker when I married him, but I had no idea how bad it would get. I don't know how long I can do this." Debra paced in Esther's kitchen while Tessa was playing in another room.

Debra's words stung. More importantly, they frightened Esther. She turned to her daughter-in-law, holding up the hands that had been shaping meatloaf. "Debra, you cannot divorce him. My heavens, the scandal! Not to mention what it would do to my granddaughter." She turned back around to the dinner, hoping Debra couldn't see the panic in her eyes or detect the fear in her voice.

"Really, Esther," Debra said, throwing up her arms. "Divorce is accepted, even commonplace." She lowered her voice. "Besides, don't you worry about what his drinking will do to Tessa? She's five years old. She doesn't understand his passing out—she thinks he's napping. And when he slurs his words, she thinks he's being funny. He's not a stoic drunk. You know it as well as I do. He's sloppy. As she gets older, we won't be able to excuse it."

"Now don't you say such things in front of the child," she admonished. "Tessa could be right around the corner."

As if Esther's fears had a voice, Tessa came skipping in the kitchen. "I'm hungry," she announced in her pretend, grown-up voice.

"Go wash your hands and Grandmother will get you a cookie," Esther said.

When Tessa ran off to the bathroom, Esther turned her admonishment full force on her daughter-in-law. "I will not have Junior talked about at the country club just because you can't handle him. He's a loving father and husband and has always provided for you. I'd think the fact that he brings home enough money for you to stay home and take care of Tessa would mean something to you. A good wife would make his home comfortable so he wants to stay more often."

Debra stared silently at her mother-in-law, the kitchen island the smallest obstacle between them.

She's usually a mouse of a woman, thought Esther, regarding the unfamiliar steel glint in Debra's eyes.

"Esther, I don't owe Arthur anything." She lowered her voice and whispered fiercely, "Yes, I loved him when we married. I love Tessa, too, and would do anything for her. She needs a stable home and that's my priority. If Arthur can't stop drinking, I can't stay. I will not risk Tessa's stability." She looked past Esther toward the bathroom where they could hear that Tessa had shut off the faucet.

Debra narrowed her eyes, and Esther could feel the challenge in them. She finished preparing the meatloaf and placed it in the pan, a diversion while she gathered her thoughts.

Debra rose a little higher in Esther's esteem. She'd never tell Debra that, of course. The woman needed to believe Esther Wilde could be a threat if she threw Junior out. Because if her daughter-in-law did that, Junior would come to live with Esther. She had no strength to address Junior's problems. Debra was better suited to handle Esther's son than Esther was, not that she'd ever admit that. "Don't underestimate me, Debra. I'll fight for custody of Tessa."

As the words left her mouth, Esther regretted them. She had never threatened Debra, never used Tessa as a pawn in keeping Junior's reputation safe, but she did it now. Instead of backing down or trying to make up for what she'd said, she dug the knife in further. "I am her blood. And I will be part of Tessa's life." Then she turned to the sink, scrubbing her hands and hoping her words would be enough.

Tessa chose that moment to come skipping back to the kitchen and stopped abruptly, looking between the two of them. "Mommy?" she asked Debra.

Both recovered quickly. Debra scooped up Tessa while Esther dried her hands then fumbled with the cookie jar for one of her Snickerdoodles.

• • •

The memory rushed back with such force tears sprang to Esther's eyes. That was the beginning of the end. Debra had divorced Junior, Esther had never followed through on her threat, and Debra had raised Tessa, taking little advice from Esther. The spirited child had grown into a girl full of her own ideas, not those Esther had imparted.

Esther had grasped her bracelet so tightly there were indentations in her palm. She loosened her hold but kept the bracelet clasped.

Someone was rustling about in her bedroom. "Who's in there?" she demanded.

The kind-eyed lady showed her face. "Just me. Mayra. I'm about finished making your bed. Today is shower day, so we'll get you bathed and prettied up. Debra will be here after lunch." She retreated, leaving Esther to ponder why Debra was coming over. She only saw her and young Tessa on Sundays for dinners or the occasional special holiday. For the most part, they talked on the phone and for specific reasons. What could she want from Esther that she was coming over in person?

•　　•　　•

Esther sat on the lanai. Puddles of water pooled on the ground and trees dripped water droplets occasionally. Had it rained? She looked up at the blue expanse, finding it hard to believe it could have. The cloudless sky shimmered. It reminded her of peach-picking days when the branches bowed low to the ground. She would trail after her father, dragging her wooden bucket, and filling it with the fuzzy fruit from the lowest branches. The air would fill with the aroma of peaches that had split open when they fell or were poked at by birds. Esther remembered sneaking a peach, trying to hide the juice that dripped down her chin and staining her overalls. The stickiness almost welded her fingers to the bucket handle as she'd traipsed after Daddy. The Overtons only had a few rows of peaches; pecans were their mainstay. But Esther had loved the sweet, juicy fruit best.

"Ms. Esther, your daughter-in-law is here."

Esther was jolted out of her memory by Not-Sally. People always invaded her sentimental moments. She turned her head slightly and caught sight of a woman approaching. A brunette with wavy, shoulder-length hair. She wore smart dress pants and a lovely, patterned blouse. Very professional, very appropriate. This face felt familiar. Esther demanded, "I know you. How do I know you?"

"I'm Debra." She clutched a purse like a life ring. Or a shield.

"Junior's Debra?"

"Yes. I—I want to talk about Tessa." She stood in front of Esther. She seemed anxious, nervous even.

Esther remembered this one. Junior's wife. She was quiet but she could handle Junior. Esther liked her. "Well, come on. Sit down." She gestured to a nearby patio chair.

Before Debra could sit, a few raindrops made their appearance. Esther looked at the sky. Just a moment ago she'd admired the baby blue skies. A sun shower, that's what it was.

Debra grabbed the handles of Esther's chair and took her onto a screened porch, placing Esther in front of a brightly patterned chair. Hibiscus flowers of red and white adorned the cushions. Debra sat down and the two women were face-to-face.

As if a curtain lifted, Esther's mind rooted itself in that day she saw Debra and Tessa at the girl's graduation lunch. The scene replayed before her like it had just happened. Maybe it had.

"Debra, you must convince Tessa to replace that silly notion of hers to seek a career. Take it from me, I thought being a writer was my future. Thank goodness, I married Art instead. Can you imagine if I'd had to travel to Woodstock or college protests?" She shuddered. "It wouldn't be safe, not to mention it's not the proper environment for a lady. No, Tessa must find a nice boy to settle down with. Perhaps take a secretarial course and get a little job where she'd have opportunities to meet nice, young men."

Debra stared at Esther. Then she sank into the cushy chair.

"You're going to have to convince her," Esther insisted.

Debra put a hand to her forehead. "You wanted to be a journalist?"

What was wrong with Debra? She knew that, didn't she?

"Before I got some sense in me, yes. A travel writer, really. Then, I realized marrying Art was a better choice. Women shouldn't seek careers for themselves." She leaned towards Debra. "You've got to remind Tessa of that."

"I'm still digesting that you wanted to have a career," Debra mumbled.

"Speak up, for heaven's sake," Esther reprimanded.

"Sorry. I said, since you once had career aspirations, surely you can understand why Tessa might have some, too. She wants to do something meaningful and independent just like you once wanted to."

Esther's voice escalated. "I most certainly have a meaningful life. Raising Junior and taking care of my home and husband is a full and rewarding life. Don't you dare think otherwise." Even though Debra spoke the thoughts that often ran through Esther's own mind, it wasn't appropriate for Junior's wife to point them out.

"I—I didn't mean that," Debra started. She sighed loudly and placed her hands on her thighs, rubbing them back and forth a few times. "Shouldn't you encourage Tessa to reach for her dreams instead of suppressing them?"

Esther sat as straight as she could in the chair. "Absolutely not. Dreams are for children and sleeping. Tessa should be practical and face reality."

Just then, the sliding glass door opened. The nice, brown-eyed lady strode over. "Hello, Ms. Esther. That little sun shower just came out of nowhere, didn't it?"

The face was familiar. Beautiful waves of black hair clung to the lady's head, ending at her neck. Such a smart look. Not-Sally.

Esther remembered her manners. "This is—" she stopped.

Who was this younger woman again?

"—Debra," the lady finished.

Not-Sally addressed Debra. "I brought something from Ms. Esther's room, hoping Tessa would be with you today." She pulled a white box from her pocket and held it out to Esther, speaking to her. "I thought you might want Debra to give this to Tessa."

Esther's memories fired up, snippets of vague recollection lacking details. But she recognized the box. "Why do you have Tessa's gift?" She raised an eyebrow at Not-Sally.

"Ms. Esther, I brought it from your room. You want Debra to give it to Tessa or do you want to save it for Tessa's next visit?" The woman stood there holding Tessa's box.

"Debra." Esther said the name to jumpstart her memory. *Who was Debra?*

She narrowed her eyes at the woman sitting across from her, willing recognition to come. Junior's wife! Tessa's graduation gift! Esther latched on to a fleeting memory before it paddled away. She took the box from Not-Sally.

"Give this to Tessa, Debra. It's a charm bracelet she can use to collect memories. The right memories. Marriage and family. She doesn't need to hobnob with those girls she runs with. They'll lead her down the wrong road. Set her straight, Debra. Before it's too late," she warned. She thrust out the gift.

Debra took the bracelet and placed it on her lap. "Is this what you tried to give Tessa at graduation two years ago?"

Graduation? Whose graduation? Esther looked at the white box. She didn't know.

Not-Sally cleared her throat and said quietly, "Lucidity comes and goes. Even within a conversation."

Debra nodded and smiled thinly, and Not-Sally moved away.

The woman turned to Esther. "Remember Tessa, your granddaughter? She's twenty years old now. She's in college and—" The woman stopped talking.

Thank God. Esther didn't know what she was going on about. Her Tessa was a child.

"Who's watching little Tessa?" Esther demanded. "She's much too small to be left alone. Now, if you bring her to the house, I'll be glad to look after her."

When Debra only frowned, Esther continued. "She loves my charm bracelet. And dressing up," Esther chuckled. "Why just the other day she modeled my mother's old fox stole and paraded in the living room. You should have seen her. She jutted her hip out, hand on top, my white gloves practically swallowing her entire arm."

Esther pictured little Tessa, the eager-to-please child. As vividly as the picture flashed, it changed. She saw an older Tessa, no longer playing dress-up but telling Esther stories. The memories switched around in her mind like pictures out of order.

Esther's voice wobbled. "She's so much like I was. So inventive and creative." Her voice trailed off.

Debra leaned toward Esther. "Some of Tessa's favorite childhood memories are playing with your clothes and jewelry." She fiddled with a white box in her lap. "It's time for the truth to be told," the woman said. She inhaled deeply and said, "Tessa said you called her 'Lou Ann.' I thought—" Debra stopped suddenly and stared searchingly at Esther. "Esther? Are you listening? Can you hear me?"

Esther had sat back in her chair, eyeing the woman warily. "Of course, I hear you," Esther answered, crossing her arms. "I'm not deaf, for heaven's sake." *Tessa* was a name that tried to poke through the bubble that kept Esther's memory from being accessible. Lou Ann was familiar. Junior's old girlfriend. This woman was not her, though.

"Now, who are you?" Esther demanded.

"I— I'm Debra, Esther," the woman finally answered after rubbing her hand across her forehead. "I'm Tessa's mother."

Esther eyed this one carefully. Her hair was wrong, her voice was wrong, her mannerisms were wrong. "No, you're not. I don't know who you are, but you can leave now." Esther used her best I'm-not-fooling-around voice. She didn't like strangers, especially ones who didn't wear uniforms.

The strange woman blew out the breath she seemed to be holding. She stood up.

Meanwhile, Not-Sally had returned with a tray of coffee. "I'm sorry. Looks like this day isn't such a great one after all." She was speaking to the woman.

The stranger held a white box in her hands which she placed in a purse. Faint bells of recognition sounded in Esther's head, but they were too distant to hear clearly.

"I'll give Tessa the gift," the woman mumbled to Esther.

Finally, Not-Sally and the stranger left.

Esther closed her eyes to enjoy her memories.

CHAPTER ELEVEN

Tessa

Tessa had just changed into her favorite jeans and a band tee shirt when her phone pinged with a text. The *Good Morning! I'm here!* was a lot of sunshine for an early Saturday morning. That was her mom, though. Bangles on her arm, hair pulled up in a loose bun, Tessa left her room and stepped on the elevator.

She'd slept poorly the night before, waking frequently and re-playing her mother's request to visit Grandmother. Tessa still believed she was right to refuse. Even if her grandmother's mind was muddled and hazy, she remembered that she didn't like Tessa.

Tessa exited the elevator into a quiet lobby, most students sleeping in on weekends. A few lounged on overstuffed couches with paper cups of coffee in front of them. Three girls were poised over laptops, concentrating on their screens. Tessa spotted her mom reading some announcements on the community board.

When her mother turned, she saw her and let out a little squeal. "How's my art restorer?" she asked, consuming her in a bear hug.

It felt good to have the comfort of her mom's hug. They'd always taken away the sting of Grandmother's barbs. When her grandmother had said, "Tessa, get a proper haircut" or "What in heaven's name are you wearing?" Mom would answer with "Leave her alone, Esther. She's sowing her oats, learning her way." And she'd always hugged Tessa or squeezed her arm in solidarity. Then Grandmother would make that clucking sound of disapproval. A sound that wasn't so painful with her mom around.

Tessa hugged her mom back. "It's good to see you, Mom."

"How about a cup of coffee at that little campus coffee shop?" her mom suggested.

They sat in *From the Ground Up* sipping their drinks. Tessa talked about the art history program to a mother who seemed miles away. "Mom, are you paying attention?"

"What? Oh, sorry, dear." She shifted in her seat, leaning on her elbows and fixating her gaze on Tessa. "Yes, you were saying how you'd asked for admission into the art history program and you're waiting to hear from the professor." She squeezed Tessa's arm. "Have I told you how proud I am?"

"Only about a thousand times," Tessa said, rolling her eyes and smiling at her mom. Despite her mother's praise, Tessa felt tension coming from her.

Her mother leaned back, biting her lip and spinning her coffee cup between her palms.

"How's Grandmother?" Tessa asked, sitting back in her chair, trying to sound casual and aloof. While she didn't care, she was curious how Grandmother had greeted her mom.

Her mother cleared her throat and sat up straighter.

Uh-oh.

"She's fine. I'd really like you to come with me to visit Grandmother again, Tessa."

Not what Tessa had expected. She opened her mouth to retort that she'd never go back, when something occurred to her. "Why are you going back? You just went yesterday."

When her mother only shrugged, Tessa's irritation grew. "You can wrap yourself in Grandmother's world if you want, but I'm not." Tessa felt heat rise to her face and tears brim in her eyes. "You asked me to check on her and I did. You said only one time. This isn't fair." She heard the whine beginning. She clamped her lips shut and blinked to clear her eyes.

"I know I did, Tessa. But when I was there, your grandmother gave me that graduation gift to give you. She's been holding on to it for two years. Two years," she stressed. "I thought we could go, and you could open it there. And thank her in person."

Tessa prepared to protest, to tell her mom she didn't want the gift and remind her that *not* visiting would be more of a gift to Grandmother than a visit from Tessa. But before she could say any of that, a shadow fell across their table.

"Hello, Tessa." Chip hovered over them.

Tessa's face flushed. How much did he hear? She stammered an introduction to her mother.

Her mom's sly smile and raised eyebrows asked all kinds of questions that Tessa ignored.

"Nice to meet you, Mrs. Wilde," Chip answered coolly, calmly, and completely at ease. "I met Tessa the other day when we collided on the student pathway."

His lopsided grin made Tessa's stomach flop.

"'Collided,' huh?" Her mother looked amused. "I don't believe my daughter mentioned that," she joked, turning her full attention to Chip. "And it's *Ms.* Wilde. Tessa's father and I divorced years ago."

Too much information, Mom! But Tessa knew her mother was enjoying herself. At Tessa's expense.

"It was just a bump on a sidewalk," Tessa muttered. "Nice seeing you, Chip. My mom and I were just leaving, though," she added as she stood up, anxious to put some distance between Chip and her mother. And herself. "We have to visit my grandmother," Tessa lied, trying to wrench her backpack off the chair. She pulled the chair over instead.

Fumbling to upright it, Chip came to her rescue. He smiled and set the chair in its place.

Tessa was certain her face flushed with heat.

"Well, Chip," her mother drawled, still sitting, "as Tessa said, we do have to visit her grandmother, but we have a few minutes. Are you a student here?"

He nodded, nonplussed by Tessa standing and her mother sitting. "I'm a graduate student in photography."

"And Tessa's an art history student who's going—"

"Mom!" Tessa interrupted. "We should go. We don't want to be late." She gave her mother a pointed look.

Ignoring Tessa, her mother asked, "So, what do you photograph?"

Tessa interrupted again, this time using her eyes to shoot daggers at her mother. "Mom. We really need to get going." The last thing she wanted was her mother grilling Chip.

Mom smiled and finally stood up, reaching for their empty cups.

"I got these." Chip grabbed their drink ware and placed them in the dirty dish bin by the garbage can. He turned. "See you around, Tessa. Have fun with your grandma."

She could only nod and smile. Why was she so tongue-tied around him?

Mom took her arm as they left the table and whispered, "He's cute. What's the deal?"

"Hush," Tessa admonished. "There's no 'deal.'" She pulled her mom out of the coffee shop and toward the parking lot.

"Well," her mother sighed. "One good thing came out of that encounter." She pointed to Tessa. "You're coming with me to Sunset Shadows," and she strode towards her car.

"What? No, I'm not!" Tessa exclaimed, trailing behind her like a recalcitrant child. "I just said that to leave."

Her mother stopped mid-stride, hands on hips. "Too bad. You just told that nice boy you were going to visit your grandmother. You don't want to be a liar, do you?" she asked with a wicked, teasing grin. "And when you run into him again, he's sure to ask about her."

Tessa refused to discuss Chip and marched past her mother toward the little Honda, waiting for Debra to click open the passenger door. She stopped and hardened her voice. "Wait until you see how mean she is to me, Mom. I hope you're happy that you're causing me such stress." She felt the tears leak and quickly donned her sunglasses.

Her mom sat in the driver seat, keys in her lap. "I'm not punishing you, and I don't want to cause you stress. She just might be a little more controlled and settled today." She turned to Tessa. "Her dementia is getting worse, and soon she won't even know herself. I want to give both of you a chance to set things right."

Tessa narrowed her eyes. "Set what right? You're talking like there's some big mistake between us that can be straightened. There isn't. And I haven't done anything wrong!" She inhaled deeply to avoid the tears that wanted to spill over. "Years of criticizing aren't going to be erased even if we have one pleasant day together."

Her mom's silence raised a red flag. "Is there something you're not telling me?" she asked.

Mom shook her head and sighed. "I just hoped you two might bury the hatchet. If that won't happen, at least accept the gift she got you. Apparently, she talks about it often. Or so Mayra, one the CNAs there, tells me."

"I've met Mayra," Tessa said. "And 'bury the hatchet'? C'mon. It's not like we had one misunderstanding that morphed into a long-standing feud. In fact, she was as mean to you, probably meaner, than she was to me. Why do you want to make nice and be all buddy-buddy now?"

Her mom sighed. "I just don't want you to have regrets. She's not going to get any better, and if there's a way to find resolution for some of your childhood experiences, I want you to have that opportunity."

Tessa exhaled her own sigh. "We're not staying long." Then, as her mom started the car, Tessa stole a glance toward the coffee shop. No Chip. Was she relieved or disappointed?

A little of both.

As they drove, Tessa's anxiety grew. "I hope she doesn't scream at me to get out again," Tessa muttered.

"She was in and out of it yesterday. And apparently keeps waiting for your father to show up and take her home," her mom said with a thin smile. She tapped the steering wheel rhythmically, a nervous habit

Tessa noticed whenever Arthur Wilde Jr.'s name cropped up. Yes, he'd been dead four years, but he'd left their lives many years before that.

Tessa had a few good memories of him. She remembered a boisterous, laughing man who whizzed into their home filling it with fun and silliness when she was a kid. As she got older, she recognized those "fun" times as her father in a good mood when the right amount of alcohol was in him. Or none at all. She also recalled the dark days when he slunk into the house, grumbling to himself, ignoring Tessa and her mom as he crept up the stairs. Sometimes, Tessa wouldn't see him for days and if he did appear, he looked haggard and unwashed. Then, he'd be off for business, barely acknowledging her. Tessa hardly felt his absence. In fact, the house seemed to relax with him gone. She couldn't say she'd ever missed him, but she missed the sense of a father figure that many of her classmates had.

She'd long come to realize that everyone has their problems. She certainly wasn't the first child of an alcoholic, and tons of other kids had divorced parents. Still, she had mixed feelings about her dad. Angry at him for being an alcoholic, even though she knew it was a disease, and sad that he died because of it.

"What do we say if Grandmother asks us where Dad is?"

"I asked the staff that same question. They suggested we 'go with the flow,'" her mom said, lifting one hand from the steering wheel to make air quotes.

"You mean pretend he's just away on business? That feels like lying."

"Maybe that's kinder. Why should we remind her that he's dead?"

"I guess that makes sense." Tessa sat quietly for the remainder of the ride.

CHAPTER TWELVE

Esther

Esther awakened in her recliner. Had someone called her name? Maybe Millie had arrived from school, anxious to begin their adventure to Savannah. By the time Esther's brain registered it wasn't Millie, she'd regained her wits. "What do you want?" she called out to the air. She looked around the room, spotting the familiar photos and movie posters. Where was Sally?

"Ms. Esther, you've got visitors today." Not-Sally stepped into view and two women lingered in the doorway behind her. "Debra and Tessa," the woman added, stepping aside to allow them to enter.

Debra and Tessa. Esther's brain fired off memories. *Junior answering the door unsteadily to usher in Debra and Tessa. Debra, fearful to leave young Tessa in Junior's care. Tessa, growing more anxious and wary around her father. Debra and Tessa morphing into a twosome leaving Junior and Esther in their wake.*

She eyed the two women.

The older one said, "Esther, I brought Tessa. Can we come in?"

"May," Esther corrected automatically. Tessa. Debra. The names banged relentlessly inside her head like a memory straining to get out of its box. A vision of an insolent, teenage girl filled her mind. Tessa. A girl who'd marched upstairs, turning her back on Esther. Who'd refused Esther's calls and invitations to lunch. The granddaughter who Esther had worried she'd alienated forever. Her heart danced a bit seeing the girl, and the name came naturally off her lips. "Tessa. My, how you've grown. You've matured quite nicely."

Tessa looked askance and answered warily, "Thank you?"

"Be assertive, dear," Esther sighed. This girl she remembered.

Debra and Tessa. Esther repeated the names to cement them in her mind. "Well, don't just stand there. Bring some chairs over and let's have a visit," Esther ordered.

Not-Sally said she'd be back later and left the room, closing the door behind her.

Esther watched as Tessa brought over two chairs. Several silver bracelets hung from the girl's arm and clanged against the chair frame. "Where is your charm bracelet, Tessa?" The girl should wear such a lovely gift.

Tessa set the chairs down and looked at Debra. Then, she addressed Esther. "I don't have one of those, Grandmother."

Esther threw her arms up in exasperation. "Of course you do. I gave you one for graduation the other day."

Debra piped in. "You gave me this yesterday." She rummaged through her purse and brought out a white box with a tattered pink ribbon.

Esther was puzzled. She remembered giving it to Tessa in the living room before lunch. How did it end up with Debra? She looked wordlessly between the two of them.

"Why doesn't Tessa open it now?" Debra suggested and handed it to Tessa who placed the box on her lap and untied the ribbon.

When Tessa brought the charm bracelet out of the box, peering at the cap and tassel charm that adorned it, Esther waited for the profuse thanks.

"Oh, I think I remember these," Tessa said instead, turning the bracelet over in her hands. She addressed her mother. "This is one of those Pandora things, right?"

Esther said coldly, "You're welcome."

Tessa's eyes darted back to Esther. "Sorry. Thank you."

Esther clasped her hands in her lap and tilted her head to her granddaughter. "Do you know what to do with this, Tessa?"

"Of course I do, Grandmother," she replied curtly. Then she inhaled deeply. "I know you collect charms to decorate the bracelet. Thank you for the—" she craned her neck close to the charm, "graduation charm."

"That's not what I mean, Tessa. This bracelet will help you put your life in perspective. Charms commemorate occasions and events. This will allow you to collect lovely mementos of important things. And you can give up those dreams that will disappoint you."

Tessa clamped her lips together to form a thin line.

Debra coughed gently.

Esther ignored both. "I know what you're like, Tessa. You and I have the same dream-filled desires and adventurous spirit. Listen to me. I have lived in your shoes. And your legs want to take you on the road to disappointment and despair. Tessa, life will not turn out the way you plan. It never does. Put your energy into building a life of comfort. Use the charms to remind you how fulfilling a steadfast life can be."

Tessa let out a deep exhale. And a sound of exasperation with it.

What didn't she understand?

"Look," Esther implored, "I thought Millie and I would slay the writing world and make big names for ourselves. But after Millie gave up the dream and I got married, well. . . I realized those ideas were ridiculous anyway. You should find a nice boy who can take care of you and start a family. I had a wonderful husband in my Art, and, of course, your father is a good provider."

Tessa narrowed her eyes. "We're nothing alike, Grandmother. I'm not looking for some guy to fix my life or take care of me. And I'm definitely not going to wait on someone hand and foot. As for my dreams, well. . . they're mine, and if I want to follow them, I will." Tessa's face was flushed, and she'd leaned forward in her chair.

Debra patted Tessa's arm as if to pacify her. And she whispered something to her.

"It's very rude to whisper in another's company," Esther said, looking pointedly at Debra.

Tessa glared.

Esther continued, "And don't put your feelings on your face. Put a mask on those escaping emotions. Boys need to see that you have dignity and decorum. And frowns are so unappealing, dear."

Esther watched as Tessa closed her eyes, seeming to gather her thoughts, and breathed slowly, deeply, like a woman in labor. Hopefully, she was digesting Esther's stellar advice.

"Grandmother, I'm going to have a career. And my ideas aren't 'ridiculous.'" She crossed her arms.

The girl before her wasn't the timid Tessa Esther remembered. But the topic was far from over. "Oh, for heaven's sake," Esther harrumphed. "That's silly. Tessa, you need to get your head on straight. Debra hasn't given you the right upbringing. Now—"

Tessa held up her hand. "Stop criticizing my mother." She turned to Debra. "How can she possibly think we are alike?"

How could Tessa not see it?

Esther said, "You're like me, and you're like your mother. Don't see much of your father and perhaps that's a blessing. But thank the good Lord for Debra. She saved you both." Esther turned her attention to the woman who'd saved Junior from himself. "You're a good woman to take on Junior."

Debra blushed and looked between Esther and Tessa.

"Oh, for goodness sake, Debra. You and I both know Tessa would've had a tough road to travel if she only had Junior and that awful—"

Esther was interrupted by Debra. "We all do the best we can, right?" She squirmed in her chair and broke eye contact with Esther.

What in tarnation was wrong with her?

Esther watched as Tessa's face clouded over with apparent confusion, and Debra glanced away, smoothing her slacks, and avoiding Tessa's gaze.

As Esther looked between the two of them, her mind slipped a little. "Where is Junior?"

Once again, the two women looked quickly at each other and seemed at a loss for words.

"Goodness gracious. Are you two imbeciles? Where is Junior? Is he traveling again?" Esther sat straight up.

Debra answered. "Well, um. . . Junior is away."

"I could figure that out. Good grief," Esther muttered under her breath. She tried to remember where he'd told her he was going. Nothing came to mind. As she looked back to the woman and the girl, neither one looked familiar. The blonde girl stared at Esther, a look of something like pity on her face. The older brunette chewed her bottom lip nervously and eyed Esther sympathetically. *What was wrong with these two?*

The girl spoke, her jaw twitching. "What did you mean by saying Mom saved both of us? Who are you talking about, Grandmother?"

Grandmother? Who is this person calling me Grandmother? I'm much too young to be some teenager's grandparent. I only have a baby granddaughter. Theresa. Tyler. The name escaped her. "What in the world are you talking about? And who's 'Grandmother'? I'm certainly not your grandmother." Esther's eyes skirted between the two of them. The older one ignoring the younger one; the younger one staring wordlessly.

"Now who are you two again?" Esther asked.

They didn't answer, but the older one stood up as if to leave.

Esther's eyes caught on a white box that the young girl held on her lap. It looked familiar. "Thank you for visiting. I'm sure Sally will be here shortly to see you out." She nodded and offered a courteous smile.

The teenage girl put something shiny into the box.

Silver jewelry?

A scene, one with a glass display case, a bracelet, and a slew of charms flashed before her and then faded.

The women returned chairs to a nearby table and adjusted a purse and backpack on their shoulders. Then they stood there as if they expected Esther to say something. So she did. "Good-bye."

The two nodded awkwardly, turned and quietly left.

How odd.

Esther turned her attention to the scene outside the window. Something caught her eye. She leaned forward, straining to see. Old people sat on her back porch. She rapped on the window and shouted, "Get off my property!" The shout sounded more like a squeak. No one responded. She knocked louder. Still nothing. Finally, Esther sat back with a deep sigh. So much about her life didn't fit into frames. Her favorite movies ran through her mind in order, events juxtaposed perfectly, chronologically, and naturally. Why couldn't she recall her own life in some kind of order, too? Instead, pictures filled her mind like scenes cut from the film of her life, dropped carelessly on the studio floor, then popped into places other than where they'd occurred. She anxiously awaited the completed movie that would reorder the jumbled scenes of her life.

CHAPTER THIRTEEN

Tessa

"Well, that was weird and frustrating and confusing." Tessa said as she and her mom walked through the halls of Sunset Shadows. The sconces on the walls gave off amber hues probably meant to soothe and comfort. It did neither for Tessa.

Her mother looked everywhere but at Tessa. "I guess it's just what that disease does."

Tessa's eyes furrowed. "You don't even seem bothered. She called me 'silly' for wanting a career. And even worse, she called us 'imbeciles' for not telling her where Dad was." As they rounded a corner, Tessa threw her hands up. "You are annoyingly calm. Didn't it bother you that she was so rude?"

Her mom stopped walking and turned to her. "I hate that she continues to treat you as if you were a child, Tessa. But I kind of feel sorry for her, too. Did you hear her say that life wouldn't turn out the way someone planned? Sounds like she had different dreams for herself that never came true. That's kind of sad that it has stuck in her mind for so long."

"I guess."

Had her grandmother given up dreams? Mayra had said something to that effect the first time Tessa was there.

Tessa and her mom began walking again. "Who's Millie?"

Her mom shrugged.

"Okay. Answer me this. Why did Grandmother say you saved me and Dad? What does that mean?"

Her mom looked sideways at Tessa and picked up the pace as they neared the reception desk. "I can explain later."

Tessa trailed along. When she opened her mouth to ask when later would be, she was interrupted again. This time by someone behind them. "Debra? Tessa?"

Tessa and her mother turned at their names.

Mayra walked up. "Thank you for visiting. I love to see family come. Especially as the memory loss deepens. I know it can be tough to watch a loved one lose so much." She smiled sadly but genuinely and looked at the little box in Tessa's hand. "She's been going on for weeks about getting that to you."

Her graduation gift. Tessa had almost forgotten she was holding it.

"It's a lovely charm bracelet," Mayra said. "Your grandmother holds hers almost every day. She treasures it. It must hold all those good memories." She smiled as if to encourage them to share some.

"I don't really know what it holds," her mother replied coolly.

Tessa frowned. That response didn't sound like her mom at all.

Mayra nodded. "Well . . . I'll leave you to your day. I hope you'll be back soon." The woman turned on her heel, probably disenchanted with them.

Once Mayra was out of earshot, Tessa said, "Mom! You were rude to her." She scribbled her name on the visitor's log after her mother did the same.

"I'm sorry, but your grandmother did unnerve me. I'm not without feelings, Tessa. Yes, it bothered me that she was so cold and callous." She sighed. "I guess it's time."

"Time for what?" Tessa asked.

"Let's get lunch and I'll explain."

Tessa saw the set jaw, the lasered eyes, and the purposeful gait that meant a single-mindedness Tessa couldn't redirect. She'd have to wait.

In the car, Tessa fastened her seat belt and peered at her mom. The creased brows and rhythmic jaw-wiggling were signs of Debra's concentration. Tessa leaned her head back trying to make sense of her grandmother's strange words and her mother's strange reactions to them. *Secretive.* The word made her heart skip a beat. That was it. Her mother acted secretively. Tessa clenched her backpack tighter on her lap.

They pulled into a local diner, one of Tessa's favorites. It sported 1950s décor and served burgers and shakes. And normally it lifted Tessa's mood when she was stressed or anxious. The juke box and checkered tablecloths reminded Tessa of old movies and television shows where teens gathered wearing poodle skirts and duck tails, talking about which drive-in to see or whose parent would let them drive the family car.

They were ushered to a table in the not-too crowded restaurant. Her mom fussed with her hair and twisted her paper napkin. Tension emanated off her like visible waves.

They ordered and once the waitress moved away Tessa pressed. "Mom, what's up? What do you need to explain?"

Her mother opened her mouth to say something, then clamped her lips, a mixture of impulse and anxiety. Finally, she exhaled loudly and lifted her chin, making eye contact. As if she had to deliver bad news.

Equal parts curiosity and dread filled Tessa. She sat up straight, steeling herself for the worst.

Her mother's breath rushed out with the words. "Okay. I'm going to tell you something. Something I should have told you already. Something that you need to hear from me before your grandmother inadvertently spills it. Please don't overreact and freak out. Be rational and calm."

Tessa held her breath, steadying her heart and nerves for whatever her mother might say. *Ohmigod. . . Was her mother sick? Were they penniless?*

Tessa tried to will herself to relax and still her mind from making random guesses.

Her mom let a few beats of silence go until Tessa exploded. "Mom! What the hell? You're freaking me out!" All semblance of maturity dissipated. She couldn't remain composed.

Debra took a deep breath. "I married your father nineteen years ago, not twenty-one like we've told you."

Tessa waited for thunder to boom, lightning to strike. That was it? That was her mom's big reveal? She had Tessa without being married?

Tessa's whole body unclenched. "Geez Mom, you had me imagining the most awful news. This is not a big deal. It's not unheard of to have a child before getting married."

The waitress appeared with their burgers. As Tessa poured ketchup on her plate, she said, "I can't believe you're having a fit about being married *after* I was born." She cocked her head. Maybe that wasn't it. Maybe her parents never married and only "lived in sin" as Grandmother would call it. "Were you and Dad never married? Is that it? Because again, it's not a—"

Her mother looked at her as if Tessa spoke in Greek. "Of course, we were."

"Then, I don't get it." She chewed a French fry as she held her arms up, palms open.

Her mother inhaled deeply, and the words tumbled out. "I am not your birth mother."

Stars swam in Tessa's eyes and the table wavered. She swallowed the last of her French fry and dropped her arms to the table and pushing her plate far away. Blood drained from her face. Oxygen froze in her lungs. She couldn't speak. She gulped the air around her trying to still her heart and catch her breath.

Time stopped.

Her mother reached across and held Tessa's hands, gently folding them within her own. "I am your mother in every other way, honey. I've loved you from the second I met you."

Met me? The only other words to reach Tessa after 'not your birth mother.'

"What?" she squeaked. Tessa inhaled and exhaled slowly, allowing the blood to settle back in all the right places. The tingling feeling left her face; her hands warmed slightly inside her mother's. *Debra's.*

"Am I adopted?"

The question felt other-worldly. Tessa knew adopted kids and thought nothing of it. But that was them, and this was her. And they knew as children they were adopted. How could parents hide this from their child?

"Not exactly." Her mother's words brought her back to the present.

She yanked her now warm hands out of her mother's. "What does that mean?" Tessa demanded. She had a right to be angry, to feel excluded from the most important fact of her life.

"Arthur Wilde is your birth father; Grandmother Wilde is your grandmother; I'm just not your biological mother." She looked Tessa straight in the eye. "We should have explained all this to you years ago, but there never seemed to be a right time. Then your father and I divorced, and he died. . ." she faltered.

"Explained *what* years ago? You haven't explained anything, *Mom*," she hissed.

The food turned cold; the ketchup ran in a watery circle, dripping into the hamburger bun and turning a once-appetizing meal into a soggy waste.

"Is anything wrong?" the waitress asked when she returned to check on them. Neither had taken a bite of their burgers. "I can take these back if—"

Her mom looked up. "No, it's fine. Can you just wrap these to go? And bring two cups of coffee instead?"

The waitress's confused look couldn't compare to Tessa's own. Confusion, anger, and disbelief competed for top billing, none of them winning.

Her mother took a deep breath. "When I met your father, he had just landed his first big sales position with the furniture company. He was celebrating at a party thrown by some of his former high school buddies. It was love at first sight. I know that sounds cheesy, but it's true."

Tessa's mind could hardly comprehend the words. And she didn't care how her parents, or those people she'd always thought of as parents, met.

"Cut to the chase—the part where you *didn't* have me," Tessa interrupted. It was sarcastic and snarky but being hurt did that sometimes.

"When I saw your father," her mom continued resolutely, "I fell head over heels. On our fourth date, he admitted to me he had a child, or rather, was going to have a child."

Tessa's mouth set in a stubborn line. Part of her wanted to plug her ears while the other part wanted to soak it all in.

"He had briefly dated a girl outside our circle of friends."

"Outside how?" Tessa asked, sitting back in the booth and crossing her arms over her chest.

"She didn't come from a family like the Wildes," her mother began, "and she didn't hang out with the kinds of kids your father and I did. She was brash and outspoken." She paused. "And beautiful and free-spirited. She also fell into a hard life of partying. Drugs and alcohol. She didn't refuse either."

When her mom paused, Tessa crossed her legs underneath the table, wiggling her foot to still her nerves. She could feel shivers starting, the kind that came from absorbing a shock. But she willed them gone. Her head spun with questions. "Was he dating both of you at the same time?" *What a cheat!*

"No. They only dated a little while. Before we met." Her mom shifted in her seat. "Arthur was dazzled by her brazenness. There wasn't a boy in a five-mile radius who could resist Lou Ann Parker's personality." She smiled sadly. "And your father was especially taken by her."

Lou Ann? Tessa's brain fired off connections. Grandmother hated someone named Lou Ann. Puzzle pieces came together. *Lou Ann*

Parker is my mother. Grandmother hated this Lou Ann and that's why she hated Tessa.

Tessa felt halved, like a machete had just torn her life in two parts: Before and After.

The only constant was her grandmother's rejection. Today and the yesterdays of childhood.

She fought the tears. She fought the urge to scream. She fought the desire to call her grandmother every name in the book. And she fought her mother's compassion. Nothing would ever be the same.

"Honey, I understand this is a lot to take in."

"No, Mom. You really don't understand. Are *you* a mistake? Were *you* born to a family who didn't want you?" That was Tessa's new truth. Her grandmother never wanted her. For years, Tessa had held onto a little hope that there was a valid reason for Grandmother's disapproval. That her grandmother had an emotional block that made her the way she was. Now, it was clear Grandmother didn't have the problem: Tessa did. Having been born to a woman Esther hated, and burdening Grandmother with the label "illegitimate grandchild," Tessa was doomed from the start. And until the end.

She leaned across the table. "I get it now. I'm undesirable because I'm the daughter of some girl Grandmother hates."

Her mom looked stricken. "No. That's not right at all!"

"You're telling me that Grandmother likes Lou Ann?" Tessa dared her mother to disagree.

"Well, no," she backpedaled. "But she never held it against *you*. Esther loves you. I know she does."

Tessa's glare was steady and hard. She knew better. Her heart hardened to petrified stone. She'd never forgive her grandmother. And she was done with her.

Her mom was talking. "She never compared you to Lou Ann or begrudged you for having been born to Lou Ann."

Try as she might, her mother would never convince Tessa. She held up her hand to stop her mom's words. "Forget it." Ruminating on Grandmother's dislike would only bring tears. She needed to hear the rest of the story. "How did you get me? And where is Lou Ann now?" Tessa couldn't even address the fact that her birth mother had never even contacted her in all these years. And like a slap to the face, she remembered Debra telling her that Lou Ann was a woman from her dad's past and that she had died.

"She's dead," Tessa confirmed softly.

When she spoke, her mom's words were soft and gentle, like she was delicately placing them before Tessa. "Arthur offered to marry her. Even though it was a passionate, brief relationship that didn't last long, he was going to do the right thing. And even though he was dating me."

Tessa saw a flash of hurt cross her mother's face.

Her mom held up her hand. "I know what you're going to say. Illegitimate children aren't taboo anymore, but he had old-fashioned ideas about what constituted a gentleman. Surprisingly, Esther didn't want him to marry someone he didn't love and someone she didn't—"

She stopped talking midsentence, but Tessa knew what the rest would be.

"—approve of," Tessa finished. "Grandmother would never accept someone who didn't check all the boxes and have the proper upbringing."

Even an unborn baby's existence wasn't enough to soften her grandmother's heart and compel her to drop her narrow-mindedness. The resentment and bitterness of what Tessa imagined Lou Ann had endured flashed through her. "I'll never be like Grandmother," she swore.

The waitress brought their coffees, and Tessa took a sip. Her appetite was gone and so was her energy. But she needed to know more. "How did I end up with you and Dad?"

"Lou Ann told him she didn't want to marry him and would raise you on her own but needed his financial support. He wanted to be a part of your life and told her so." She added quietly, "And they weren't a couple when you were born. I was his girlfriend. Your father was trying to be a good father."

Tessa knew her mom was trying to paint a picture of an involved, loving father, but that was not the man Tessa knew, and she wasn't willing to hear glowing reports of a dedicated Baby Daddy. Too little. Too late.

"Your father and I continued to date throughout Lou Ann's pregnancy. I was smitten with him and he with me." She smiled wistfully. "I told him I would be a supportive partner and a kind stepmother. That was our plan. He asked me to marry him; I said yes, fully intending to welcome you in our home every other weekend or whenever he and Lou Ann had set up visitation." She paused.

Tessa bit back the question that hung at the end of her tongue. What happened to Lou Ann? She wanted to know; she didn't want to know.

Her mother fiddled with the paper napkin and blinked back tears. "Your father and I married, and for a few months shared you with Lou Ann. Actually, we had you more than Lou Ann did. Your father asked her for full custody, but she said no." Her mom hesitated.

Tessa pushed her mom to continue even while her heart hammered in her chest. "Keep going."

"Lou Ann asked your father for more money." She took a deeper breath, and the words tumbled out. "Because he had no more to spare, Lou Ann went to your grandmother. Esther refused, claiming it was blackmail, and Lou Ann left in a huff. A few days later, she was on a binge and wrapped her car around a tree. She died instantly. The autopsy showed cocaine and alcohol in her system."

Her mother seemed to have run out of steam, shoulders slumping and eyes downcast.

Tessa sat perfectly still, having set the coffee down. Her mother was a drug addict. Tessa felt as if her heartbeat was loud enough for anyone to hear. Nothing existed but those words *she died instantly*. No time for answers, no chance for reparation.

"I want to go back to my dorm now." It was time to give her brain a rest, unravel the tangle of emotions balled inside.

Her birth mother wanted Grandmother's money.

Her grandmother didn't want Tessa because she was Lou Ann's daughter.

Her father and her moth—Debra—*had* to take her when Lou Ann died.

She needed alone time to weed through these revelations.

The ride back to campus was quiet and pensive. Several times her mom asked Tessa if she was all right.

"As right as I can be, Mom." Tessa felt her throat thicken when she said the word. She put in her ear buds and tried to let Phil Collins's "Misunderstanding" settle her racing mind and breaking heart. There were a lot of new truths to absorb. Not really misunderstandings as much as misinformation. Or lies by omission. That was at the heart of all Tessa's emotions: she'd been kept in the dark, hidden from her own birth story, lied to. That last one summed it up. Her parents and grandmother had lied all her life. Every time they looked at her, they knew where she came from while she didn't. The anger simmered, mixed with hurt and rejection and grief for a woman she never knew.

They arrived at Tessa's dorm, and her mom turned off the engine.

Tessa picked up her uneaten dinner, boxed and bagged, and held it in her hands. She didn't know when she'd have an appetite. "I need time to process all this."

"I know. I'm sorry. I don't know what else to say other than I love you." Her mom looked forlorn, like a child who'd shattered an irreplaceable, unrecoverable family heirloom.

Tessa loved her mother—was she still her mother? Of course, she was. Still, she kind of became a stranger in that diner. And Tessa became a stranger to herself, too. No one could understand her complicated feelings, least of all the woman who'd caused them. In part. It would take time for Tessa to understand. If she ever did.

Debra might have ended the Lou Ann Secret, but in Tessa's eyes, the mystery had just begun.

CHAPTER FOURTEEN

Esther

Her eyes flew open. She absorbed the quiet of the room. She didn't hear the chirp of her beloved cuckoo clock or the hum of Art's electric razor, staples of her morning wake-up world. The wallpaper had disappeared, too. Her bedroom walls were supposed to show off a blue-feathered pattern, an Art-and-Esther compromise. She had wanted a nod to floral and he demanded something in blue, preferably not flowers. The result was cornflower blue feathers. The walls that met her gaze now were off-white, a shade she'd never liked. It was dingy laundry and stale sheets. From the corner of her eye, Esther spied the framed photograph of her childhood home surrounded by the Georgia pecan groves in summer. Junior had enlarged that photo and framed it for her birthday. One of her birthdays.

She looked at the other side of the room. The open bathroom door displayed a shower with a chair in it. Wasn't that for old people? Hand grips rested on the walls of the shower and next to the toilet. *Get it together, Esther. Figure this out.*

Suddenly her bedroom door opened wider, and a lady breezed through. Familiar yet unfamiliar, Esther wasn't as startled as she might have been. The feeling that she was supposed to know this person resonated within, keeping fear at bay.

"Good morning, Ms. Esther," the lady said. Carrying a tray with white, mini-paper cups, she approached Esther as if it were a regular occurrence. "I've got your medicine here. Hot coffee on the table behind me."

Esther peered around her to see steam coming off a small steel pot that rested on a movable cart. Coffee. The knowledge placated her briefly. The mornings she sat at the old, pine table in the kitchen with her favorite coffee cup rushed back. *Junior racing around her before heading to the bus stop. Art dodging the corner edge of the table as he stole a kiss before work. Tessa fitting under the table until she grew tall enough and smacked into it, surprising herself too much to cry.* Esther pictured the stainless-steel percolator that ran faithfully every day. Until it didn't. She remembered replacing it with the new Mr. Coffee machine and being amazed how quickly coffee was ready.

The woman handed her a tiny, ruffled paper cup with two pills in it. And a glass of water. And smiled. "How about you take your pills and then I help you into the recliner?"

Esther felt warmth in the woman's smile, comfort that belied the fact that she was a stranger. She allowed herself to be propped against the bed pillows and swallowed and drank. This one wasn't her beloved Sally, but she was kind.

"Let me help you up and we'll get dressed for the day," Not-Sally said.

"I certainly don't need help to get out of bed," Esther exclaimed, as dignified as she could be wearing a flowered nightgown. Esther Wilde could place her feet on the floor and walk to a chair, for God's sake. She folded down the bedcovers but startled as she caught sight of her hands. Why were they mottled and wrinkled? Esther let her gaze roam up her arms. Scrawny, saggy with little muscle. Where was the elasticity she remembered?

Not-Sally took a step towards Esther. "How about you let me hold on to your arms while you swing your legs to the floor?"

Confused by her own appearance, Esther let Not-Sally do so. Her legs were as spindly and as old-looking as her arms, and a deep sadness took over.

"Oh, Ms. Esther, please don't cry. I'm here to help."

Esther wasn't crying because she needed help; she cried because she was old.

When did old age arrive?

She accepted Not-Sally's help and soon was led by wheelchair to another room.

Esther's eyes sought the familiar recliner and Not-Sally settled her into it. After she brought Esther's coffee, Not-Sally left.

Sipping her coffee, Esther appreciated the familiar taste. Every cup was better than the last. Esther would never give that up. Even while pregnant, she'd had coffee throughout the day. Of course, that was before the medical community considered caffeine dangerous—like smoking and alcohol. Although she'd never smoked, Esther had enjoyed an occasional cocktail, even pregnant. Could that have been what caused Junior's problems?

Her heart ached when she remembered discovering Junior's love for alcohol.

• • •

The smell of Junior's room almost gagged Essie. Why were teenage boys immune to their own body odor? She picked up clothes, sorted clean from dirty shorts, and stripped Junior's bed, all while holding her breath as much as possible. It was in the pillowcase that she found it. The bottle of vodka pilfered from their own bar cabinet downstairs. Essie sat heavily on his bed, odor forgotten. For months she'd thought Art had been drinking after she'd gone to bed. That he was the reason their alcohol cache was shrinking. She'd assumed he'd been medicating his worry. Losing the position of sales manager to a younger, fresher salesman took a toll on a man. He had denied it; she pretended to believe it but kept an eagle eye on Art every morning. No wonder he seemed well-rested and alert. He wasn't the culprit.

"Oh, Junior," she sighed, "what have you done?"

Essie picked up the bottle, its contents practically gone, and wondered about all the other missing liquor bottles. A quick but thorough search of his closet turned up three more—a gin, a vermouth, and a scotch.

She stood light-headed, her heart pounding. These bottles were less than a month old. What to do now?

She took several deep breaths to steady herself and gathered the evidence. Both Art and Junior were out—Art at work and Junior at school.

For heaven's sake, he was only a high school sophomore!

How could he drink so much?

Why would he drink so much?

She rechecked his room for anything she'd missed—she didn't find any more, thank God—and wondered how to approach this. She decided that Art should be the one to address their son.

At first, her husband brushed off her discovery as "boys will be boys," but Essie insisted this was more than normal, teenage exploration. Art sighed but agreed to talk to him.

Essie stood near but out of sight, straining to hear, worried that anger would consume both of them. Curiously, she heard little. Art's occasional raised voice, Junior's lackadaisical attitude. When he returned to their room that night, Art relayed Junior's defense. His friends had a party and according to Junior, he'd only agreed to take what was left to protect the others from being found out. He claimed Essie and Art were "cooler" than the other parents. Only Essie saw through Junior's flattery and weak argument. Art heard what he wanted to hear. When she challenged what Junior had said, Art insisted she was making a big deal out of nothing. She let it go.

But she shouldn't have. Junior's drinking continued. She knew by the minty breath when he came home chewing gum that he never liked, or the tight grip on the banister as he walked up the stairs. Determined that she and Art would intervene, life did instead. Her husband died. A sudden heart attack left Esther grieving and alone. A single parent, Essie had to become Esther. Junior became surly and angry, a bull unable to be corralled. His drinking continued, and Esther hadn't the energy to face it. Junior graduated high school but barely, his charm overriding his poor grades. His natural charisma became his value, his shield, and his weapon. Junior strutted when managers praised his sales techniques, talked his way out of public spectacles that his drinking created, and blamed his father's unexpected death for his binges. Before Esther knew it, Lou Ann and Tessa had come along, and she had bigger things to worry about.

•　　•　　•

She thought of the man Junior had become. She'd made excuses for him. He'd made promises to her. The tears they'd shed and apologies they'd both made created a hamster wheel of a relationship. She never could get him to stop drinking. She'd thought Debra would be the answer.

Debra. The name came unbidden, then whiffed away in the wind. A picture arose of a woman sitting next to her on a porch. Was it a dream or a memory? They blurred together. *Lou Ann.* Why in heaven's name would she think of that money-grubbing tramp? Esther closed her eyes against the confusion, the jumbled images, and the anxiety pulling at her heart. *A wild-eyed, blonde girl banging on Esther's screen door. A newborn in tow.*

Her eyes traveled towards her posters hanging on the apartment wall. She found solace in the familiar. *The Big Sleep.* Now, that was a movie worth watching. Junior was never interested in movies she liked. But Tessa was. *Tessa.* Esther closed her eyes. She had big plans for little Tessa. No chasing elusive dreams. She'd direct Tessa to follow the path that would give her security and safety. More images sprang. *Sweet, adoring baby Tessa. Compliant, eager-to-please child Tessa. Frowning, eye-rolling, adolescent Tessa.*

She blinked her eyes a few times. Those images seemed so real, seared in her mind but she just couldn't place when or where they'd happened. She felt for the bracelet that was usually on her lap and picked it up like a fragile egg. Memories captured in a piece of jewelry.

She closed her eyes, choosing a charm to hold. Bringing the bracelet to her chest, she brought forth the tire swing memory that brought her the most joy. When childhood dreams were untamed, and the future was limitless. She drifted to sleep, thoughts of children churning in her head. Junior. Tessa. Herself.

She awoke later. The television in front of Esther flashed pictures of a happy family gathered at a table. They reminded Esther of Sunday dinners after church. Mother's roasted chicken with mashed potatoes and fresh green beans. Esther leaned her head back and sniffed, imagining the pleasant aromas of yesteryear. The yeast of just-baked rolls wafting in the breadbasket, the buttery steam almost visible on the heaping potatoes. Her mouth watered in anticipation.

"Good afternoon, Ms. Esther," a sing-song voice called, disturbing her journey. She turned her head toward the voice. Not-Sally.

The woman stood next to Esther's recliner, hand on hip. "You up to going to the dining room for Sunday dinner, Ms. Esther?"

So it was Sunday. She wasn't so mixed up. Esther smiled to herself, proud of her connection.

"Can we go to Sunday dinner?" Not-Sally repeated gently.

Esther shook her head. She hated leaving this little enclave, wherever it was. She just wanted Junior to return and take them home. She thought she heard Not-Sally sigh.

"I'll bring a tray in here then."

Esther looked sharply at the woman. "When is Sally returning?"

Not-Sally's face softened with a gentle smile. "Tell me about Sally." And she pulled over a chair next to Esther.

Esther searched Not-Sally's kind face for telltale signs of trickery. Was Not-Sally trying to trap her? Too many strangers had asked Esther questions about what she ate, where she lived, or what day it was. Esther narrowed her eyes. She wouldn't be fooled by polite questions. She'd had enough of that at the country club with those biddies. "You know her. She hired you temporarily. Don't you be trying to fool me." She wagged her finger at Not-Sally.

Not-Sally drew her eyebrows together. Then she said, "Do you have a favorite memory with her you'd like to share?"

A memory with her housekeeper? Like the television, pictures flashed in her mind's screen. But the images were partial or blurry or came and went so quickly she couldn't hold on to them. *A chubby toddler boy teetering between Esther and Sally's outstretched hands. A sullen, scowling boy glaring at Sally . . . and Esther. A confident Junior strutting past Sally ushering his friends to the kitchen.*

She reminded Not-Sally, "I do expect Junior any day now, so you be on the lookout for him." Esther pointed at her with the hand that held her precious charm bracelet.

Not-Sally said, "Of course. I'll be back soon with your dinner, Ms. Esther."

Esther barely registered the words. The charm she'd grasped was a deck of cards. Much as she loved the game of bridge, the small reminder dredged up a less favorable memory. It was the last committee she'd ever joined.

•   •   •

Esther hung up her navy-blue cardigan in the coat closet of the lobby next to some of the others: Beatrice's velvet blazer that she thought matched everything; Henny's white sweater with the pearl buttons she believed gussied up any outfit; and Nancy's coat of many colors—a lightweight jacket she swore complemented any piece of clothing.

"Hello, Esther," she heard over her shoulder.

Esther backed out of the small cloak room and turned to the familiar nasal sound. "Good morning, Amelia." Esther always felt scrutinized under Amelia Sutton's gaze, probably because the woman was married to the son of one of the founding members of the Sutton Country Club. And because Amelia treated her with disdain. When Art was alive it was easier to brush off Amelia's condescending tone; Art had connections with important people in town and Amelia wouldn't step too close and risk their criticism. Now though, Esther had to hold her own.

"I'm surprised to see you here today, Esther," Amelia said, practically bouncing on her toes with a smug look on her face.

Esther watched the pale-faced, rail thin woman smirk. Amelia's bony shoulders poked out as her arms crossed in self-satisfaction. Esther fantasized about knocking her over with a tap of a finger, but she wouldn't give cause to be kicked out. Nor would she take the bait Amelia offered. "Amelia, will you be joining the bridge club meeting this morning? I don't remember seeing you actually work before."

It was snide, but oh, so deserved.

Amelia unclasped her arms and stood still, her limbs dangling.

Clearly, she was itching to say something to Esther. What was the woman up to?

Amelia opened her mouth then shut it quickly. She looked past Esther to the open doors behind.

Esther turned her head, watching the women inside the room pull up chairs, preparing for the meeting.

"After you," Amelia said. She cocked her head to indicate Esther should go first, forming a wicked smile.

Holding her head high, Esther strode to the circle they had formed, bringing a chair with her. The ladies stilled and eyed each other. Esther stood for a moment, just outside their sanctum, unsure why the air had cooled several degrees.

Amelia cleared her throat. "Ladies, do you have something you'd like to share with Mrs. Wilde?"

Red flags waved like a matador in Esther's mind. Something was up.

"How dare you show up here, Esther?" It was Beatrice, the one Esther felt was the most genuine of the pretentious group. Beatrice's arms were crossed, a hardened glaze in her eyes, hurt shining through.

"What?" Esther began.

She was interrupted by Henny. "We have no need for your services with this group, Esther Wilde. Take your high-handed opinions and find another group to insult." Henny's eyes flashed as she leaned forward in her chair.

Esther's heart pounded. What in heaven's name could they be talking about?

Behind her, Amelia snickered.

Esther spun on her heel and addressed Amelia. "What did you do?"

The woman put her hands on her chest as if shocked. "I did nothing." Then she set her beady eyes on Esther. "You got yourself in trouble. Well, you and that lush of a son who got himself sloshed at the bar."

Esther stuttered, unable to formulate the questions that raced in her mind.

Amelia squared her shoulders. "Apparently, you're unaware of your son's antics last night."

What had Junior done now?

She crossed her arms, a smirk on her face. "Allow me to enlighten you. Junior sat at the bar last night, several scotches down the hatch, and told my Elliot the things you've said about us." She waved her hand to include the others who sat stone-faced with accusing eyes.

"I've never said anything—" Esther claimed. But Esther lied. She had gossiped about them. Calling them out as conceited, image-conscious, social climbers. But she'd never told a soul. Except Junior, her only confidante now that Art was gone. He'd betrayed her. First by his constant drinking; now by his lack of inhibitions.

Beatrice stood up. "Calling me a woman who wants power and prestige. According to your son, I only get invited to committee groups because I have the most money." The accusation burned.

Esther considered telling them she had been joking, but she knew those words weren't funny.

Henny voiced what Esther supposed they all thought. "We've been kind to you since Art died, God rest his soul, and we've put up with that obnoxious son of yours as well. He's a degenerate who fathered a child out of wedlock. Chances are that the baby will grow up to be as willful and single-minded as he is." Henny's eyes softened, hurt replacing anger.

"And he laughed as he told Beatrice's son exactly what you think of all of us."

There was no way Esther could salvage this. She did the only thing she could—she fought back. Turning to Amelia first, she raised her head high and added enough steel to her voice to hide her desperation. "Amelia Sutton, you might carry the name of this illustrious club, but you'll never carry the class or the respect it does. And you cannot get rid of me. You know Art and I are lifelong members; read the fine print your father-in-law wrote when we joined twenty-five years ago. You will see my face all the rest of your days here at Sutton Country Club."

Then she addressed Beatrice. "We all say things we aren't proud of. Including me. I apologize to you." And to Henny, "It will never be acceptable for you to insult another woman's child. If you had any, you'd understand. You will not disrespect my son or my granddaughter. You are not welcome in my home for bridge ever again." Esther turned to Amelia. "You're the worst one of all. Your father-in-law would be ashamed of you running the club's reputation into the ground." And with that, Esther marched out the doors.

She'd be back and when she returned, it would be with Tessa in tow. She'd make an upstanding, Amelia Sutton-worthy member out of Tessa if it were the last thing she did. She'd show them—the Wilde name would be revered once more.

•   •   •

Esther did return to Sutton Country Club—for fund-raisers, social events, and dinners. Sometimes she took little Tessa but most times she didn't. The spirited girl had difficulty sitting properly for long spells.

Esther glanced at the bracelet now, still clasped in her fist, fingers wrapped around that deck of cards charm. Some memories seared like scars in her mind. She saw them regularly, felt the ache of them as if they'd happened yesterday.

New images popped up. *A blond girl in this very room taking a bracelet in a box.* Was it a movie or real life?

Life had become difficult. Esther was running out of time. Tessa would soon be all grown up, too old to shape, too stubborn to change. She had to show Tessa how to mold her own life and encapsulate those memories in charms like Esther had done. Tessa was more like her father than Esther wanted to admit. Was it too late to rein her in?

CHAPTER FIFTEEN

Tessa

Tessa eyed the students who passed her on the walkways, wondering if they saw her differently, like she saw herself. She was an orphan. Maybe she was being dramatic, but she didn't know how else to think of it. Lou Ann was gone before Tessa could even know her, and of course, her father was dead, too.

Students passed by, smiling and laughing. She bet none of them felt the sting of a grandparent's rejection.

She brought up her playlist on her phone. Matthew Wilder's "Break My Stride" might give her the determination she needed. She had to focus on her gains. She'd found a major. She needed to revel in that victory.

Dark clouds moved in, and Tessa picked up her pace. Winter thunderstorms weren't as common as summer ones, and not usually as intense, but Tessa didn't take them casually either. After all, there was a reason Florida was the lightning capital of the country.

Her phone rang. She suppressed a sigh and tapped the green button. "Hey, Mom." Regardless of the new information, Debra was still Mom. While Tessa blamed her mom for never sharing the truth about her birth, she felt some sympathy for her. She had been thrust into motherhood when she'd just gotten married and was forced to raise a baby who wasn't hers. Although Tessa had to admit that her mom never gave off vibes that Tessa was anything other than her own.

"What are you doing?" Her mom sounded breathless and a little frantic.

"What's wrong?" *Please, no more surprises.*

With one eye on the skies and the other on the path in front of her, Tessa stood under a huge live oak at the path's edge. She spotted the fine arts building ahead and could make a quick run for cover if the clouds unleashed their pent-up frustrations.

"It's your grandmother. She fell earlier. They've taken her to the hospital for tests."

It was hard for Tessa to feel sympathy. She asked coolly, "Is she getting admitted?"

"I don't know yet. She insisted she was fine, but of course she didn't know where she was and asked repeatedly for your father or her former housekeeper Sally. She thought she was still at her old home."

Nothing new there.

Tessa heard thunder growling. "I'm sure the hospital will admit her if they need to," she said as she hustled toward shelter. She felt a twinge of guilt for sounding heartless, but she owed her grandmother nothing. The old feelings of hurt and rejection had come back exponentially once she'd learned how Grandmother had discarded Lou Ann like a used tissue.

"I know they will, but—" Her mother paused.

Tessa took the bait. "But what?"

"Do you think you should try to patch things up with your grandmother?"

Tessa's stared at her phone as if her mother could see her. "Are you kidding?" Her voice had escalated, and she was aware of other students nearby, most of them hurrying into the building to escape the imminent storm.

She stood under the overhang of the arts building and lowered her voice. "There's nothing to patch up. She sees me as an extension of Lou Ann and will never like me." *Let alone love me,* she thought.

Tessa pulled the door open and walked to a corner in the building's lobby area for privacy.

"I understand, honey. I really do. But you need answers that only she can give. I don't know if her mind is even capable, but she's your only source. Only Esther can explain why she was so—" She hesitated and then said, "difficult."

"I've told you, Mom," Tessa hissed, "I know why she was 'difficult'."

"Honey, Esther is a lot of things, but carrying resentment or hatred toward you is not one of them. All she ever wanted was to spend time with you. When you were little, she begged to have you for sleepovers or take you to the country club—"

Tessa interrupted. "I remember, but how about later? Once I stopped wearing the clothes she approved of, she never took me to the club. And she only wanted me around to try to change me. She never accepted that I was different from her. *Am* different. I don't want a husband and a membership at a country club and a pretty house in the suburbs." As her voice wavered, she furiously blinked back tears and drew deep breaths to stop the torrent of hurt that wanted to escape. "Anyway, that's old news. I'm not going to subject myself to her insults anymore. And maybe she doesn't hate me, but she damn sure doesn't like me."

With a look at the big wall clock, Tessa added, "I can't talk now, Mom. I have class," and she hung up, swallowing the pain for another time, and taking the steps carefully. Windows comprised one wall of the three-story building, to the right of the staircase. Looking through them, she saw the clouds open, the rain pouring like overturned buckets. A storm unleashing. Almost unconsciously, she remembered dress-up days with Grandmother. A favorite pastime in stormy weather. Wearing Grandmother's clunky charm bracelet. Dressing in her stuffy clothes. As a child, Tessa loved the feel of silk scarves and smooth cotton gloves on her skin. Grandmother would laugh and clap her hands at Tessa's frivolity. But it didn't last long. By age twelve, Tessa preferred a clothing style which was met with frowns and shakes of the head. And Grandmother began to pummel Tessa with how she should dress (like a middle-aged woman), do her hair (like a little girl—straight and down), and even walk (as demurely and quietly as possible).

But for a little while, Tessa had felt loved.

She pushed the memories aside and slipped into class. The classroom was one of the bigger ones, large enough to hold about ten round tables that would seat six to eight each. Charmaine waved Tessa over to hers. This was Tessa's first day in the class, although the semester had started a month ago.

Professor James stood in front of a huge screen. Having met him last week, Tessa found his familiar face reassuring. In his office, she had felt immediately at ease. Instead of a disheveled, absent-minded, cardigan-wearing professor, he'd been sharply dressed in pressed jeans and button-down shirt. His hair had been slicked back, dark and sleek, like a newly paved blacktop. A photo of several young children flanking him on an Adirondack chair had rested on his desk with the frame "World's Best Grandpa." Tessa had been surprised that he was old enough to be a grandfather.

Comparing him to her stuffy Grandmother had almost made her laugh out loud.

He'd said that he appreciated her interest, approved of her prerequisites, and saw in Tessa a little bit of his young self. He'd admitted her to the program. Score one for Tessa Wilde.

Now her attention jumped to the slide on the screen beside him titled *What Were We?* She leaned over to open her backpack when Charmaine nudged her side. "Isn't that the guy from the cafeteria?" and she tilted her head toward the front of the room.

Standing there with the professor in the shadow of the lighted screen was Chip. Tessa was already rattled from her conversation with her mother. Now this.

The professor addressed the students, a microphone pinned to his lapel. "This is Chip Foster. He's one of the department's TAs. Chip's studying for his MFA in Photography. He'll be assisting me today."

Tessa's heart skipped a beat as Chip scanned the classroom. His eyes settled on her.

Charmaine muttered, "He remembers you."

Tessa tried to ignore the glow burning in her belly.

Chip turned back to the slide show presentation as Professor James kept talking. "One of the skills of an art historian is to pay attention to detail. Today, you'll examine photos of popular items. With your table partners, research what is necessary to preserve each one and prevent spoilage. Chip here," and he turned to his assistant, "photographed these objects in close detail. One day these may become obsolete, just pieces of history."

The professor instructed everyone to take out their tablets. Tessa fumbled getting hers out of her backpack, almost dropping it in her flustered state. *Of all the classes to assist, Chip had to be here.*

Professor James clicked the remote and pointed the laser to the first slide, an iPad.

Several students chuckled at the idea of that being an outdated, unused item.

Tessa tried to concentrate on the task but found her eyes sliding toward Chip, who worked the room talking and advising students. His tall, lean frame moved effortlessly. When he approached her table, waves of masculinity wafted off him, testosterone and spice.

"Notice the iPad screen," Chip addressed the students. "For preservation, a curator . . . or art restorer . . ." he smiled slyly at Tessa, "would need the proper cleaning solution. She'd also have to ensure the iPad remains in a temperature-controlled environment, free from humidity, especially in a place like Florida."

She might have imagined his lingering gaze or hoped it, she didn't know which. She did know that his attention unnerved her, made her self-conscious. And she had too much going on than to think about Chip Foster.

When class ended, she didn't dawdle. She grabbed her backpack to leave, but before she could, Professor James called her name. She saw him signal for her to come over.

"Yes?" Tessa called out, hoping the professor had a quick question that would allow her to escape quickly.

"Got a minute? I want to introduce you," Professor James said. He beckoned her like one would encourage a reluctant child to enter the grown-up party.

She walked over. "Hello, Chip." Then to Professor James she said, "We've met." Hoisting her backpack further on her shoulders she said politely to Chip, "Nice to see you again."

Chip raised his eyebrows and regarded her with apparent amusement.

The professor cleared his throat. "Ah, well, good." He clapped his veiny hands together. "Ms. Wilde, I'm making Chip your personal mentor, so to speak. You're new to our program, and Chip is knowledgeable and experienced. He can answer questions, get you up to speed, and help you become immersed in our world."

Chip bowed elaborately. "My pleasure, Ms. Wilde."

Tessa rolled her eyes, and the professor seemed oblivious. "Chip will meet you for lab work when necessary and inform you of community art events that I'm sure you'd like to see."

She recalled the art exhibit that Chip had mentioned last week.

Plus," Professor James held up a finger for emphasis, "Chip will be here this summer and I won't. I know you're taking a few classes then to catch up. He'll answer any of your questions." He began gathering his materials, leaving Chip and Tessa to stand awkwardly.

While Tessa pondered the appropriate response—*Thank you. Okay. I won't need his help.*

Chip turned more serious. "Tessa, I want you to feel comfortable reaching out to me. I'd love to show you around our art community."

She compelled her beating heart to still itself. Tessa Wilde would not swoon over a boy. *Wow, you sound like Grandmother.* That last thought was enough to squash any romantic inclinations. She answered as neutrally as she could. "Sure. I appreciate your availability." Then she added, "I catch on to new things pretty quickly, so you shouldn't have your hands too full with me." He'd probably prefer photographing more trees than babysitting a college sophomore.

"I wouldn't mind if you need me," he said.

Was he flirting?

"Summers are pretty slow," he added.

Not flirting. Just preparing for a boring summer.

"Shall we go?" Professor James asked, not waiting for them as he strode to the door.

The three of them left the classroom. The downpour that had begun earlier hadn't let up. Professor James peered at the relentless rain and said he'd go upstairs to his third-floor office.

She and Chip descended the stairs, Tessa cautiously avoiding slippery spots and slick, muddy tracks.

"I don't know about you, but I'm parking myself on that bench until the rain stops," Chip announced pointing to one of the black, vinyl-covered benches that dotted the lobby area. "Care to wait with me?"

Tessa took a quick peek at the skies. The rain had slowed to a steady rhythm. Clouds were everywhere though, with no end in sight. Besides, she should get used to being around Chip. Tessa wasn't stupid; she recognized attraction for what it was. But like all shiny new toys, the fascination would recede in time. She was convinced of it.

For a few moments, they watched their peers. Rain-soaked students about to enter paused outside on the porch, shaking umbrellas or limbs that dripped with water. A few kids laughed as they grasped handfuls of their own hair to wring out. They pushed their way through the double doors, some giggling at their drowned rat looks, others grimacing or grumbling about getting caught in a storm.

Chip leaned forward, elbows on his knees. "You know, Tessa, rain makes phenomenal pictures."

"How do you figure *that*?" she asked. "Wouldn't the pictures come out blurry?"

"If you crawl into the brush, the palmetto and palm fronds provide covering and you can mostly stay dry. Pictures of rain droplets dripping off new spring leaves or frogs blinking as water cascades over their hooded eyes are cool."

Chip was so comfortable and confident talking about things most guys wouldn't even notice. His self-assurance made him more attractive, but Tessa ignored the thought. Instead, she said, "I've never thought of it that way."

"A lot of people forget there's more than one way to see the same picture. Sometimes you gotta change the lens. You know what I mean?" He looked directly at Tessa, and it was as if he could see her history, the struggle with Grandmother, her secret birth story. Even though that was impossible for him to know.

She refocused. "Like those optical illusion pictures. You might see the frog while I see the rabbit." She sat up straight. "No, it's more than that. Even abstract paintings take on different meanings when someone looks through the eyes of their own history. I think that's why art can be so powerful." She looked down, a little embarrassed to reveal a philosophy she didn't even know she had.

"Exactly." Chip tilted his head toward her, his brown eyes seeming to study her. In a good way. With respect and understanding.

She felt her breath hitch as the world around her shrank and all she noticed was Chip Foster. The fluttery feeling when he talked to her and the skipping heartbeats when he held her gaze disturbed her. This hadn't happened with any boy—guy—before.

"Hey, look at that!" and he pointed to a ray of sun slicing through the glass panes, breaking the spell. "When all you see is clouds, sometimes nature surprises you with the light."

Tessa pulled herself back to reality. Sure enough, she could see the watery sun poking through dark clouds.

Chip stood up. "We should probably head out. Looks like more rain is coming."

She stood with him.

He touched her arm giving it a gentle squeeze. "I'll give you the details about that exhibit downtown as soon as I get them."

Tessa's mouth felt dry and her throat tight. Her arm tingled. She didn't trust herself not to squeak when she talked so she only nodded.

He held the door open for her and they both walked outside. He took off towards the parking lot while Tessa headed toward the dorms. Tessa knew she was attracted to the kind, confident, college graduate student. However, Chip Foster would not be a distraction from her future.

Nor would her grandmother. Or her mother. Or any new information she had to absorb.

And nothing would convince her she'd gotten her perspective wrong.

She put in her earbuds, choosing "Never Surrender" to refresh her resolve and accompany her to the dorm. Corey Hart's voice trilled in her ears. She would stick to her guns. Refuse to see Grandmother again. With time, the hurt would fade, her life would resume its course, and she'd be Tessa Wilde, future art restorer. With her head down Tessa didn't see Kendra approaching and almost bumped into her. She apparently had a bad habit of doing that.

"Hey, girl, you ignoring me? I'm waving my arms like I'm trying to make it rain again, and you're lost in Tessa World."

Tessa took in the glittery headband, jumbo hoop earrings, and bright pink shirt that defined Kendra today. She removed her earbuds. "Sorry, just thinking about stuff."

Kendra turned to walk with Tessa. "Care to share, chickadee?"

Tessa had first seen Kendra on the night of a Get-To-Know-You social event. Tessa hadn't planned to attend. Large social gatherings were not for her. Tessa had held the door open for a group of girls entering the lobby with boxes in their arms. When a box slipped, its contents scattering in the lobby, Tessa had helped retrieve everything. Before she knew it, she was setting out drinks and food and taking orders from a girl with hot pink hair and flashy, mismatched clothes. Kendra, as the girl introduced herself, had barked directions to others. And they'd willingly obeyed. Tessa had never met someone so confident, comfortable, and commanding so she'd stayed for the party. She and Kendra had clicked, and a friendship had begun.

Now she appeared just when Tessa could use an open ear. Even though Tessa was private and not prone to spill her life story, she could use a sounding board. And there was no better one than Kendra. "I saw my grandmother again."

"Yeah?" Kendra asked.

"And I got way more information than I wanted. None of it good."

Kendra stopped short. "I think this conversation needs coffee." She took Tessa's arm, and they walked off the main path to one that led to the Student Union. "You sit there." Kendra directed her to a couch in a semi-private corner. "I'll be right back with drinks."

The sun had disappeared once again, the clouds banding together as if in cahoots with Mother Nature. *Cahoots.* Such a Grandmother word.

"What happened with your grandma?" Kendra asked when she returned with two frothy cappuccinos and had wiggled into the couch cushions.

Tessa provided a detailed account, starting with that first visit and ending with the last. And sharing her birth details. As she talked, the story seemed less shocking and more like a sad secret.

But she sipped her coffee drink, which reenergized her, and watched as Kendra's mouth gaped open and stayed there. Finally, Kendra said, "Dang, girl. You don't need the Real Housewives of Wherever show. You got reality TV in your very own life." Kendra sat back and looked at Tessa over the top of the cup. "So, what do you want to do about it?"

Tessa shrugged. Her bruises wanted distance. Her psyche wanted answers.

"Well, the next move belongs to you."

Tessa loved and hated Kendra's directness. It made her squirm. It made her accountable. It made her pay attention. And now, it made her angry. She pointed to herself and said, "*I* don't have to do anything."

Kendra set her coffee down and leaned toward Tessa. "You're just gonna let the story end here? Smack dab in the beginning where it started?" When Tessa didn't answer, Kendra continued. "Lou Ann might not be alive, but your grandma is. And she's the key to any closure you might get." She pushed. "Look, either you can mope and feel sorry for yourself, or you can get some answers. Use Grandma's love for the past. Let her talk." She picked up her coffee and relaxed into the sofa again. "Once she's gone, it'll be too late, and you might never learn anything."

Tessa looked at her friend. She had essentially mimicked what her mom had said. Why did it sound so logical and clear-headed coming from Kendra?

Kendra delivered the punch. "Alzheimer's only gets worse. No one recovers from that disease, you know. If you want to learn anything, you can't wait."

CHAPTER SIXTEEN

Esther

Not-Sally sat on the bed next to Esther. "You took quite a fall yesterday, Ms. Esther. Good thing you didn't have to stay in the hospital. Just bruises and soreness for you, ma'am." She patted Esther's legs gently which were tucked under a rose-colored blanket.

Esther didn't remember falling. But she hurt. Aches and pains accompanied her most days; today was no exception. But they told her she was alive.

It's a great day to be alive, Essie! Art's voice sang through her thoughts. Every morning after his shower, he'd proclaim the goodness of the day. Art was the early riser. Watching the sun rise kick-started his day. Esther had always believed it was the two cups of coffee that provided his excess energy so early in the morning.

"You ready to get up?" an unfamiliar voice asked her.

The strong voice boomed with positivity. Esther frowned. She didn't answer the lady. Words seemed to lodge themselves in her mind, trapped behind invisible doors. They crowded each other so much she couldn't tell one word from another.

"It's late. Just about time for lunch. I hear it's pot roast today. Sound good?"

Lunch already? Esther thought she was just getting up from a night's sleep. But the sun was bright through the slats of the window blinds. How did time slip past her?

Pot roast. Sally's pot roast? That made her mouth water just thinking of the tender beef that fell apart with a fork. The subtle spices caused Esther's taste buds to spring to life. Nothing too crazy, just the right amount of peppery flavor. When Esther opened her mouth to reply, all that came out was "Spot post." *What?* She knew the right words. Why weren't they dancing off her tongue?

Not-Sally smiled and caressed Esther's legs. "Yes, pot roast. I'll get your brush and we'll get ready."

The bed squeaked when Not-Sally got up, reminding Esther of the noisy crib mattress she had for baby Tessa. That baby monitor Junior had bought her picked up every sound from that crib. Tessa was a sweet, if not busy, child. Esther's heart both lifted and sank when she thought of the golden-haired child. Walking unsteadily but determined to motor herself around Esther's house, Tessa was always on the move. Even in her sleep, baby Tessa tossed and turned. A vision appeared of a darker blonde girl, gangly and awkward, still on the move. An older child, Tessa had started to show signs of independence. Esther worried Tessa's unconventional streak would keep her apart from the path of security. That she'd scare boys away and be alone. Her heart tightened. Giving Tessa a charm bracelet and explaining how to make it significant might shift the girl's focus from living wild adventures to capturing important ones in charms.

From the corner of her eye, Esther spotted her own charm bracelet on the side table. Like a pacifier soothing a fussy Tessa, Esther's bracelet transported her to a place of serenity and joy. She stretched her arm to retrieve the bracelet, but banged into a cup of water, knocking it to the floor and missing the bracelet altogether. Why was her arm jerky and uncontrollable?

She cried.

Not-Sally came out of the bathroom nearby. She placed Esther's hairbrush on the table and said, "Don't you cry over that, Ms. Esther. I'll get that cleaned up lickety split." And she left the room only to return momentarily, a roll of paper towels under her arm. "I've found myself bashing or bumping into items in my own house every day." She shook her head and chuckled, all while bending over to wipe the water off Esther's bedroom floor.

Once Not-Sally stood up, a wad of damp towels in her hand, Esther said, "Bracelet?"

After Not-Sally placed it in her hand, Esther closed her fingers and pulled her beloved bracelet close to her chest. She closed her eyes, letting memories of the past fill her with comfort.

Beep-beep-beep. The sound emanated from Not-Sally's pocket somewhere. She pulled out a square device and looked at it. "Ms. Esther, I'll be right back and we'll head to the dining room." Then she left.

Esther felt the charms, her fingers lingering on the baby rattle. *Junior. Tessa.* Both names linked together. She tightened her grip, wishing the names brought blessed relief instead of heightened anxiety. Babies. She'd traded one dream—writing and traveling—for another. She'd intended to become a mother of a brood on whom she could impart her love for words, both written and read. It would be her new calling.

•   •   •

"Art, I have something to tell you." Unlike her husband, Essie wasn't so good at surprises.

"Hmm?" he asked, the newspaper open in front of him.

She sat across from his favorite recliner and cleared her throat. Sunday mornings were usually reserved for lengthy newspaper reading followed by church but today would be different.

"I don't think I'll go to Sunday sermon this morning," she started.

This garnered her a lowering of the paper and a curious gaze.

"Why not?"

"I don't feel well. I'm nauseous and it comes and goes in waves, so I'm never sure when it will hit me." She raised her eyebrows in a Do-you-understand? kind of way.

"Might be the flu. Best if you sit it out," he agreed, returning the paper to its original position in front of his face.

"Except I've felt this way for several weeks."

Now her husband wasn't a stupid man, but he was slow to pick up her not-so-subtle hints. It had been fifteen years since they were married with no pregnancy to show for it. They'd both assumed it wasn't in the cards for them.

"Art, are you listening?" Essie walked over to him and pushed the paper down, so he was forced to give her his full attention.

"Yes, dear. Sick, flu. That's fine. I can go by myself. I'll bring you some soup."

When it became clear subtlety wouldn't work, she said, "Art Wilde, I get nauseous in the mornings, food is unappealing, and sometimes I crave pickles!" The last part wasn't true, but she wanted to drop an obvious hint.

Realization dawned slowly, but it did happen. She watched a grin spread from his mouth to his eyes. He threw the paper down and jumped up from his chair.

"Esther Mae, are you telling me what I think you're telling me?"

Essie could only nod, tears welling in her eyes. She wasn't a particularly emotional person, but the worry of not providing him a child had had her in knots for years. It wasn't something either of them discussed, too uncomfortable or afraid to broach it, but joy hit them now as if they'd been waiting for this moment. The relief was like a dam breaking.

He swung her around the living room, yelping with delight. "Really? When? What can I do? Sit down! How do you feel?"

She laughed, surprised at his silliness and relieved the tension of childlessness had been lifted.

"Let's celebrate! Today is the last day of the carnival. Let's ditch church and go walking through the fairgrounds. Check out the booths and rides for next year. We'll take little Wilde on all of them!" Art shouted.

He grabbed their coats before Essie could say anything and hustled them out, still creating scenarios of carnivals and fairs of the future. "This is the start of our big family, Essie!"

He opened her car door and planted a big kiss on her lips as she reeled from the suddenness of it all. It was a time for celebration, and the morning was a spectacular spring one. She couldn't stop his happiness if she wanted to, which she didn't. She willed the nausea away and off they went on a spontaneous adventure.

Essie felt like it was the start of a beautiful family.

•   •   •

She'd only had one child. It wasn't for lack of desire. Esther had learned life's disappointments never stopped but she'd always been a believer in the lemonade-out-of-lemons theory. As Junior aged and no more children came, she had energized herself trying to build a small but strong family. Then Art died. Junior drank. She thought she'd lost control. Then came Tessa. Tessa was her do-over, her chance to shape someone who wouldn't be a victim of her own self-absorption. Wouldn't strive for the impossible like Esther did or drown in her own problems like Junior did. Someone who set realistic, achievable goals and recognized the value in that. Tessa would be her salvation.

Not-Sally strode into her room and broke into her remembering. "Okay, let's get you up and in the wheelchair."

Esther allowed herself to be moved and settled like a doll placed on a shelf after someone played with it. That's how she felt often—like someone's plaything, moved at their discretion. Esther couldn't direct her body where to go sometimes, speak for herself on occasion, or even take care of herself. Like she was trapped in someone else's world.

Not-Sally pushed Esther in a wheelchair down a carpeted hall. Pictures of scenic beaches, sea grass, and dunes lined the walls. Sconces gave off subtle lighting. Tasteful, but Esther missed her old house with its artifacts and wall hangings. A blend of traditional and historical, Esther and Art's house encompassed Esther's childhood favorites, her mother's dining room set and accompanying china, and Art's father's workshop tools. Surprisingly, some of the old-fashioned tools made wall hangings that gave a flair of workmanship to their home.

Although this building was pretty, she missed the solidarity of over fifty years' worth of sameness, reliability, and comfort. Uniformity had soothed her when Art died.

She had decorated her three houses similarly. She had no need for new "stuff" as styles changed, no need to replace what was dependable and functional. Her homes manifested her spirit of thriftiness and convention. She loved them all. This place however…

Esther sighed as Not-Sally opened a set of doors. The clattering of utensils, the shrill squeaks of elderly voices that have lost their timbre, and the uniformed staff hustling from table to kitchen and back were sure signs she wasn't home. Oh, how she missed Sally.

Her wheelchair stopped at a four-person table. She smiled at the other three, who returned the polite gesture. As she placed her napkin on her lap, a waitress arrived with soup. Turning slightly to pick up her spoon, her eyes caught a glimpse of familiarity.

A young man of about thirty-five, Junior's age, sat at the table diagonally from her. He had a full head of thick, black hair and a short beard. Esther gasped. It was Junior!

Her mind tumbled down the road of the past, tossing any sense of the present aside. She lost sight of where she was and who was around her. All she could see was her son.

"Junior! Where have you been?" Soup forgotten, Esther placed her hands on either side of the table, ready to give her son a real talking-to a few tables away.

He ignored her. A few others turned their eyes her way, then slid them back to their respective meals.

The gall of him to pretend he didn't hear her.

"Arthur Junior, come over here right now!" Esther delivered a firm message that she was not to be ignored this time.

Lots of heads turned her way, including Junior's. Nearby chatter stopped and confused expressions met her eyes, especially those of Junior's tablemates.

He stared at her, surprise registering on his face. Then, he did the strangest thing. He looked around him as if he had no idea Esther was addressing him.

"Son, whatever is the matter with you? Come over here and let's have a talk."

She prepared to shoo her seatmates away, to make room for her beloved Junior, but he remained seated where he was. One of those helper people in the teal uniform approached her as did the familiar lady. The one whose name she forgot. Sally's new hire?

The lady spoke softly blocking her view of Junior. "Ms. Esther, that is not your son."

How dare she stand in Esther's way? And how dare she claim Esther didn't recognize her own son!

"Miss, you need to move immediately," Esther demanded, shifting in her seat to see around the woman.

"Ms. Esther, that man's name is Benjamin. He's Mr. Jeremiah's grandson."

Junior hadn't risen from his seat. In fact, he seemed rooted there in defiance of Esther's order. As she glared at him, daring him to ignore her, something nibbled at the edge of her mind. Something sad and empty.

"Ms. Esther, Junior isn't here," Not-Sally said, and Esther heard the sadness and regret her voice.

Something like recognition or remembrance tickled her memory. The feeling was laced with bitterness and sadness. She dropped her shoulders and tears pooled behind her eyes threatening to spill in front of all these strangers.

Stiffening in her chair, she pushed back from the table and raised her chin. "I'm ready to go now," she said to no one in particular.

"I'll take you back to your room." The voice contained enough kindness to make the tears spill over.

Esther didn't even try to wipe them away. Junior was gone. The dead kind of gone.

The wheelchair muffled its way back down a hallway. Esther's mind was a perforated box—it was large enough to hold things but filled with holes that let those same things slip away. It bothered her. Bothered her enough to get angry. Esther didn't do pity.

The chair stopped in front of a door that held little sentiment for Esther. Her place? She didn't know, but when Not-Sally opened it, Esther spied her blanket on the back of a recliner.

When the wheelchair stopped at her recliner, Esther's tears had dried, and her anger spilled out. "I can do it myself!" She almost slapped the lady's hands away when brown arms reached out to help her up.

"Okay, Ms. Esther," that same kind voice said.

"I'm not a child; don't pacify me," Esther answered.

Not-Sally ignored Esther, guiding her into the chair anyway. Esther's nerves were on edge. She needed a break. A break from forgetting and remembering, a break from the past and present intermingling, a break from strangers/not strangers entering her life.

She pictured Tessa in this room, sitting in that chair, talking to her. But Esther didn't trust her mind—was it a memory or a dream?

Oh, Art, how I miss you.

"Ms. Esther, I'll be right back with some dinner," Not-Sally called out as she left.

Esther closed her eyes and rested her head. Life had become difficult. She was once so certain of a day of the week, a season of the year, a decade. Then, it all vanished like the fog as day broke.

When will you come for me, Art? It was a wish more than a question.

CHAPTER SEVENTEEN

Tessa

Tessa tried to immerse herself in her classes to catch up and escape the oppressive pain of Grandmother's and Debra's betrayals. But when time allowed, her brain played the scene in the diner over and over. She was someone else's daughter. A drug addict, a wild girl, an outcast. *And yet,* a nagging voice said, *you were loved.*

Grandmother, however, was a different story. And despite what her mom or Kendra said, Tessa didn't know if there was a way to find closure. Or answers. Or to patch things up.

Kendra had suggested she engage Grandmother in the past. But why should Tessa do what Grandmother wanted? *She* was the one with the bombshell news to swallow.

Her mother pushed her to make amends. But how could she do that with a woman who didn't even know who Tessa was?

She strolled around the school grounds. Mexican heather lined the pathways, bursts of purple blossoms making a nice contrast with the dark green palmettos and shrubs behind them. But her thoughts were far removed from flowers or school. So deep in thought, she barely heard her name. After the third "Tessa!" she turned around.

Chip jogged toward her.

Tessa's breath quickened and she willed herself to play it cool. And mature.

He wore a plain tee shirt tucked into faded, pressed jeans. The picture of casual sophistication. With his hair pulled back in a short ponytail, he looked dapper. She mentally eye rolled. *Dapper.* Another Grandmother word.

"What are you doing here on a Sunday?" she asked, going for casual nonchalance.

He stopped next to her. "I've got a photo class study session. I was just getting ready to text you, though. The show is next weekend. Photographers and sculptors. Do you want to go?"

Yes. No.

Chip unnerved her, made her feel goofy and silly when she so wanted to be mature and composed. But she needed exposure to the art world and the experience of being around other students and artists.

Her silence lengthened into awkwardness.

Chip shrugged. "It's okay." He smiled and turned to leave.

"No, wait!" She grabbed his arm, then let go quickly as if it burned. "No. Yeah. For sure. I'd love to go." Tessa stuttered her response.

Speak clearly and hold your head up high, she heard in Grandmother's chastising voice. In spite of it being Grandmother's advice, she did just that. "Exactly when and where is it?"

"I'll text you the details." He consulted his watch. "I've got to go help some photography students with their perspective." He winked. "Talk to you soon, Tessa." And he sauntered away.

Chip Foster probably thought nothing of asking Tessa to an art show. Wasn't that exactly what Professor James told him to do? It was nothing more than that.

Perspective. The word reverberated in Tessa's head. One definition meant a kind of two-dimensional drawing that gave the impression of other elements—height, width, depth and relation to each other—when viewed a particular way. Like looking at the layers of an object. Or person. If someone were to draw Grandmother as a perspective drawing, would they see her other than how Tessa did? Was there more to her grandmother than Tessa knew?

Just then her phone buzzed with a new text message:

Checking that you didn't give me a fake number the other day. Text me back 😊

Tessa smiled. Should she say something or just send an emoji?

Haha. It's me. LOL

She resumed her walk. She put in her ear buds and was lost in her music until Kenny Loggins sang about the danger zone. Not this one. Then Simple Minds chanted "Don't You Forget About Me." Both songs brought the face of Chip in front of her. Tessa turned off the music and took in her surroundings instead. She loved the unspoiled nature of the college grounds. Thick palmetto trees almost hid the marshy ponds. Spanish moss hung from the branches of live oak trees like an old lady's stringy hair. After a few minutes the dense scrub brush looked familiar. Unintentionally, Tessa had walked to the spot where she'd first met Chip.

She peered into the brush. Chip had taken those pictures in that clearing—where a person could stoop with palm fronds as shelter. It was kind of cool. Glancing quickly to her right and left, Tessa ducked underneath low hanging branches and pushed shrub leaves aside. She climbed into the gap, shedding her backpack and placing it behind her. Then she crouched down.

Chip had told her it was important to see things from a different perspective.

Looking up, the underside of palm fronds blocked her view of blue sky. A thatched hut came to mind. Back in the day, Tessa imagined these leaves would be roofs for primitive people. As her gaze traveled down, she paused to see what greeted her at eye level. Or knee level. She spotted sawgrass, nature's weapon and shield. She smiled as a childhood rhyme returned to her:

"Sedges have edges,

Rushes are round.

Grasses are hollow,

What have you found?"

She remembered that sawgrass wasn't grass at all. The blades had tiny teeth even though they appeared to be tall, soft grass. The razor-sharp edges provided safety for animals of the marshes and protection against predators. The rush of information transported Tessa back to field trips. As tour guides and teachers prattled on, Tessa had imagined what life was like before someone turned the park or historical site into a destination. Maybe her love of history and all things old wasn't so far-fetched after all. And maybe Chip was right about perspective.

Just then the sound of laughter broke through her thoughts. On the path right next to her. She peeked through the foliage to see a group of students lingering nearby.

One voice rose above the others. "One of the best spots to utilize different lighting and an unusual perspective is right through there."

Chip!

Her heart raced. She scrambled to think of a different exit. Or an excuse to explain her presence. *What was he doing here? Didn't he say he had a study session to lead?* She groaned inwardly. Why did he bring them here?

She tucked herself into a ball as much as she could and held her breath. Maybe they'd leave. *Please don't come in, please don't come in,* she repeated silently to any god who might listen.

"Hello? Is someone there?"

A quick glance behind her showed Tessa that her backpack was in plain view. She might as well have lit an SOS fire. Where was Harry Potter's invisibility cloak when she needed it? Like a cornered animal, her eyes darted everywhere searching for a hiding place. Nothing.

She heard the leaves rustle.

"Tessa?" Chip was bent at the waist peering through the palm fronds.

Crap.

"What? Oh. . . um. . . hey, there!" She grabbed her backpack and climbed out as if it were natural to pick her way through shrubbery.

Then she spun around searching the ground for a pretend lost item. "Yeah, hi. I was—" She didn't know what in the world could be a reasonable excuse for hiding in an isolated spot off the beaten path. Literally, off the path.

He grinned. "So glad you got here first." He rocked back on his heels, clearly enjoying her discomfort. Then he turned to the group of students. "Tessa is a newer fine arts student. I told her about this place." He turned back to her. "See what I mean about the way you can perceive something differently?"

She nodded, not knowing what else to do.

As she stood awkwardly, trying to think of something to say that would explain her presence, he addressed the group. "No matter where you are, look for a different viewpoint. Seeing leaves through new eyes, for example, might make a person appreciate them. Right, Tessa?"

"Yes, it's a great exercise in point of view," she said lamely. She hitched her backpack up and made a show of pulling her phone from her back pocket, checking the time. "Oh, gosh. I've gotta bounce. Hope you all enjoy picture-taking," she said, noting the camera equipment each one carried.

If she could have run without bringing any more attention to herself, she would have.

She felt Chip's eyes watching her. She'd only gone a few steps when he stopped her. "Hey, hang on a minute." To the others, he said, "Go ahead and set up your cameras for close range and find a spot within the brush or any other area that feels good to you."

Steeling herself for the teasing that was sure to come, she stood ramrod straight.

"What brought you out here?" he asked once the others had moved on.

His directness surprised her. She sighed, relaxed her stance, and answered honestly. "I really don't know." Then she blurted out, "My grandmother has Alzheimer's. To be honest, we don't get along well, and things between us have always been awkward, even before . . . the disease. I guess I just wondered about the whole perspective thing. If I could get into her head, I might see what compels her to say the awful things she does."

Tessa ran out of steam. *And where the hell had that come from?* Embarrassed, she cleared her throat and lifted her chin to say goodbye.

Chip put his hand on her arm. "Alzheimer's sucks. Especially when people don't make sense. And relationships are hard. I have an uncle who puts down my photographs all the time. I think he's jealous. At least, that's what I tell myself." He chuckled at his joke.

She smiled more to break the tension than because he was funny. Still, she wasn't quite so humiliated.

"I give you credit for trying to figure it out, Tessa Wilde. It means you care."

His understanding eyes made Tessa want to jump into them. In fact, she leaned towards him, caught up in his kindness. The movement shifted her weight, and the backpack slid sideways, knocking her off balance. Chip grabbed her before she fell. He held her arms steady in front of him. In an awkward moment, Tessa lifted her shoulders to realign her backpack, and Chip gave her a hug at the same time. The result was a stiff embrace with Tessa's shoulders scrunched to her ears.

He loosened his grip on her arms but still held them. "Don't give up on your grandma. Maybe she had a tough life that made her the way she is." He dropped his arms and shrugged. "That's how I explain my uncle's rudeness even if it's not true." He offered her a wry smile.

The hug-but-not-a-hug had left her feeling awkward and stupid. She was sure a blush was vining its way up to her face. She could only nod.

He either didn't notice or ignored it. "Look for my text with the art show details." He smiled before heading back to the students.

Her heart pounded as she walked away. He had saved her from embarrassment in front of those other students. He didn't even call her out when they were alone. Chip was different from other guys she'd known. Like a big brother.

No. Her feelings were definitely not those of a little sister.

Chip brought out the heart of her. The qualities of herself that she most cherished and kept bottled up. Honesty and openness. The ones that made her the most vulnerable. She was sure the mystique would end soon, and then he'd be just another guy she'd crushed on. Even in high school, she'd flirted a little, gone on a few dates, but the fun faded quickly. She was not a "relationship" person. But he was the third person to urge her to try to repair the broken relationship with Grandmother.

Tessa set off toward her dorm with a new idea. She didn't necessarily want to repair the relationship—some things couldn't be fixed—but she did want to know as much as possible about Lou Ann. Even if Grandmother spewed only venom, Tessa wanted to know something about the woman—girl—who'd given her life.

It was Sunday afternoon, probably a quiet time at Sunset Shadows, a day of visits. Maybe her grandmother would be coherent. If not, Tessa had a plan. She'd ask about Grandmother's charm bracelet and pick out a charm that might have meaning, like her own birthstone. Maybe she could influence the right memories to spill out. At the last minute, Tessa grabbed the charm bracelet Grandmother had given her and threw it into her backpack.

She jumped in her car and headed over to the assisted living facility. As she walked to Grandmother's room, her confidence wavered. Was she setting herself up for more rejection?

She knocked on Grandmother's door without hesitation this time and heard a faint "Come in."

The television was on, an old show from the 1980s. A woman writer who solves mysteries, Tessa remembered. She couldn't remember the name of it. But it was something she and her grandmother had watched a few times together.

Grandmother was in a recliner, the quilt over her legs, watching the TV. Who knew if she really saw what was projected in front of her?

"Hello, Grandmother." Tessa stood in the hallway leading to the living area, hoping her grandmother would recognize her.

"Dinner?" her grandmother asked. And she threw off her afghan and leaned forward as if to stand up.

Tessa rushed to stop her, wondering at the one-word question. Usually Grandmother was formal and proper. "Um. . . no. It's. . . uh, too early for dinner, Grandmother."

While her grandmother settled back into her chair, Tessa placed her backpack on the floor and rummaged through it. She held up her own charm bracelet. "Do you recognize this? It's a bracelet you gave me for graduation."

Her grandmother stared at it and then at Tessa. She seemed to struggle to make the connection.

"It's similar to yours," Tessa added. When her grandmother continued to stare between the bracelet and Tessa, Tessa brought over a chair. "I'd like to ask you a few questions about my mother." She felt her breath hitch, the unpredictability of her grandmother bearing on her.

"Who?"

Tessa noticed the lack of emotion, more curiosity than animosity and took that as a good sign. "I know Lou Ann is my mother. I know she died."

Grandmother looked out the window and Tessa worried she wouldn't answer anything. "She was no good. Ran wild. Off the rails. Took no responsibility." Then she turned to Tessa. "You're stubborn like her. Restless. Reckless."

Tessa felt her stomach drop and her head pound as the blood rushed to it. Would her grandmother only spout rancor and anger, hatred and disgust?

Her grandmother continued talking. "She made Junior laugh for a while. And she gave me my granddaughter." Her brows furrowed and she narrowed her mouth into a straight line. She leaned forward toward Tessa. "Now, who are you again?"

This time Tessa heard the suspicion. Before she could answer or ask anything else, Mayra entered. "Hello, Tessa. I brought your grandmother's medicines. How are you?" She bustled about with a steel cart and put some pills in a white paper cup. "Oh, darn it. I'll be right back. I forgot your water," and she scuttled out the front door.

Tessa stood up in front of her grandmother's recliner, intending to leave. She wouldn't get any memories from Grandmother today. Just more rejection. Exactly what she'd feared. She prepared to pick up the chair and return it to the table when her grandmother grabbed Tessa's arm. "This is the last bit of cash I give you. Junior pays you well. You either make do with that or give me Tessa. I'll raise her right." She looked past Tessa. "Where's my pocketbook?" Her eyes grew frantic, and she whipped her head around, searching the room. "Did you take it, you little thief?" Her voice had escalated to a screech.

Tessa tried to back away, but her grandmother's grip clutched her arm. She shook her head. "It's me, Grandmother. Tessa!" Oh, how she wished Mayra would appear. Tessa had no idea how to handle this outburst. Without thinking, she held up her bracelet in her other hand. "See, the bracelet you gave me."

"You've stolen Tessa's bracelet! Help, help!" Her screeches turned to shouts.

Mayra burst through the door, water sloshing out the top of a pitcher. "Okay, Ms. Esther. Let's settle down. What's going on?"

Although she was swift and efficient, Mayra's voice was soothing and calm, apparently a perfect balm for Grandmother because she released her death grip on Tessa.

Tessa rubbed her arm protectively and grabbed her backpack. "I can't do this," she said and she raced out the door.

CHAPTER EIGHTEEN

Esther

Esther sat at the little pine table in her room. Today, she had dinner, or lunch—Esther didn't know what time it was—in the apartment. She swallowed the salty chicken noodle soup the nice lady with the wavy flat hair brought to her. Too bad Sally was on vacation or wherever she was. She made a perfect soup, seasoned just right with loads of noodles and pieces of chicken.

The Not-Sally woman puttered about Esther's kitchenette. The odd kitchen without a stove or coffee pot. Esther remembered baking in her old kitchen. Until Amelia Sutton's nastiness, Esther had provided dessert for the bridge luncheons at the club. The memory of gooey, chocolate chip cookies made her mouth water, and she looked for her favorite cookie tin on the table. It wasn't there. Nothing familiar was there.

Esther watched Not-Sally wipe the counter, rinse out a cup, and straighten the odd stray item nearby—salt and pepper shakers, a decorative napkin holder, a bottle of hand lotion.

Esther's brain had let her down. Why was she here? Where was "here"? When was she whisked away from her home? And Junior had yet to show up.

She pushed the soup bowl away.

"Ms. Esther, can't you eat a little more?" Not-Sally asked as she came over. The woman pulled out a chair and sat next to Esther. "You aren't eating nearly enough. I worry you're gonna fade to nothing," she joked.

But Esther saw Not-Sally's brows furrow with concern.

"Blech," Esther responded, crossing her arms and turning away. Sometimes she felt like a child. Words often failed her. She resorted to using them only when necessary. She gripped the bracelet in one hand. The only link to feeling like herself.

Not-Sally put her hands on Esther's crossed arms. "Unfamiliar things are scary, Ms. Esther. And I know the soup isn't what you're used to. When I first moved here from Miami, I couldn't find a decent Cuban restaurant for miles." She chuckled and released her hands, sitting back. "No one could make a satisfactory Paella around here. And plantains." She made a face. "No taste at all." Not-Sally said quietly, "But I had to eat something, so I pretended I was back in Havana with my family, trying to make Mama's dishes." She leaned towards Esther. "How about a few sips of soup? Pretend you're tasting some new and exotic dish from a favorite place."

Plantains! Esther remembered those. She and Art had tasted them in Jamaica. The only out-of-the-country trip they'd ever taken. She uncrossed her arms and opened her palm, searching for that charm. The bongo player. She caressed it while the memory swept her back.

• • •

Art dragged Essie through the streets of downtown Montego Bay, browsing the street vendors' wares. Her sundress stuck to her back in the humidity, but Essie wouldn't complain. With Junior back at home and Art's best friends watching the one-year-old, she enjoyed a few days without child-minding. It was the first time she and Art had been out of the country, and the five-day trip had been freeing. Bright sunshine sparkled off the turquoise water, a color of blue she'd never seen at the Georgia beaches. And the white, soft sand practically glistened in the sun. They'd laughed and eaten unfamiliar food. Dirty rice which was spicy and plantains which were kind of like bananas. They drank coconut milk straight from the shell and ate mangos while swinging in hammocks at the hotel. Blue skies greeted her each morning as she took her daily walks. Strolling shoeless, sand filtered between her toes. And the salty spray from breaking waves tickled her browning skin. Essie felt like a young girl again. Like she could ride the wind anywhere she wanted. Reality tugged the edges of freedom, though. She loved her husband and son and was committed to the life she'd chosen. Still, the carefree attitude of the islands left her with a bit of longing for what she once thought would be her life. Traveling. Writing. She pushed that aside and concentrated on the present. She had a few days of abandon left.

"Essie, let's get a charm for that bracelet of yours. You don't wear it enough, and maybe if we load it with memories, you'll show it off more." Art wanted a remembrance.

"I love that bracelet, Art," she wanted to reassure him, "but with a baby to mind, it gets in the way. I save it for special occasions."

"Hmm . . . well, that pearl necklace your daddy gave you never seems to get in the way," he answered casually.

Her hand automatically felt the small beads at the base of her throat. Was Art jealous?

More likely, he worried that his gifts weren't as special to her as her father's. She'd have to work harder to show him that wasn't true, although she knew her heart's spot for Daddy was probably larger than that for her husband. Daddy had always encouraged her girlish ambition, her unrestrained dreams, until practicality became necessary for their family. When she'd married, he was pleased for her—for them— but he'd never mentioned her career aspirations again. When Daddy died a few years back, she'd vowed never to take off the necklace. And she hadn't.

"Yes, Art, I'd love a charm."

He beamed and they sorted through all the vendors, the smiling faces, and enthusiastic offers. She finally settled on a bongo player and drum. It was the music she'd first heard when they'd landed on the island. The thrumming beats were unfamiliar but bold; the joy of daily living played out in the rhythm of the drum.

Since she didn't have the bracelet with her, she tucked the charm away in her pocketbook. She vowed to affix it once she returned home.

•   •   •

That trip had been the beginning of her silent promise to choose specific charms as reminders of the best parts of her life. A way to record special events. Like a diary. Especially when she wanted to revisit past dreams. Esther had pledged to find happiness in what life gifted her: Art, Junior, and any more children to come. When she and Art had returned home, they were ecstatic to find she was pregnant once again. The hope for a bustling family was coming true. A few weeks later, nature had disrupted that plan. Pregnancy never happened again, and they were left with a three-person family forever.

She heard Not-Sally sigh. "Okay, Ms. Esther. Maybe tomorrow will be better." She scooped up Esther's unfinished meal.

Esther knew the woman meant well. She would've said as much but her mouth couldn't be trusted. Words fluttered like pieces of confetti someone shot in the air. They fell randomly. The result was nonsensical syllables or random words.

Not-Sally brought Esther's wheelchair over, another unwanted appendage of old age. And dependence. Not-Sally helped Esther from dining chair to wheelchair and then to the recliner. Then she pulled out a re—re—something. The thing turned on the television. *Murder, She Wrote* popped up on the screen.

Angela Lansbury scurried about Cabot Cove solving the latest murder. Esther thought of the life she'd once envisioned chasing down stories. She felt the self-pity rising and pushed it down. *No sense crying over spilt milk,* as her mother would say.

Esther watched the determined television character as she followed clues. TV never held the same appeal to Esther as old Hitchcock movies or classic romantic comedies. She had introduced Tessa to *Paper Moon.* Truth be told, although the child had laughed and smiled at the antics of Ryan and Tatum O'Neal, she preferred the silliness of *The Bad News Bears.*

She felt her eyes closing as thoughts of Tessa, scooching under the cover of the quilt on movie days, filled Esther with longing.

A rapping sound startled Esther. She must have been dozing. "Come in," she called sleepily. She shook her head of the dream, at least she thought it was a dream, of dancing on the sand at nighttime, next to a moonlit ocean, swaying in her husband's arms.

The Not-Sally lady came in. "I've got your medicine," she announced in a sing-song voice.

Esther couldn't remember why she took medicine, but she swallowed the pill and the water anyway. As she lifted her arm, her charm bracelet fell onto her lap.

"I've never had a charm bracelet, Ms. Esther. Maybe I should have. Seems like quite the treasure for you," the woman said, turning to a metal cart she'd pushed into Esther's room.

A flash of a young girl with a bracelet flitted in Esther's memory. "Your daughter here earlier?"

Not-Sally puzzled her brows and shook her head. She came to stand in front of Esther. "Tessa was here."

How in heaven's name could a child come alone? Although Esther had a vision of someone asking about Lou Ann. She brought a hand to her mouth. Had Lou Ann visited? "Sally, if Lou Ann comes by, you tell her to leave."

"Now, Ms. Esther, I don't know who Lou Ann is, but Tessa came—"

Esther shook a finger at Sally. "That girl is trouble. Junior just about ruined his life for that girl. She's nothing but evil. You hear me? You make sure she leaves!" Esther could hear her voice escalate but couldn't stop. She was determined to make Sally understand the severity of Lou Ann's wretchedness.

But the lady wasn't Sally. Not-Sally.

Not-Sally murmured some kind of shushing noises and Esther forced her breathing to regulate.

"Oh, this damn disease," Not-Sally muttered. "Takes over everything. I wish I could've told Tessa that your fingers had minds of their own, that you couldn't have released your grip on her arm even if you'd tried." Then she sighed deeply. "Do you want to talk about Lou Ann?"

Esther had no desire to discuss Lou Ann Parker anymore. And she was so tired.

CHAPTER NINETEEN

Tessa

Tessa drove to campus, still shocked over what had happened in Grandmother's room.

She touched her bruised forearm. Her grandmother had never physically hurt her before. How did Tessa trigger such anger?

Tears spilled over her lids. Tears of anger. Some of her anger was directed at herself for thinking things could be different between her and Grandmother. Another part of her was angry with her mother for suggesting she try, with Kendra and even Chip for thinking Tessa had a relationship to salvage. She and Grandmother had nothing but bad blood between them. And it would only get worse as Grandmother's mind spent more time in the past. As far as Tessa was concerned, the past only brought about bad memories.

With one hand, Tessa wiped the tears away. *Enough. You've let Grandmother hurt you for too long. Your instinct was right. Let it go. Let her go.* She pulled into the campus parking lot, relieved to be in familiar territory and ready to forget this awful afternoon. Her phone rang. A generic ringtone that signaled someone she didn't know. She sat in the driver's seat, fumbling for her phone in her backpack.

"Hello?" she answered.

"Hey, Tessa, it's Chip. I wanted to give you the details of the art show on Saturday. It's easier than trying to text it. You got a minute?"

"Sure," she answered as casually as she could. Thankfully, he couldn't feel her palms sweat or her heart race.

"Do you know the Leland Galleria on Brick Avenue?" he asked.

She nodded, before remembering he couldn't see her. The velvety tone of his voice had her tongue-tied, and it was a soothing balm to the day. "Um, yes," she said, clearing her throat and her head.

"Parking is limited. It's probably best if we ride together. I can pick you up and you can help with the setup. See what's involved in prepping for a show."

Tessa's heart flipped with the thought of riding with Chip and being a part of the art show, even if it was just prep work. And she had no worries that he was a serial killer.

Be assertive and enunciate. Grandmother's childhood directives played relentlessly in her head. "Yes, that sounds great."

"Excellent, I'll meet you in your lobby at noon. Which dorm?"

"Osprey Hall." Tessa hung up and a wave of exhaustion hit her. Whether it was because of Grandmother's bizarre behavior or Chip's invitation, she didn't know. But her head spun thinking of both uncharted territories she'd entered.

Rubbing her arm, she walked into her room and wondered again about her grandmother. Especially how she'd grabbed Tessa's arm and wouldn't, or couldn't, let go. Tessa sat at her little desk as the evening sun was setting. And she searched the Internet for Alzheimer's. What she knew about it was culled from her friends' observations and interactions with their own grandparents. She looked at the symptoms of the early stages and remembered that brief moment at graduation lunch when Grandmother seemed to forget her place. Was that the beginning? Or just a not-so-well-hidden lapse. Mayra had said Grandmother was in the middle stage of the disease. From what Tessa read, there was no timetable. This could last months or years. The only certainty was that it wouldn't get better. There was no cure, no going backwards or controlling the progression of this disease. Grandmother's memories were subject to the whims of her brain.

Unlike her grandmother, Tessa's brain could conjure up information at will, but it had nowhere to go. Lou Ann was a dead end unless Tessa could find out more about her. Her mother and father had grown up in the town Tessa was raised, so maybe Lou Ann had, too. And Spring Break was just a few weeks away. She'd be going home. She'd find out all she could about Lou Ann Parker then.

•　　•　　•

Tessa peeked out her mini blinds that Saturday morning. A cloudless blue sky was a good sign. Lying back on her bed, she fantasized about the day ahead. She'd help Chip set up his display and impress him with her intelligent observations about his photos. She'd mingle effortlessly with the other artists.

Outside the fantasy, reality painted a different picture. Would there be awkward silence on the drive downtown? And what if she asked stupid questions? Then Chip might regret being stuck with her the whole upcoming summer. And he might tell Professor James that Tessa was a poor choice for the program. Oh, God. Then Grandmother would be right about the pursuit of silly dreams.

That last thought forced Tessa to grit her teeth. *Stop it.* Grandmother was not part of this.

Tessa swung her feet to the floor. *Go with the flow. Take each moment as it comes. Just be yourself.* She waited for the long-standing mantras to give her strength and confidence. Nothing. She'd lived by these in high school, and they'd worked. But she'd also not had much at stake then. Now, her whole future was going to be affected by her choices.

Trudging down the hallway, Tessa pep-talked herself. *Concentrate on learning. Be present and observant. Ask people about themselves.* Grandmother's mantras. The same sayings she'd pushed out of her mind in high school came roaring to life now.

After showering, she padded back to her room, past the closed doors that housed sleeping students and those just rousing for the day.

She scoured her closet for the right outfit. Pushing hangers aside, she dismissed a sundress—too little girl-y. She rejected pants and a blouse—too matronly. Standing in front of her tiny closet, rummaging through the assortment, she hoped the perfect ensemble would jump out. No such luck. Finally she chose a patterned shift dress and ballet flats. Securing her hair in a clip and draping it over one shoulder, Tessa declared herself ready. *Dressy without being overdressed,* she decided. *Classy but casual.*

Her phone chirped. Chip was downstairs. Slinging her purse on one shoulder, she headed toward the lobby, telling the butterflies to simmer down.

Chip stood just inside the front doors checking his phone, hair slicked back and secured in a man-bun. He was a mature presence in a space usually filled with barely-out-of-the-teenage-years kids. The dark jeans, fitted and ironed, creased sharply from knee to foot. A pale blue, slim-fit shirt hugged his six-pack abs, and tan shoes were perfectly laced. His brows pursed in concentration.

Tessa's heart skipped a beat. She inhaled, raised her chin, and walked over.

Chip immediately pocketed his phone, eyes on her. His smile widened.

"M'lady, your chariot awaits," he said with a little bow.

Tessa laughed, relieving some initial tension. "I hope this chariot is air-conditioned," she said as they walked out into unusual February humidity. Tessa silently applauded her choice of hairstyle. Had she left it unclipped, the damp air would have made it a ball of frizz in no time.

In the parking lot, Chip pressed the car key, and Tessa followed the chirp to a small, black truck. It glistened and flaunted a blue tarp covering the open bed.

As Chip opened her door, he nodded to the back. "I got roped into bringing some of the others' work since I have a truck," he admitted. "You'd think I run a moving company," he joked.

Small talk flowed easily on the drive. Chip was a newbie to Florida. Originally from North Carolina, he'd come for college and had never left. She learned he had two sisters, both younger, and they lived in Charlotte with his parents. His father was an artist, his mother an attorney.

Before she knew it, they'd arrived. The designated exhibition hall was a spacious, bright room, one side with floor-to-ceiling windows. The view of a pond and fountain added charm and serenity to the space. Once the truck was unloaded, Tessa unpacked easels and sorted information cards that contained facts about the piece and the artist, photographer, or sculptor. It wasn't too difficult to match them up.

Tables scraped the floors as the exhibitors moved them around. They opened boxes and placed objects in strategic spots. Chatter was at a minimum and Tessa felt the tension of the artists hoping to receive favorable reviews. Maybe a few sales. It was exciting to be part of such anticipation.

As the first visitors entered the door, Tessa became the invisible fly. She observed which displays attracted people and which ones were overlooked. She paid special attention to Chip's photos. Tessa was too far away to overhear comments, but she saw people nodding their heads approvingly as they passed several of his displays. Only a few picked up the information cards.

She wandered over to one of his photographs. The picture was of a cresting wave, tall with froth building, just as it broke over itself. She scanned the information on the little white card. The sentences were factual and vanilla. Tessa turned the card over in her hands and mentally rewrote the information:

Droplets of sea water gather and prepare to pop as one of St. Augustine's waves builds in the Atlantic Ocean. One can almost taste the salty spray as the ocean meets the shoreline, crashing on unsuspecting sea life and sending shells, seaweed, and debris onto the beach.

Tessa's thoughts broke as Chip hustled over. "Hey, you doing okay? I feel like I'm answering the same questions over and over. And the answers are right there." He pointed to the card she twirled in her hands.

Tessa blurted out, "You could rewrite the cards to make them more appealing and interesting."

He said nothing.

Oh, great. She'd overstepped. And insulted him.

Tessa quickly put the card back in the holder next to the wave picture and faced him. "I'm sorry, I—"

"What do you mean?" he asked.

Chip didn't sound offended, simply curious.

She explained, "You can give the same details but narrate it differently. Almost like a mini-story or a tale highlighting the features of the sculpture or the scenic landscape in the picture."

"Hmmm," he said. Chip cocked his head and beckoned her with a nod.

She followed him to a spot where he pointed to another one of his pictures. It was a palm frond with a small spider situated in a web that ran from one side of the leaf to the other. "So, just on the fly, no pun intended, what would you do for this?"

Tessa scanned the information. She cleared her throat and stared at the picture a few moments. "Um, well." Then she remembered the one piece of advice her grandmother might have been right about. She straightened her shoulders and closed her eyes to get a visual of what she imagined from the perspective of the spider. With a strong, confident voice Tessa said, "Florida palms are symbols of warmth and happiness, but to a small-sized creature, they're more. They offer protection. The gritty texture allows Spidey to move from side to side, building a secure home. Trapping unsuspecting mosquitos and gnats in its web, Spidey bounces along the weightless palm, safe in the shelter of the green frond."

Tessa opened her eyes to find Chip staring at her. His face was blank. Whether it was from incredulity, or embarrassment on her behalf, she couldn't tell.

Without warning, he burst into laughter, covering his mouth to hide the sound.

Her confidence dissipated. Heat crept from her chest to her face, reddening everything in its path. Tears pricked her eyes. He was making fun of her. Her only recourse was to turn and run, but she was rooted to the spot.

After a few moments, Chip's laughter quieted to a chuckle.

Tessa, meanwhile, bit her lip to prevent the tears from falling and gathered her dignity. She turned on her heel intending to flee to the bathroom and summon Uber.

Chip gently grasped her arm. "Wait!"

She faced him and made her expression as impassive as she could.

He looked alarmed. "I'm not laughing at your idea. It's amazing! But 'Spidey'?" The smile took over again and he shook his head with disbelief. "Spiderman might not appreciate being an actual spider," he joked.

"It's the first name that came to me," she said stiffly, trying to decide if he was being honest or pacifying her.

He turned his attention to the photo. "Your story gave this palm frond life and purpose. It seems so important in nature when you explain it from, um, Spidey's perspective." Chip grinned. "This is a great idea. Want to do that for all my photos before a show? It might be a game-changer for me. Bring more interest and sales. I could pay you. A little, but something at least."

Tessa had gone from hope to despair and now pride in the span of five minutes.

"Gosh, Chip. It's easy to do. You don't have to pay me. I'm happy to help."

"Tessa, if you write those cards your way, people will look at my pictures with a fresh perspective. And—" He looked around the hall. "I bet the sculptors and artists would benefit from your help, too." He snapped his fingers. "You know, this could be a niche, a way to get involved in the art community while you're learning."

Tessa listened incredulously. "Are you saying I should charge to write up the information cards?"

"That's exactly what I'm saying."

She heard excitement in his voice. Excitement for her, not himself.

"You'd make a little money and get some contacts, too." At her skepticism he urged, "You have a way with words. You can bring fresh life to old pictures and create great stories for the modern pieces."

She looked at Chip in wonder. Having someone think about her future rather than his own was unfamiliar, as in, it had never happened.

He clasped her arm gently. His touch started the heart-thumping again.

She didn't notice the people milling about, the strangers staring at two people engrossed in conversation. She only noticed him and his fire.

"We can meet one day next week and talk more about it. What do you say?" Chip looked interested, hopeful.

Tessa nodded, smiling slightly while her pulse raced. All she could focus on was how tender his touch was, how comforting and safe it felt to have him look in her eyes. She broke eye contact before Chip could see her crush. She admitted it to herself. She had a crush.

"It's a plan, then," Chip said with a lopsided grin.

She could only nod like a bobblehead.

He pulled his phone out of his back pocket and the screen lit up with the time. "Looks like we need to clean up."

Tessa went into action gathering the information cards, while her heart fluttered with the prospect of next week's meeting. A crush was a harmless schoolgirl lesson in flirtation. It wouldn't come to more than that, and Tessa was a little relieved that she could name it as such. It sounded less threatening to her independence. A crush she could handle.

CHAPTER TWENTY

Esther

Esther unwrapped the foil covering her chocolate candy. Lately, she'd had such cravings for the sweet treats. Not-Sally had come earlier and left these chocolate delicacies for her. Esther used to ration her desserts, back when she minded if extra pounds crept on. When Art was alive. She'd always believed a woman should keep herself at her best for her man.

Esther was not one for spa treatments or massages. All that unnecessary touching. She had learned to appreciate the benefits of manicures and pedicures, though. The warmer weather of Florida meant open-toed shoes. And that meant her toenails had to be as pretty as her fingernails. She held up one hand to admire her nails but saw only swollen joints and arthritic fingers. And plain, buffed nails. When did she get so old?

Her bracelet dangled from her wrist. She didn't often wear the old charm bracelet but today she'd asked Not-Sally to clasp it on. It was still clunky. Esther toyed with the charms, letting them jingle together, remembering how little Tessa loved that, too.

And it had meant so much to Art when Esther wore it. After he'd passed, she'd found herself wearing it more often. Whether it was as an accolade or an albatross she didn't know. She missed him so. Not as a woman should miss her true love, but as a sister misses her favorite brother. Esther's guilt in not loving him as deeply as he loved her had never abated.

She set her arms purposefully in her lap. Tessa's name sat in her mind. Esther remembered her granddaughter, but specific conversations and words evaded her. Esther wanted to smack the memories loose, like she used to bang the saltshaker to unclog it on humid days.

She stole a glance at a tiny, rough-edged, rectangular charm. The wavy lines mimicked a newspaper, a charm she'd bought herself many years ago to symbolize her love for writing. Normally, a writing memory would bring joy. Not today. Maybe it was the thoughts of Tessa. Tessa and her illusions. Tessa and her unrealistic expectations. Esther and her wanton musings. Esther and the mistake she'd like to take back.

•   •   •

It was a whim, really. Just a last-ditch effort to rid herself of childish dreams.

Essie answered a want-ad for a freelance writer. With Junior in middle school, she had so much time on her own. At forty-seven years of age, Essie felt the stirrings of restlessness. Art traveled often. Essie was increasingly lonely. Loneliness turned to bitterness for a career she never had.

That raw morning in Florida, rainy and ugly like November days could be, Essie opened the local, weekly newspaper Shout It Out! *to the Help Wanted section. Like a beacon directing her or a neon sign yelling at her, Essie saw the little ad:*

NEW: Research writer needed for destination travel section right here at Shout It Out! No travel necessary just an adventurous spirit, writing ability, and less than twenty hours. Perfect for college students, retirees, or anyone looking for a little extra income. Apply in person at the office.

It was like sunshine pecking at the heavy, charcoal skies. She marched herself to the office that morning, interviewed, and landed the job. Even Art was impressed with her gumption.

For the next four days, she researched ski resorts and authored an article on the merits of snowboarding—a winter sport like skiing but using one very wide ski. One article morphed into more. The problem occurred when Shout It Out! *brought in another writer.*

Joseph was a few years older than Essie, far more worldly, and, unbeknownst to her, a reputed ladies' man. He willingly copyedited and proofread her articles in his spare time, meeting her at the library or coffee shops.

She did nothing inappropriate; she wasn't that kind of woman. But she found herself relaxing as they pored through articles on the newfangled World Wide Web. Essie had a hard time containing her amazement as they sat in front of a big computer, striking keys on a keyboard and watching information pop up in front of them. Essie and Joseph still used the microfiche machines in the library's basement to access old local newspaper clippings as needed, but this concept of information that could appear at an instant befuddled and excited Essie.

Over time Art objected to her side job. Initially, he made subtle references to her "hobby," more curious and teasing than anything else. But once he met Joseph, Art became less pleased with the way she spent her mornings. He cautioned her, saying Joseph seemed a bit shady, overly attentive to Essie. Essie chalked up Art's concerns to jealousy. She even accused Art of wanting to keep her home-bound and a slave to his needs, something that came out of nowhere. Art had never demanded she be at his beck-and-call; she did so willingly. Essie realized later she was projecting her own concerns, unfulfillment, and itchy feet.

For weeks she had argued with Art. He claimed Joseph had lurid intentions, saying a man could tell. Essie defended Joseph's attention as work-related, denying his amorous comments, telling herself it was harmless flirting. One beautiful spring morning, holed up in the library basement searching through old microfiche, Joseph pinned Essie against the wall. In that second that seemed to freeze time, she realized how wrong she was.

"Stop it," she told him through clenched teeth, as his hot breath pummeled her neck and ears, coming faster and faster as he pressed her harder into the wall. His body weight clamped her upright and she couldn't push him off. He slipped his hand to her breast, whispering, "You know you want it."

When Essie repeated "No," it only served to make him more aroused. She felt his desire through his trousers and full panic set in. She didn't know a way out.

She was released suddenly from his grip, and Essie watched as Art made a fist and hit Joseph square in the mouth. She yelped, covering her mouth with her hand, then slunk to the ground, back against the wall.

Her husband panted, wild with rage, and he shouted at Joseph to get out or he'd call the police. Joseph crawled to the door, burst through it, and practically ran up the steps to the main library.

Essie uncovered her mouth, still in shock at what had almost happened.

"You okay?" Art said, sliding down the wall next to her. No recriminations, no I- told-you-so's, no lectures.

What a wonderful man.

"How did you know he was here?" Essie asked, dumbfounded that Art showed up when he did.

He gave a lopsided smile. "I didn't." He pointed to the wicker basket upended on the other side of the room.

Essie took note of the sandwiches, fruit, and wine bottle now strewn about the Research Room floor. She looked up in wonder at her husband.

Leaning his head back on the wall, he gently took Essie's hand. "I took the rest of the day off, packed us a picnic, and thought I'd surprise you. I heard you yell, "Stop" as I came down the stairs. He looked imploringly at her. "Essie, I thought something horrible happened. I guess it almost did. I wouldn't have forgiven myself if that guy had hurt you."

"Forgiven yourself?" Essie echoed. "It was my fault. I didn't listen to you. You were right; you were absolutely on the money about him. He's

a lech, a horrible man." Her breath caught in gasps as she tried to reckon what she'd escaped.

Truth be told, she was afraid she'd brought it on with her flirtatious actions. She'd never do anything stupid like that again. That day she quit the newspaper. Art never mentioned it again.

The little bronze newspaper charm, while also a reminder of her love of writing, warned her how dangerously close she'd come to losing it all.

•   •   •

Esther returned to the present when she smelled the delicious aroma of coffee. Not-Sally placed a Styrofoam cup of steaming liquid next to her. "Good afternoon, Ms. Esther. I brought you a treat. If you ask me, there's nothing like an afternoon cup of Joe to pick up your spirits." She put a napkin on Esther's lap. "Mmm . . . the smell of coffee always transports me back to my childhood. Mama seemed to keep a pot of coffee brewing all day." Not-Sally shook her head.

Esther didn't answer, but Not-Sally didn't seem to expect it. She had turned away already.

Esther heard cabinet doors in her bathroom open and close. She supposed Not-Sally was taking stock of provisions. She seemed to do that frequently, checking for God-knows-what in Esther's vanity and under-the-sink cabinet. The woman kept Esther well-stocked in toiletries Esther didn't even know she needed.

She took a sip of her favorite drink, the bracelet she held gently hitting the Styrofoam edge. Her eye caught on a tiny teacup charm, the memory of luncheons, fundraisers, and volunteering. And Tessa.

•   •   •

"Like this, Grandmother?"

Tessa held the plastic teacup in the air, pinky out and mouth pursed for the pretend drink. Her feet bounced off Esther's couch, little white socks and Keds grazing the edge.

"Yes, dear. That's exactly how a young lady drinks her tea."

"But you don't drink, tea, Grandmother. You drink cofkee," the six-year-old responded.

"CofFEE," Esther corrected, biting back a smile at her granddaughter's pronunciation errors. "Whether it's tea or coffee doesn't matter. You must learn all the proper manners of young ladies, Tessa. You'll want to fit right in at the club, you know." Esther might not feel at home there anymore, but her granddaughter would be welcome. She'd make sure of that.

"Daddy said fakers and wannabes go there. Why do they want bugs at a club?"

Esther clamped her lips in a thin line, annoyed with Junior's labels. She furrowed her brows at her granddaughter. "Bugs? Dear, what do you mean?"

"Wannabes. Are they like bumblebees or wasps?" Tessa wiggled her feet in the air and continued to hold her teacup. The picture of a little girl wannabe grown-up.

Esther leaned forward on her own chair and clasped her knees. She couldn't withhold the laughter. First "cofkee" and now "Wanna Bees." Laughter didn't flow easily or often, but now it spewed. And it was a welcome distraction from her son's frequent misspeaks.

As Esther hooted at Tessa's mistake, the little girl stopped swinging her legs. The happy-go-lucky expression that had filled Tessa's face vanished. She scooted off the couch and ran out of the room, dropping her teacup as she dashed off.

What in the world?

Esther stopped laughing immediately. She sat for a moment, trying to understand the mind of a child.

Junior opened the front door. "Hey, hey, where's my girl?" he sang as he shut the door.

Esther closed her eyes and breathed deeply. The singsong tone told her what she didn't have to ask. His balance was unsteady, and Esther turned her face away. It was painful to watch him try to pretend he hadn't been enjoying the club. The place of fakers and wannabes.

"Junior, Tessa is in the playroom." She assumed so anyway.

"Well, let's get her and go out for ice cream!" The slight slurring told Esther he'd had just enough to be jovial.

She treaded carefully. "I think we should have some dinner first, dear."

He brushed his hand over his face, a telltale sign of trying to clear his thoughts. "Why? Can't we just forgo the traditional and have ice cream for dinner? C'mon, Ma. Tessa'll love it."

"Tessa!" he called. "Come on down, darlin'. We goin' for ice cream." Sounded more like eyesch-cream.

"Junior, I really don't think—" Esther's heart sped up. She had to stop him from getting in the car, stop Tessa from leaving her house, convince Junior to put on the brakes. But Esther had to do it in such a way as to make Junior think it was his idea. Otherwise, a blowup would ensue.

"Daddy!" Tessa flounced down the stairs. Usually she was tentative, hesitant to run to her father. Today she seemed anxious to see him. Esther saw the tear-streaked cheeks and noticed how Tessa avoided looking at Esther.

"Well, now, that's the way I like to be greeted!" Junior said, leaning over to pick up and swing the little girl. "How about a big dish of chocolate ice cream?" he asked her, his face close to hers.

She wrinkled her little nose and craned her neck away from him. She squirmed as she said, "Put me down, Daddy."

Instead, he held her tighter, and his smile faded. "Why?" A hardness came over him, his eyes changing from glassy frivolity to glassy suspicion.

Tessa went still in his arms.

Esther interjected. "Now Junior, Tessa and I were just about to fix dinner together. Right, sweetheart? We have a roast beef ready to go into the oven." She held out her arms to Tessa, trying to encourage Junior to loosen his hold and added, "I need her to help me peel the potatoes. We'll be ready to eat in about an hour."

Junior's grip loosened and his posture stiffened. "Fine," he said. He let Tessa slide down from his arms, and she stood there practically immobile.

Tessa didn't question Esther's made-up story. The last few months Esther had noticed Tessa altering her own behavior depending on Junior's mood. She adjusted her actions to fit her father's mood swings.

It saddened Esther that Tessa couldn't be the same child in front of Junior that she was for Debra.

"C'mon, Grandmother," Tessa replied, taking Esther's hand. "Let's make dinner." She tugged Esther away.

Junior turned on his heels and headed up the staircase.

The little girl never mentioned Esther's lie, never explained her sudden escape from the room earlier, and never asked why her father didn't appear for dinner.

Esther realized the six-year-old had lived as a grownup too much already.

That night, she called Debra and blessed her daughter-in-law's upcoming divorce.

•   •   •

As she sipped *cofkee*, Esther's own sadness deepened. Tessa would never know the security of a strong, solid father. Never know how a daddy's arms could ease a rough day. Like Esther's father's had. Her hand wobbled, coffee sloshing inside the Styrofoam cup. She set it down on the side table. How could she convince Tessa to find someone who could offer her safekeeping from her own impractical and idealistic aspirations? Give her the security she missed as a child.

Esther's heart pounded wildly. A memory, broken like gaps of time torn apart, leapt in her mind. *A mature Tessa sitting right in front of her. Esther clenching Tessa's arm.*

Esther hit the arm of her chair, frustration banged out in each thump. Why were memories just lumps of clay that never shaped into something relevant?

"Ms. Esther," Not-Sally's calming tone accompanied Esther's whacks as she walked over to Esther. "I can see you're frustrated and that's okay. Does anything hurt?"

Esther shook her head vehemently. She was desperate to tell Tessa about the comfort of a good, trustworthy, responsible man. But all she could do was to thrust her arm out, her bracelet jingling. Raising her eyebrows questioningly, she shook the jewelry at Not-Sally, silently begging her to understand.

Not-Sally sat in a chair directly in front of Esther. "Is there something about the bracelet that bothers you?"

Esther gave her head one quick shake. She jiggled the bracelet again. "A story about one of these charms?" Not-Sally guessed.

Kind of, but not quite right, so Esther sighed and put her arm back on her lap. She had no way to break through to Not-Sally.

Not-Sally stood up and strode to Esther's bookcase. She leaned to one side as if reading book titles. She brought something to Esther and placed it on Esther's lap. A photo album.

Esther opened the pages and saw her own childhood. *Mother and Daddy. Pecan fields. Her graduation.* She closed the book. Where was Tessa's graduation? She tried to stand.

Not-Sally held out her arm. "Whoa, Ms. Esther. Your legs aren't as sturdy as they once were. Let me get your chair."

Esther let out a garbled "No" that sounded more like "nuh." She pointed to the bookcase.

"Want a different one?" Not-Sally asked.

When Esther nodded, Not-Sally brought out several. She held them up one at a time.

Esther shook her head until the one that contained baby pictures of Tessa appeared. She reached for it and set it gingerly on her lap, as if it might break. Here was her special girl. Her Tessa. She flipped it open. A blonde-haired girl of about two stared at her from the page. Esther caressed the picture lovingly. As she thumbed through the pages, she watched Tessa grow older. From pleasing child to wary teen. *Where was Tessa's graduation? Didn't Esther give her the bracelet?* Her hands whipped through the pages so fast that she heard a few rips.

Not-Sally placed her hands on Esther's. "It's okay. Are you upset with Tessa?"

Esther stopped her frantic searching and shook her head. Not-Sally had mentioned Tessa's name. Did she know Tessa? Esther tried to explain how important it was that she tell Tessa to find a reliable, steadfast man. But her mouth made syllabic sounds that didn't resemble words. They only made sense in her head.

Not-Sally asked her to slow down or breathe deeply or something.

Esther cried, not knowing how to make it all coalesce properly.

"I'll call Tessa, Ms. Esther. Maybe she can visit."

Esther's heart resumed its steady rhythm; she leaned her head back with a deep sigh. Not-Sally would take care of it. Just like Sally once did.

CHAPTER TWENTY-ONE

Tessa

A crush. That's what she'd called her feelings for Chip. So long as she reminded herself of that, Tessa could handle her heart's flutterings and palpitations. As if to challenge her, her phone chirped with a text. From Chip. Suggesting they meet the following day at the coffee shop. Her heart flipped and flopped.

Tessa promptly called Kendra.

"Whoa, the hot photographer guy wants to meet you for coffee? Sounds like a date to me," Kendra said confidently.

"No. I told you—he has a business idea he wants to discuss." Tessa swiveled in her dorm room chair and twirled her hair absent-mindedly.

"Hmm . . . I don't know, girl. Listen, I'm coming to your room now."

Before Tessa could protest or question or even agree, her friend was knocking on the door. Kendra rubbed her hands together in classic preparation mode. "Let's find an outfit for this date-not-a-date tomorrow," she insisted as she barged past Tessa. She opened Tessa's closet, surveying clothes with various murmurs of "hmm" or "uh-uh" and even a few snickers. She turned to Tessa who had returned to her chair and was watching the closet inquisition helplessly from the sidelines. Kendra put one hand on a paisley-patterned hip and tilted her head questioningly.

"Really, girl? You've got nothing remotely sexy in that wardrobe."

Tessa's eyes widened. "I'm not going for sexy, Kendra. It's just a meeting. Not a date."

Kendra sighed. "You are so unworldly. Be right back. Don't go anywhere." She left before Tessa could react.

While she was gone, Tessa stood and examined her clothes choices. *They're not bad,* she told herself defensively. Although Kendra was right. There was nothing close to *Come hither.* Tessa rolled her eyes. *Hither. Really?* Then she slid the closet door shut decisively. She was not trying to lure Chip Foster.

The door burst open with Kendra carrying a pile of clothes. She tossed them on Tessa's bed. "Let's go through these. I picked out the quietest ones. I figured I couldn't get you into a hot pink silk blouse with a deep V-neck even if I paid you. But . . ." she gave a flippant wave towards Tessa's closet, "I know I've got something better than those."

And the fashion show began.

Tessa said no to the Lily Pulitzer neon green and pink dress. She shook her head to bell bottoms that Kendra said would lie snug and low across Tessa's hips. She crossed her arms defiantly when Kendra thrust the black faux leather mini dress on her.

Finally, Kendra whipped out a leopard print, three-quarter length sleeve sweater. It was subtle, for animal print. Tessa tried it on, turning this way and that in the full-length mirror on the backside of her door. The scoop neckline was daring enough.

Kendra rummaged through Tessa's closet again until she found a pair of skinny, black jeans that she demanded Tessa pair with the sweater. Kendra also ordered Tessa to strut in some black boots of Kendra's. Tessa had to admit she liked the look. She felt mature and confident, like she could shop at boutique stores or have dinner at a nice restaurant. And she didn't feel fake.

Kendra walked around Tessa as if she were appraising a mannequin. She nodded. "I'll be here to do your hair, and then you're good to go."

What's wrong with my hair? Tessa self-consciously touched it.

As if she could read Tessa's thoughts, Kendra said, "Your hair is great. I want to put a little curl in it. You know, just a wave to give it some bounce."

Tessa looked sideways at her friend. "I swear, if you make me look like I'm trying to impress him . . ." She let the sentence hang.

Kendra held her hands up palms forward. "I promise." She made the cross-your-heart symbol. "Just a little something different. It will help you feel the part of a start-up business owner. Okay?"

Although still suspicious of her friend's motives, Tessa agreed.

Kendra picked up the rejected clothes and draped them over her arm. "Um," she began.

Tessa cocked her head Kendra's way. "What now?" She was certain her friend was going to offer suggestions in the art of flirting.

"Anything new with your grandmother?" she asked. "I mean, since your last awful visit when she grabbed your arm? Have you tried again?"

"No, I haven't. Honestly, Kendra. I think I have to accept that my relationship with my grandmother sucks and any attempt to fix it would be a bust. I did, however, decide to try some sleuthing on my own when I get home for break. Or at least, bug my mom about what she knows about Lou Ann. I'm sure she knows more than she's saying."

Kendra pursed her lips.

"What?" Tessa stopped short of opening the door for Kendra. "You have an opinion, I'm sure."

"I'm all about learning who this Lou Ann person was, but don't forget—" she hesitated and said, "Your mom and your grandma are the only family you've got left. Real family. Even if Lou Ann gave birth to you, Debra raised you and your grandma tried to help. I'd hate for you to give up patching what you can before. . . you know, your grandma dies."

"I hear you, Kendra. But it's hard to be around someone who sees only disappointment when you walk in the room."

Kendra nodded and reminded Tessa she'd be back tomorrow before Tessa's date. Not a date.

• • •

Tessa headed for the coffee shop, hair gently cascading over her shoulders, huge curls that reminded Tessa of Chip's ocean wave picture. And it did bounce a little when she walked. She couldn't help but smile.

Tessa opened the door and scanned the place. Chip was seated at a four-person table in front of his laptop. He wore a Florida Coastal hoodie, and his hair was pulled back in a ponytail. His focus was on whatever his computer screen showed. Tessa noticed his feet crossed under the table, casual and comfortable. He seemed much more relaxed than she felt. She took a breath for assurance and walked over.

He spotted her, looked twice, and grinned. "Looking nice, Tessa. I hope I didn't interfere with any plans. Or date later?"

She put a smile on her face, even as disappointment flowed through her. She vowed never to let Kendra pull even the tiniest bit of romance from Chip's words ever again. She pulled out a chair next to him. "No. Just ran a few errands," she said vaguely. *Lame,* she chastised herself. *Just get this over with so you can go back and hang your head in shame.* "So how would this work?" she asked, waving her hand in front of the computer.

"Let me get you a coffee before we start. Room for cream and sugar?" he asked.

She nodded.

He sauntered to the counter while Tessa chastised herself for letting Kendra encourage her . . . crush.

When he returned, he had packets of sugar and containers of various creamers. And a large cup of coffee.

And she'd regained her sensibility.

She fixed her coffee to her liking, took a big gulp, and filled herself with caffeine and focus.

For the next thirty minutes, Chip detailed his idea. They sketched a website, *The Art of Words*, and discussed marketing strategies. She was so engrossed in planning that she didn't hear her phone ring.

Chip tapped her arm and pointed to her phone sitting on the table.

Tessa didn't recognize the number, but the area code told her it was local. "Hello?"

"Tessa, this is Mayra from Sunset Shadows."

Despite Tessa's sworn vow to disentangle herself from Grandmother, a chill swept through her. "Is everything okay?"

"Ms. Esther's feeling a bit distressed. She can't communicate well, but she wants to see you. At least, I think she does."

Mayra stopped talking, and Tessa filled the space. "Are you sure it's me she wants to see?" And did Tessa even care?

"Ms. Esther's been looking at photo albums. She says your name repeatedly, pointing to pictures of you. Then she tugs on her charm bracelet," Mayra added.

The charm bracelet that held all her grandmother's memories. The one that might be a conduit to the past. To Lou Ann. But Tessa didn't relish another unpredictable encounter with Grandmother. Their previous one had ended with Tessa's bruised forearm.

"If you have time, I'm sure she'd appreciate seeing you," Mayra said.

Tessa was sure she wouldn't. Yet a war raged inside: her inner child wanted to please her grandmother; the surly teenager wanted to snub her. But the college sophomore recognized an opportunity to learn more about Grandmother's past, more about Lou Ann. It might be her last chance to get anything out of her grandmother. "Okay. I'll come over, Mayra."

She hung up and turned to Chip. "My grandmother is asking for me."

"Is she okay?" He gently touched her arm, sending electric shocks through her body.

Tessa nodded. "I think so; she just wants to see me." She didn't add that it might be to yell at her more. Nor did she add that she might try to control the narrative of the visit herself.

"Go. We can talk more about your business later." Chip gave her a quick hug, and Tessa's breath seemed to freeze in her lungs.

This was some crush she had.

•   •   •

The little Volkswagen zipped along the backroads to Sunset Shadows. Thunderclouds appeared as she drove, announcing that a late afternoon storm would soon arrive. When she had returned to her room to get her car keys, she'd also grabbed her charm bracelet and put it on. It swayed from her wrist now and she gripped the steering wheel tighter as a thought occurred to her: *Were there more secrets to shed?* As much as she would like to know more about Lou Ann, she feared it, too.

She pulled into a parking spot. Droplets of water plopped from the heavy clouds. Like a warning of what was to come.

Tessa approached her grandmother's door, a huge clap of thunder accompanying her. She inhaled deeply and lifted her fist. Confidently and assertively. *Rap-rap.* Tessa waited for her grandmother to call for her to enter. Nothing. She knocked harder. *Rap-rap-rap.*

Mayra had told her that Grandmother was agitated, repeating Tessa's name. But it was quiet in there now. Tessa turned the knob. Stepping into the foyer, she called out, trying to make her voice resonate over the thunderclaps and drumming rain. "Hello? Are you here?"

She heard a startled cry and followed the sound to Grandmother's bedroom. She was resting in bed. She'd apparently been napping. But now her eyes were open, and she looked around, a blanket clutched to her chin, her eyes soaking in the room.

"Agh! Argh!" Grandmother sounded scared, her words nonsensical sounds.

Tessa had never seen her grandmother so upset. *Was it the storm? Or was Grandmother having a heart attack or stroke?*

Before Tessa could ask, her grandmother narrowed her eyes and held her hands up as if to ward off danger. "Stranger!" she called weakly.

Tessa stopped. A wave of pity washed over her. "It's Tessa, your granddaughter. I won't hurt you." She stayed still with her hands at her sides, trying to reassure her grandmother she was not a threat.

"Junior?" Challenge replaced fear in her voice.

We should go with the flow. "Dad's not here, but I came to visit."

"Dad?" Her grandmother repeated Tessa's words. "Who . . . you?"

"Tessa," she answered quietly. As she scrambled to think of a way to jog her grandmother's mind, she spotted the old bracelet on the nightstand. She pointed to it while holding up her own wrist, the silver chain dangling innocently. "Grandmother, look. I have a bracelet like yours."

Grandmother's facial features relaxed, and she released the death grip she had on the blanket. "Tessa?" It was a mild question couched in what sounded like wonder and hope.

Tessa clung to the lifeline and nodded.

Just then, Mayra rushed in. "I had hoped to be here as you arrived, but I had another resident to attend to," she said to Tessa. "These storms cause all kinds of panic." She paused and looked between the two of them. "You good?" she asked.

Tessa nodded slowly while her grandmother continued to stare at Tessa.

Mayra addressed Grandmother. "Okay, Ms. Esther, let's get you in the other room for a proper visit with your granddaughter." She lifted Grandmother, placing her in the wheelchair located next to the bed. Mayra whispered to Tessa, "She seems better after a little nap."

But Tessa didn't think of Grandmother as *better*. She was as frail as a rag doll and was led about like a puppet. Completely unlike the woman she'd known. And Tessa felt sad for her.

Mayra fussed about, settling Grandmother in the recliner and placing a quilt over her legs.

Her grandmother's gaze darted around, as if she were searching for a lost item.

Mayra held up one finger. "I know what she wants." She left the room and returned holding Grandmother's bracelet.

Tessa watched her grandmother hug it to her chest like a long-lost treasure. She whispered to Mayra, "Why isn't she talking?"

Mayra beckoned Tessa to follow her to the medical cart she'd placed in her grandmother's foyer. "As the disease progresses, it attacks language as well as memory. She struggles to put sentences together and sometimes even words come out nonsensical. Just be present and patient." She poured a cup of water from a pitcher and turned to walk back to the living area. "And sometimes she spouts a story like she's a kid again," she whispered over shoulder.

Mayra pulled a chair over from the table and gestured for Tessa to sit down. As she did, Tessa's bracelet caught briefly on one of the chair's spindles. "Oh, darn it," she muttered.

Mayra exclaimed, "Look, Ms. Esther, Tessa is wearing her charm bracelet."

Grandmother eyed Tessa's bracelet, scrunching her eyebrows, and cocked her head to one side. "Yours." Then she pointed to her own. "Mine."

Tessa looked to Mayra, raising her eyebrows with a silent question.

Mayra reminded her, "You might have to do all the talking, or she might suddenly speak pages. Just follow your gut. And if you need me, poke your head into the hallway. I'll be around." With that, Mayra left, taking the medical cart with her.

Tessa wasn't sure how to proceed.

Grandmother's eyes glazed and she turned her attention from the bracelet to the window. "The farm seemed to stretch for miles beyond our house."

Surprised by the string of words, Tessa sat there not knowing how to respond. She had no idea what Grandmother saw.

Her grandmother continued. "When you're a child, everything seems larger than it is. I thought we had the most land in all of Georgia, with the best pecans in the state, too." She closed her eyes but kept talking, her hands folded around the bracelet. Grandmother seemed transported somewhere else in time.

"I'm sorry, Millie," Grandmother said quietly. "I let you down; I let myself down. But I had to do it, you must know."

Grandmother opened her eyes and stared at Tessa, so deeply that Tessa had to look away.

"Millie, I had to grow up. We had such dreams, you and I, to travel the South dancing the nights away, riding in convertibles, and trudging through city streets for the next story. But I realized they were the stuff of little girl fantasies. Will you forgive me for forsaking our dreams?"

There was such longing in her grandmother's eyes that Tessa could only nod.

"Millie, I've kept your secret this long. I'll never betray you; you can trust me. I'll never tell a soul about the baby."

Baby? Tessa stifled the gasp that wanted to escape and closed her mouth that flopped open.

Grandmother reached for Tessa's hand and gripped it firmly. "I know it was hard for you. I pretended it was practical and wouldn't cry with you. I let you think it was no big deal and that you'd be better off without a child to saddle you at seventeen, but I was wrong."

Grandmother squeezed Tessa's hand, almost feverish in her words.

Tessa felt the urgency in Grandmother's grasp, but it was different from anything she'd witnessed before. The passion and emotion moved Tessa. It was as if Grandmother was unburdening herself. Like feelings had been stuffed in a closet and her grandmother had wrenched the door open. The same grandmother who'd told Tessa to hoard her own feelings, present an image of decorum and control at all costs. Tessa felt like she was seeing those costs now.

"Oh, my girl," Grandmother was saying. "Motherhood would have fit you to a T. I'm ashamed. I encouraged you to get rid of the baby because I was selfish. I wanted a companion to conquer the world with; I only thought of my needs. And afterward, you were never the same. Our friendship suffered, and the light went out of your eyes. I was so selfish."

Tessa sat still. 'Get rid of the baby'? Like adoption?

Or abortion? That rarely happened in those days. And her grandmother wouldn't have risked the notoriety such a forbidden action would have brought. Unless she was a very different girl than she was a woman.

Aware that her grandmother seemed to search Tessa's face for a response, Tessa said lamely, "It's okay." She looked at their hands still entwined. The grip wasn't desperate now, just secure.

But Grandmother wasn't done. "I threw all our dreams away to marry Art." Grandmother's breath came out faster and she almost gasped between sentences. It was like Pandora's box of words had just been unlocked and they all vied to get out at the same time. "I saved my parents' farm, but I didn't save us. I want you to know Millie, that ever since that day I swore I'd never let anyone who I love become fixated on dreams that might ruin her. I think of you every time I pull down someone else's pipe dreams."

Her eyes seemed to implore "Millie" to understand.

Tessa's brain scrambled for connections. There were a lot of missing pieces. How did Grandmother save her parents' farm? How would dreams ruin someone?

She unwound her fingers from her grandmother's. In some weird way, maybe Grandmother thought she was saving Tessa from whatever broke hers and Millie's friendship when she continually crushed Tessa's dreams. But that only led to more questions. If her friend's dream was motherhood and her grandmother somehow ruined that, why wouldn't Grandmother have tried to atone by helping Lou Ann?

Tessa fiddled with the bracelet on her own wrist. She didn't know what to expect but it wasn't this. Secrets were powerful, and they seemed to have taken up a lot of Grandmother's heart. Tessa didn't want to follow that path.

Grandmother's gaze softened. She'd turned her head to the window, a wistful smile playing on the corners of her mouth. Her fingers curled around her bracelet.

"Grandmother?" Tessa gently touched her arm.

She turned and looked Tessa up and down. "Well, dear, that's a lovely outfit you're wearing today. Do you know my Junior?"

Seventeen-year-old Grandmother was gone. But Tessa just smiled. It was okay. She'd gotten a glimpse of a girl who'd made decisions that changed her life. Maybe for the worse. And she felt a wave of sympathy wash over her. And something else. Maybe love. Quietly, she stood up, returned the chair to the table, and gathered her backpack.

CHAPTER TWENTY-TWO

Esther

Esther eyed the strangers in her home. Three people dressed in white coats huddled nearby whispering and consulting a hand-held television device. What were they doing? Why were they here?

She turned to the window. Butterflies hovered over the hibiscus outside. Oh, how she longed to join them, free to flutter among the flowers.

The intruders approached Esther. "Mrs. Wilde, I'm Doctor Caroll," one of the women said. "We're making a plan to help with your agitation." She waved her hands to acknowledge the others.

How dare she? "I'm not agic—agit—agim—" The word wouldn't come. Esther knew the lady was trying to say she got irritated. And she did. As the days grew interminably long, so did Esther's aggravation. She willed the night to arrive, anxious to escape to dreams of yesteryear where life made sense.

What was the word?

Esther turned away from her, wordless.

"Mrs. Wilde, you have what we call Sundowners Syndrome. You might feel more agitated or restless as the day goes on. We're adjusting your medications to help with that."

Esther couldn't follow the woman's words, but she didn't want to let on. Her confusion was often the start of her irritation. So she stayed expressionless and quiet.

The strangers trickled out and, blessedly, Not-Sally came in.

"Doing here?" Esther said. Absent were the words "what" and "were" and "they." She tried to piece the sentence together. Her efforts resulted in isolated words, disconnected thoughts, and abundant confusion. Stuck in her brain. She tried again. "Were what" is all she got out.

Not-Sally put her hand on Esther's arm. "Don't worry, Ms. Esther. We all get our words twisted up sometimes. The doctors have changed your medications. I think you'll be happier." She smiled reassuringly. "I'm going to tidy up a little."

Esther rested her head on the back of the recliner. Millie had been on her mind. Her childhood best friend. The polka to her dots. The pair of them were nearly inseparable until that fateful day.

• • •

Millie and Essie strolled through the pecan grove that January morning. Harvest season had ended, leaving only a smattering of pecans on the ground.

When they reached the tree stump at the end of the grove, Millie sat on it. She'd been so quiet on their walk, not even mentioning her favorite landmarks in the orchard—the tree they'd loved to climb years ago; the huge rock they used to race to and stand atop, each claiming she was the queen of the pecan grove.

"Mil?" Essie asked as she sat on the ground next to her.

"Yeah?"

"What's been going on with you? I feel like you've been avoiding me." Millie had been more reserved the past month, more withdrawn. They were seniors in high school and classes were demanding. But it didn't explain Millie's behavior. Whenever Essie had asked her to come over after school, Millie would mutter vague excuses about being busy. Essie was busy, too, dating Art, but she always made time for her best friend.

Today she'd find out the truth.

"I've hardly seen you the past few months; you always say you're busy with . . . well . . . I don't even know what." Essie tried to keep the hurt out of her voice.

Millie turned her face away, but Essie caught the furrowed brows and the trembling lips.

"Please, Millie. What's wrong?"

"I can't travel the world with you, Essie," Millie said quietly.

"Why not?" This was their dream. What could Millie mean? "Look, we won't do anything crazy. I know I talk about trekking through the Big Apple and knocking down the doors of Life *magazine, but we'll start slowly. I won't push you—"*

Millie's cries stopped Esther's plea.

With her head almost buried between her knees, Millie's voice broke. "I'm pregnant."

Essie withheld the gasp that caught in her mouth. What? How? When? The questions tumbled through her mind, one after the other. But she bit them back. "Millie." She touched her friend's arm. "What happened?"

"Essie, I'm just so stupid! I couldn't tell a soul about George, not even you. I met him at the drugstore; he's twenty-five and had just moved here with his wife. He was sophisticated and mature. He had a car and a real job and planned to become a president of a big company one day. He told me I was fresh air in his stale world. That his wife was boring, and I was exciting and bubbly, and he loved my energy. I can't believe this has happened!" The words had come out in a rush.

She wailed and dropped her head to her knees again.

Essie stared at the watery teardrop circles on Millie's knees, spreading into the fabric. Questions bounced around in her head. How could Millie date a married man? And how could she keep this from Essie?

Essie struggled to keep emotion from her face. She didn't want to judge her friend, but she was angry with Millie's carelessness and irresponsibility. Why did she fall for such obvious pick-up lines? She and Millie used to make fun of all the dumb things men said to get girls *in movies and on television. Especially married men. Millie had risked her whole future. Their future.*

Now wasn't the time to scold Millie, though. It was time for logic. Something Essie had scads of. "What is he willing to do for you?"

Millie's head popped up. "What can he do? He's married. He was shocked when I told him. He thought he was careful. Oh Essie, you should have seen his face. Horror mixed with disgust." She closed her eyes as if reliving it. "He paced the room. He muttered to himself. He finally looked at me like I was a problem, a useless problem." She opened her eyes and faced Essie. "I felt like a gnat, Essie. Like an annoying, irritating insect who he wished he could get rid of."

Essie sympathized with Millie but . . . Why would Millie expect him to be any different from all the other married men who had affairs? Did she think he'd leave his wife for his eighteen-year-old fling? Essie and Millie had always talked about girls who did that, how they were living in a fantasy to think older, married men would take them seriously. Oh, Millie, she thought.

Essie's thoughts jumped back to the present. Millie was talking. "Then he said he had to think. But he didn't say he'd take care of me—us—or even that he cared." Her voice hitched and tears built in her eyes. Her face paled to an ashen hue and her voice escalated to near panic. "I'm going to have to tell my parents and go away somewhere to have this baby."

Essie remained quiet, trying out solutions in her mind.

After a few moments, Millie lifted her chin. "I can't give it up. I'll figure out a way to support the both of us. Graduation is just a few months from now; I can do my work at another school far away, and they'll mail my diploma."

Essie heard a new hardness in Millie's tone. Resolute and determined. Essie appreciated the toughness, but Millie's decision would not put her back on track to the future they'd always dreamed about.

"Millie, it's 1959. It's not the Stone Ages. Girls who get pregnant don't always have to keep them."

"I already told you, Essie. I'm not giving it up for adoption."

Essie heard the stubbornness creep into Millie's words as well as the desperation. "That's not what I mean," Essie said.

Millie turned her head toward Essie and raised her eyebrows questioningly. Both girls sat straight up.

Essie took a deep breath. She looked around the fields for anyone hovering nearby. "We both know there are doctors who can help. I don't know of one in particular," she was quick to add, "but I know other girls who do." She watched Millie's face for signs of comprehension.

Millie's eyes widened into round circles. She leaped from the tree stump and leaned toward Essie, pointing her finger accusingly. "Are you proposing what I think you are, Esther Mae?" Millie's face hardened and saddened at the same time. "I could never." She turned on her heel.

Essie stood, too. "Please, Millie. Wait a minute. Think about it. No one knows. He can't marry you even if he wanted to. You're only eighteen years old! You can just make it all go away and move on."

Millie whipped around to face Essie. She shook her head, staring at Essie as if she didn't know her. Then she turned and ran out of the orchard.

Essie's heart ached. Had her bold suggestion been too much? Was their friendship over?

·   ·   ·

Esther's own startled cry brought her back to the present. She couldn't get her bearings, though. She scanned the room looking for Millie. The sights, sounds, and smells were wrong— walls bleached of color and absent of photos; voices unrecognizable and distant outside the door; aromas of lemon and antiseptic colliding in the air. Her heart fell.

Esther didn't know where she was, but she knew where she wasn't. She wasn't home.

She'd been lost in a memory. Lately, her memories had not been pleasant. The miscarriage, the newspaper job, and now Millie's pregnancy. That January day still pressed on her heart.

•   •   •

A few days passed. Millie had dodged Essie at school and had avoided their usual hangouts. She'd refused to answer the phone.

Millie's mother would always say Millie was busy, but Essie had known better.

She decided to go see her, but before she could act, Millie came to her.

"Hello, Mildred," Essie heard her mother say. "I'll tell Esther you're here."

Essie's mother always used Millie's and Essie's full names even though both preferred the shortened versions.

"Hi, Millie." Essie had heard the doorbell ring and now stood on the landing, peering over the railing. Although Essie was relieved to see her, she remained aloof, trying to gauge Millie's mood.

Millie was pale, her skin sallow, and, surprisingly, she had lost weight.

Maybe it was all a false alarm! Maybe Millie had come over to tell Essie just that.

Essie looked at Millie hopefully. Millie returned a watery smile. Essie couldn't tell what that meant. It was time for a private conversation. "We'll be up in my room, Mother. We have to work on our senior science project," she lied.

Millie brushed past Essie's mother, tears in her eyes.

"Would you like some cookies? I'll bring up a plate, Esther," Mother said, looking up at Essie.

"Not yet, Mother. I'll come down if we get hungry. Thank you," she added as Millie reached the top landing.

Essie pulled Millie into her room and shut the door, making sure the latch caught. Closing her bedroom door didn't ensure that her mother wouldn't surprise them with cookies and milk, but it was the only defense Essie had against a mother with a sixth sense for trouble.

Millie sat on Essie's bed and grabbed a pillow, holding it against her abdomen as if she were both protecting and hiding her stomach. She rocked a little, like a child comforting herself.

"What's going on?" Essie whispered, fearful of saying anything too loudly in case listening ears could hear through the vents of the room.

Millie spoke in hushed tones, too. "I decided to ask him if he would help me. I went to his work to leave a note for him. The lady at the desk said he quit suddenly. I rode my bike to his apartment. There was nobody there. I even peeked through the windows. Nothing. No furniture. He left. He left . . . me. He left his ba—" She couldn't seem to say the word. Her sobs were muffled by the pillow.

Essie remained quiet, not sure how to soothe Millie or repair her best friend's life. Millie had turned Essie's world upside down, too. She didn't want to be selfish, but Essie couldn't help the slew of feelings that had kept her awake at nights. Disappointment in Millie and in their fading dream; anger at Millie's secretive side—she'd never kept something this big from Essie before; and bitterness that Millie had risked so much for so little.

Eventually, Millie raised her head. Her sobs became quiet tears. She sniffed and finally held her chin up. "Who do you know who can fix this?"

Essie's eyes widened as she realized what Millie was asking. In the couple of weeks that Millie had been avoiding Essie, Essie had done her research. Two girls from their class had sisters who got pregnant when they were in high school. Both opted to end the pregnancies. Although abortion was illegal, those girls knew a doctor who would help.

"Millie, it won't be easy or cheap. I have some money saved. I'll help."

"I've got money too, Essie. And thank you," she added. Sadness seeped from her words.

Essie put her hand on Millie's. Between the two of them, they would put the pieces of Millie's lost childhood back together.

It took lying, sneaking around, and providing false information, but Millie's pregnancy finally ended. She'd come through it without any permanent physical damage, but not without some emotional cost. Millie lamented losing George. Even though Essie was sure George wouldn't have been the Prince Charming Millie had fantasized, she didn't say a word. She let Millie vent her emotions. Millie survived, and that was all that mattered to Essie.

What didn't survive was their friendship. Esther felt Millie's resentment the rest of their senior year. The chasm between them widened until they gradually turned to their own paths. Millie spent more time with a group of girls Esther hardly knew, and Esther grew closer to Art. Esther blamed herself for Millie's struggles—years later she'd learned her friend was hospitalized for a nervous breakdown. She never learned if Millie had any children.

•   •   •

Now Esther clenched the bracelet in her palm. She opened her hand and saw the pearl charm, sitting in the middle of her palm. When Tessa was born in June, Esther had purchased her granddaughter's birthstone. Junior's daughter would be atonement for Millie. Although Esther had insisted Junior not marry Lou Ann, she'd demanded he not abandon his responsibility like Millie's George had. Esther would help her son raise this child in honor of her friend who didn't get the chance to raise hers.

Where was Tessa now? In her mind's eye, an image flashed of a teenage girl sitting across from the recliner, right there in that strange living room with Esther's familiar things. But she couldn't trust what she thought she remembered. Memory? Hallucination? Wishful thinking?

It was too tiring to figure it out. Sometimes, it was just too tiring to go on.

CHAPTER TWENTY-THREE

Tessa

Spring Break arrived and Tessa headed home. A change in scenery might help unravel the tangled events of the past several weeks. A budding . . . something . . . with Chip. The information, or jumbled bits, of Grandmother's past.

Tessa had spent her teenage years pushing her grandmother away. By age twelve, Tessa had stopped trying to please a woman who'd she'd determined could never be satisfied. In fact, she'd put heroic effort into becoming the opposite of Grandmother's vision. Tessa had flaunted what Grandmother had criticized—manners "unbecoming of a young lady," declarations of independence; and refusals to attract a boyfriend. She'd bubble-wrapped herself against Grandmother's disapproval. And now—Tessa almost snorted aloud—she wasn't quite so angry or convinced that Grandmother was all bad.

As she drove the mostly rural Route 40 through central Florida, Tessa marveled at how the scenery changed. The live oaks and dense scrub brush of her Ocala school home gave way to the varying palms trees of the east coast—foxtail, queen, and royal palms. Tessa couldn't identify the exact spot where one tree replaced another. It was as if she'd blinked and the environment changed. People were like that, too. Rarely could someone identify when they became different from years before but only that they were. Even Tessa. At five she was meek and eager to please her grandmother but by twelve she'd turned her back on compliance and embraced defiance.

And now, she was somewhere in between. Pieces of Grandmother's life revealed more of her. Different sides than Tessa imagined existed. Sides that her grandmother seemed to have kept secret. Those secrets have grown heavier with time, taking on lives of their own. And when secrets are kept hidden for so long, they begin to shape the person hiding them. Often without their knowing. Grandmother's friend Millie had gotten pregnant. Whatever happened to that pregnancy affected her grandmother all her life. And the secret of Lou Ann being Tessa's birth mom must weigh even more. Eventually, skeletons clamber to get out of the closet, even without Alzheimer's help.

She turned onto busy A1A, almost home. The area exploded with new construction. A cinder block building advertised a new memory care facility. *They're popping up more and more,* thought Tessa. *Grandmother's not alone.*

Tessa rolled into the gravel driveway and soaked in the air. With the windows down, she smelled the salty ocean and heard seagulls squawking in the distance, a few blocks away. She marveled at the brightness of the bougainvillea bordering the front porch, the pink as bold as Kendra's hair. Lantana blossoms lined the little walkway giving bursts of pink and yellow as she walked up to the door.

"Hey, Mom!" Tessa called as she unlocked the front door of the house. She heard the refrigerator humming and the grandfather clock ticking, the same one that once stood in Grandmother's house.

Tessa closed the door, putting her duffle bag of clean clothes and laundry bag of dirty ones in the foyer. "Mom?" she called, walking further into the house.

She could hear her mother talking. Tessa followed the sound and found her on the lanai, laptop open, ear buds in while she typed and talked.

As she listened to her mother suggesting colors and fabrics and furniture to someone, Tessa smiled inwardly. Her mother had taken to her career like peanut butter to jelly.

Tessa waved, catching her mother's eye. Her mom ended the call, pulled out her ear buds, and closed the computer screen. Jumping up, she came to Tessa, arms outstretched. Tessa accepted the hug.

Kendra was right. This was Tessa's home and her family, and her mother's hug would never stop comforting her, despite the lingering resentment in her heart.

"Hi, honey. I'm so excited to have you for a whole week. I hope you want to do some flea market shopping. For old time's sake."

"It's been a while since we've wandered those flea markets," Tessa said, not quite answering her. This week would be a journey for answers, not a trip down Memory Lane.

They walked into the house. Debra rummaged through the cubby holes of her antique writing desk. She retrieved a map marked with red circles and held it up to Tessa. "I've found some of the better markets that specialize in artifacts and antiques. I thought we could see them tomorrow. What do you say?"

The hope that shined in her mom's eyes softened Tessa's resolve. "Sure, Mom."

Together they lugged Tessa's clothes to the loft upstairs. The little bungalow was a perfectly designed house for mother and daughter. The top floor was all Tessa's, a bedroom and bath, and she loved the coziness.

Tessa looked around her bedroom. She'd had the same décor, green and white, for years. It felt like home. She understood Grandmother's discomfort in the unfamiliar assisted living facility. And how the bracelet was a steadfast reminder of all she knew. Tessa felt the security of her own well-worn furnishings and reveled in their comfort.

Her mother puttered in the hallway, putting away linens and towels in the closet outside the bathroom. She poked her head into Tessa's room. "Oh, I have such fun plans for us this week." When Tessa just smiled, her mom came in and sat next to Tessa who had settled on the edge of her bed. "How have you been?" she asked softly.

"Distracted," she answered honestly. Between Grandmother's revelations and her own heart's callings around Chip and her newfound birth story, her mind was a puzzle of mismatched pieces. "Are there any Parkers left around here?"

Her mother looked at Tessa for a moment and shook her head.

Tessa wanted to believe her. But trust was a little hard to come by right now.

Her mother absently rubbed her thumb over Tessa's knuckle, and she smiled sadly. "I'm not lying."

No one could read Tessa quite like her mom.

"Lou Ann lived a different life from me. Or your father. She was poor; she fought for what she wanted, whether it was boyfriends or justice. I know she had an older brother—much older—but he died in the Gulf War. Lou Ann lived with her mom and dad in a trailer park outside city limits." She put one hand on top of Tessa's. "When she died, her parents up and left. At least, when your dad went to their trailer, it was deserted. He knocked on a few doors, but no one knew where they'd gone."

"Dad looked for them?"

Her mom gave her a half-smile and nodded. "He didn't want you to be estranged from Lou Ann's side of the family."

More puzzle pieces that needed a home. Tessa would never have pictured her father knocking on trailer doors to find his ex-girlfriend's family. Then again, she couldn't have pictured him taking in an infant, even his own, and raising her. But he had. In his own way.

Maybe she should drive to the mobile home park and introduce herself. Maybe someone would be more open to telling her about the family if they knew she was a relative. The word sounded funny in her head.

Her mother continued. "When your dad returned from the trailer park and told me and your grandmother that they'd left, we all vowed to give you the best life we could." She shrugged. "That's all I can tell you. Honestly," she added.

Tessa nodded, her head swirling with more questions than answers, none that her mom could help with. But a little pride toward the family that rallied around infant Tessa rose in her heart.

Her mom patted Tessa's hand and stood. "I'm going to finish up a work call. Come down when you've unpacked, and we'll run out for dinner."

"Sure, Mom," Tessa replied automatically. Once her mom left, Tessa lay back on her bed and let her mind wander where it may. Lou Ann was the first path it followed. Grandmother had called Tessa reckless and restless. That wasn't true. What her grandmother described as reckless was Tessa's free-spiritedness. And that was Tessa's attempt to be everything Grandmother was not. She did the opposite of whatever Grandmother advised: finding a boyfriend, dressing and acting demurely and stately, and keeping her opinions to herself. As for being restless, that part might be true. Tessa didn't want the life Grandmother espoused, but she didn't know what she *did* want. Until now. She'd found a career that fit in her heart and soul like a hug.

While Tessa didn't know if she'd inherited those traits from Lou Ann, she wondered what she did inherit. Was there a part of Tessa that was Lou Ann? Did Lou Ann like art or restoring things? Then a thought hit her. Dad was an alcoholic and Lou Ann was an addict. She'd read somewhere that kids of addicts had a higher propensity to become addicts themselves. Could Tessa have a genetic disposition to that?

She rolled over and groaned. Thoughts led to new questions. Oh, why did she ever have to find this out? Maybe her parents and grandmother were right to keep it a secret. She banished the thought immediately. Grandmother's disjointed memories from years past taught Tessa that secrets had no benefit in the long run.

There had to be someone who still knew the Parker family in that trailer park, so she went downstairs, intending to find out where it was.

Her mother was finishing up her phone call and held up one finger to have Tessa wait. She did, leaning against the granite countertop in the kitchen, jingling her bracelets restlessly. Restless. Maybe Grandmother was right.

Once her mom ended the call, Tessa asked, "Where's the trailer park? I just need to see it for myself." She stood straight, primed for an argument but she wouldn't let her mom detract her from this. Tessa needed to find some answers. Closure, it was called.

"The old trailer park was bought years ago. Developers made a parking lot out of it. It's part of the new amusement center on Gull Avenue."

Tessa's heart dropped. The small bit of hope she'd focused on dissipated like a popped balloon. She sat heavily on the kitchen bar stool. And realized that the Parkers had abandoned her as well. They hadn't tried to see her or even left a forwarding address with her dad. Her heart hardened toward Lou Ann's family.

Tessa was rejected at birth. And her grandmother rejected her in adolescence. The realization was a reminder that she would never depend on anyone for acceptance. Chip's face flashed in front of her. Especially not a boyfriend or husband.

·   ·   ·

"Tessa, let's go!" Debra's voice rang up the stairs Saturday morning.

It was like being in school again. *The bus driver is honking the horn, Tessa.* Or if she finagled a ride out of her mom, she'd hear, *The train is leaving the station in five!*

"Be right there!" she called.

A while later, a fidgety mother stood at the front door, car keys jangling in one hand, a bulging backpack in the other. "Ready for some antique fun?"

"Mom, we're not camping!" Tessa laughed and pointed to her mom's stuffed bag.

"Don't laugh. You never know when we'll need water and snacks."

Tessa rolled her eyes. They were going flea-market trolling not Wild West hiking.

The day was warm. In the car, her mom started the engine and turned on the air conditioner. She shook out her map. Tessa peeked over from the passenger seat to see three red circles along a highlighted route.

In addition to over-preparing, her mom had a reputation for jumping in while the pool was still filling up. Tessa had barely dipped her toes into her new major and her mother had them chasing down the next big art find. As her mother rambled, Tessa couldn't hide her smile.

Nor could she deny her mother's love. Lou Ann, the Parker family, and even Grandmother might have rejected Tessa, but her mom never had. In fact, Tessa realized what her mother had sacrificed for Tessa: she'd taken in a baby who wasn't her own and raised her as if she were. And loved her unconditionally despite sharing no genetics. The realization softened the edges of Tessa's resentment.

"So, what shall we search for?" her mom asked as she drove to their first destination.

Tessa laughed as the old game was resurrected. Someone would choose the object of the search, and the person who found the best example of it chose the ice cream flavor for the night.

"How about an old-fashioned camera?" Tessa said. She blushed, knowing Chip had been on her mind.

"Well, that's an interesting choice." Her mom gave Tessa a sidelong glance as she maneuvered through the Saturday beach-going traffic.

Tessa merely shrugged and consulted the map. "You've got about $1/8^{th}$ of an inch before you turn into Find It Here market. It will come up on your right."

Her mother chuckled. "Nice math skills."

"I see the sign, Mom. Up ahead."

Debra turned into the grassy parking lot and secured a spot. She unbuckled her seat belt as Tessa did the same. "I noticed the camera hanging from Chip's neck in the cafeteria," her mom said. "Is he the reason you want to find an old camera?"

Tessa saw the corners of her mom's mouth twitch with a restrained smile. Tessa had already told her mom about Chip's suggestion to write up the information cards. She'd also told her about him being a TA in one of her classes. She'd mentioned him quite a bit. Apparently, Debra

Wilde was reading between the lines. But Tessa Wilde was ignoring the page.

"Mom, stop. There's nothing between us except friendship." If she said it enough, maybe Tessa would accept it. And even if there was a growing something, Tessa wouldn't allow it to become anything more than a schoolgirl crush.

Her mom held her hands up in mock surrender.

They exited the car and walked to the first booth of goodies. For the next half hour, Tessa and her mom scoured the offerings in search of the perfect camera.

Most were too new for the rules of their game.

Her mom picked up an old-fashioned viewfinder. It reminded Tessa of the Disney viewfinder she'd had as a kid. She'd put a cardboard circle in a slot. When she turned the circle, pictures would emerge through the binocular lens. But this one was much more rudimentary. It had binocular lenses to look through and a stick protruding from the middle, where her nose would have rested. At the end of the stick were two wire slots.

"What is this?" Tessa asked.

An elderly man limped over to them from behind the table. "Well, little lady, it's a stereoscope," he said. "An old-timer's camera," he added with a grin.

He took the object from her mother's hand and picked up a pair of nearly identical black and white photographs. He placed them in the slots, side by side. "I know they look the same. They're not. Each was taken a few inches to the side of the other, probably sometime in the late 1800s. When you look through the lens, it creates an illusion of an almost 3-D picture. See?"

Tessa took the stereoscope and peered through the lens. He was right. Instead of two pictures of men building a railroad, Tessa saw one. The railroad was right in front of her, and she could practically feel the sweat that showed on the backs of their shirts.

She handed it to her mom to try out as the man continued his spiel. "Yeah, these died away in the 1920s to make room for cameras." He patted the stereoscope. "But back in the day, this was information." Then he shook his head. "Now people don't hardly use cameras! They got their smart phones. Who knows what'll be next?"

"How much do you want for it?"

He seemed surprised. "You interested in photography?"

Tessa only shrugged. Chip might appreciate it. Not that she had an occasion to give him a gift. Still . . .

"Tell ya what," the man said. "Forty bucks gets you this and that box of photographs."

Before she could answer, her mother piped in. "Twenty-five," she bargained. Her mom looked at Tessa as if to say, *It IS a flea market, after all.*

The man chuckled and shifted his weight. His jowls jiggled a little when he laughed, and his eyes sparkled. He was spunky, Tessa decided.

"Deal," he said offering his hand.

When Debra nodded at Tessa to complete the deal, Tessa shook his hand and took out her wallet.

They walked back to the car. "Interesting purchase, Tessa," her mother said.

Tessa could feel a blush arise, but she wasn't ready to talk about what she felt for Chip. She didn't even really know what she felt for Chip. A crush felt too superficial and too immature. But to say she thought he could be more. . . well, she wasn't ready for that, either.

CHAPTER TWENTY-FOUR

Esther

Millie. Tessa. The names clanged in Esther's head, blending then moving apart. She watched the shadows of the palm fronds off the lanai wave on the ceiling above her recliner. They looked like they were dancing in the late afternoon. She caressed her bracelet, toying with each charm, then stopping on the miniature dancer with the billowing skirt.

•   •   •

"Oh, c'mon, Esther. Get your dancing shoes on. Britt's is putting on a real New Year's celebration tonight. You won't want to miss it."

Esther smiled at Penny, her quasi-friend from the local library. As volunteers, they stacked the shelves and sorted videos. They'd push the Book Return cart through the carpeted aisles, placing books on the cherry shelves that always gleamed and never seemed dusty. They'd alphabetize the old videos and new DVDs and sort them into genre, something Esther loved to do. She'd stumble upon an old classic like The African Queen or Pillow Talk and find herself stopping at the check-out desk before her shift ended.

Esther and Penny had developed a comfortable acquaintanceship. Esther didn't have close girlfriends. Not since Millie. Penny was bubbly and often invited Esther to join her and her husband Tom to various events. Esther rarely accepted. Being a third wheel was worse than missing out.

Now, she looked at Penny and shrugged.

What was a fifty-four-year-old widow going to do at a New Year's Eve party full of youthful exuberance and giggles?

Junior had started his new sales job this past fall and traveled often. If not working, he was out with his gang of friends. He'd already told Esther that he was going away for New Year's Eve. She wasn't thrilled with the company he kept. Esther was searching for a suitable girl to introduce. The one he was running about with now was too loose for Esther's liking. A petite blonde with a spitfire personality.

The elbow to her arm startled Esther from her daydreaming.

"I'll pick you up," Penny offered. "With Tom out of town, we'll both be single ladies." She chuckled.

Esther took the bait, tired of being lonely, unwilling to spend another New Year's Eve alone since Art died. "Okay, I'll go."

Penny's eyebrows shot up and she took a step backwards, looking at Esther incredulously. "You will?" She poked her with her elbow. Again. "Good. You know, Ricardo is single." She did a Groucho Marx imitation.

Esther rolled her eyes but also felt her heart skip a little. The owner of Britt's was a debonair gentleman with perfectly coiffed salt-and-pepper hair and sharply pressed suits. Whenever Esther had an occasion to dine there, usually for lunch with a group of ladies, he greeted their table, spending a few minutes in polite conversation. She was much too old for girlish flirtations, but Ricardo would've challenged that ideal if she were so inclined. In the five years since Art had passed, loneliness had compounded daily.

"Ladies, can you gather the materials from the Teen Club Room?" the head librarian asked. Olga was fastidious and the teenagers were not her favorite patrons. It usually fell to Penny and Esther to clean up after them.

"I'll take care of it Penny," Esther told her friend.

"Thanks. I'll pick you up at 8:30 tonight," she whispered as Esther walked away.

Esther waved in acknowledgment. But as she straightened the Teen Club room, she second-guessed her decision. Wasn't she just too old for late-night parties?

She sighed and picked up discarded magazines, displaced books, and against-the-rules plastic water bottles usually hidden behind the fake plants. Maybe tonight Esther could find a fake plant to hide behind, too.

• • •

Later, she and Penny entered the restaurant. They were greeted with a sparkly gold and silver banner wishing them a Happy New Year! *Esther peeked at her watch. 9:00 p.m. She certainly couldn't leave before midnight, but she already felt the discomfort of social gatherings. Penny took their coats to the cloak room while Esther waited.*

Ricardo appeared at Esther's elbow. He wore a black tuxedo with a silver handkerchief in the pocket. His shoes shined like he'd polished them just that moment. Not a speck of dust or crumb of food lingered. He was GQ perfection.

"Ms. Wilde! I'm thrilled to see you here. I hope you'll save me a dance. Perhaps the midnight one?" His eyes sparkled mischievously.

Did he say this to all the single women?

Esther forced a laugh. Her hands were clammy and the heat in the room jumped thirty degrees. But she did feel pretty in her shimmery, burgundy dress that swished just a little at her shins. It reminded her of the yellow dress she'd worn when she'd first met Art.

Just then Penny returned, saving Esther from a response, and Ricardo excused himself with a lingering look at Esther. Or so she thought.

Apparently, Penny did, too. "Mr. Suarez seems mighty interested," she remarked. With a wicked grin and a lift of her eyebrows, Penny made Esther blush.

Esther stammered a response. "Don't be ridiculous. Let's go to the bar." She quickly moved off before Penny could see her reddened face or her trembling hands. The main restaurant was decorated with gold and silver balloon centerpieces. Tables were littered with confetti and champagne glasses adorned each place setting. The festive décor prepared customers for elegant fun.

After a delicious dinner paired with a scrumptious wine, Penny and Esther mingled. They chatted with those they knew and nodded politely at those they didn't. After some time, Esther suppressed a yawn. 11:45. Esther stole a glance around the room. Was Ricardo going to seek her out for the big dance?

Penny had excused herself for the restroom, leaving Esther standing alone and thinking of excuses to leave.

A hand touched her shoulder.

"It is time for our dance, I believe." Ricardo's fingers trailed from her shoulder to her wrist. He tugged her gently towards the makeshift dance floor where the band began playing Auld Lang Syne. Standing there with his arms open, Ricardo smiled and drew her towards him. She smelled his aftershave of spice and smoke. Musky and appealing. He stood six inches taller than she and gazed at her with intensity. Esther's heart pounded.

Ricardo pulled her tight and they danced like no one else mattered. Who was this version of Esther Wilde? She pressed herself against him with her head on his shoulder. She didn't dare look him in the eye. He'd see her undeniable attraction. And laugh. Or ignore it.

When the song ended, the countdown began. Esther's heart hammered as she wondered how Ricardo would celebrate midnight. Would he kiss her? Before she could wonder long, confetti dropped from the ceiling, the kazoos blared, and Ricardo kissed her. Chastely, on the cheek. A wave of disappointment rushed through her.

He extricated himself, saying he had to check on something but would be back. It was like a cold cloth thrown in her face. She hurried off to find Penny and get the hell out of there. Esther stopped in her tracks when she saw Ricardo talking to Penny near the exit. Should she flee to the bathroom or sashay past them nonchalantly?

"Esther," Penny beckoned. "Ricardo was just telling me you don't need a ride home. That he would escort you. Is that right?" The twinkle

in Penny's eye told Esther she'd have a lot of explaining to do at the library.

Esther nodded, a thrill passing through her. She felt reckless and daring.

"Ms. Wilde, if you'll give me a few moments, I'll prepare my staff for closing. Perhaps we shall go for a drink? Would that be acceptable?" The formal question mixed with his tuxedo-clad appearance made Esther feel like Cinderella with her Prince Charming.

Ricardo's green eyes captivated her. She simply nodded again.

Penny winked and walked away. Ricardo sidled back to the kitchen. Esther was alone in the foyer. What had she agreed to? Esther Wilde was not the kind of woman to spend late nights with strange men. Yet she was absolutely taken with this one. Something other-worldly had come over her. She willed Ricardo to return before sensibility reclaimed her.

They skipped the drink. Esther invited him to her house and all that entailed. It was passionate, fulfilling, and completely out-of-character. Never had any man given her the freedom to act without thinking.

The next morning, Esther awoke to the smell of her favorite coffee brewing. When she went to the kitchen, she found a note and a coffee cup waiting by the pot. But no Ricardo. His note said he'd call. Esther spent the morning in doubt. Surely Ricardo was used to smart and polished women of the times. Esther was just a Southern girl. Plain and possibly boring. In fact, the more she thought, the more Esther decided it was a poor decision to sleep with Ricardo. He'd probably gotten what he'd wanted from her. She pictured it now—she'd become enamored with him, and he'd toss her aside when the newness wore off. Then she'd be left with a broken heart. Because she could already tell she would fall hard for him if given the chance.

She needed to end it before it really began.

The next few weeks she avoided the restaurant, quit the library feigning busyness to Penny, and ignored Ricardo's calls. They finally stopped. Esther might be lonelier than before, but she still had her pride.

•   •   •

With a start, Esther wondered if she'd made a mistake all those years ago. Could Ricardo have provided a spark of love to carry her through her elder years? Art was a wonderful husband, but the spark was not strong. Their relationship was fueled by practicality and mutual respect, important for a lasting couple. But what of the passion that ignites that fire?

A voice interrupted her introspection. "Hi, Ms. Esther." It was Not-Sally. "I've got your evening medicine here."

Esther grunted. She was tired of taking medicine. Couldn't she just sit in peace with her treasured memories?

Not-Sally came over with a miniscule paper cup. Esther peered in and saw two capsules. She raised her eyebrows questioningly at Not-Sally.

"It's okay, Ms. Esther. You take these every day."

Still suspicious, Esther eyed Not-Sally. She was reassured by Not-Sally's kind eyes. Esther swallowed them down with the proffered glass of water.

"I'm going to finish my medication rounds and then I'll be back to help you get ready for bed," Not-Sally said.

After Not-Sally left, Esther resumed her watch outside. The dancing shadows of earlier were gone, leaving a charcoal darkness in their wake. Esther patted her bracelet, running her fingers over the curves and edges of each charm, lingering on that dancer. Buying the dancer had reminded Esther of her flirtation with wild abandon. When she saw it in the jewelry store, she bought it on impulse. Now fragments of scenes starring Esther flitted through her mind. *Swaying with Ricardo, her heart as weightless as cotton candy on that New Year's Eve night. Standing next to the answering machine listening to his smoky, voice of velvet when she refused to answer. The stab of heartache when the calls stopped.*

She touched another charm. A heart. Once a locket that hung from a necklace, the small gold-toned heart was one of her most prized and most heart-wrenching charms. Something she and Millie had bought so many years ago. Art had had the locket made into a charm for her. There was a matching heart locket somewhere . . . wherever Millie was.

•　　•　　•

"Hurry up, Essie," Millie called as Essie stopped to adjust her shoes.

Blisters formed on Essie's heels from the new penny loafers she'd begged her mother to buy last week at the department store. Essie and Millie would start high school in a few weeks, and Essie was excited to flaunt a more mature wardrobe. Mother had said no to the tight sweater Essie wanted. At least she got the shoes. Now they pinched and rubbed against the skin.

"I'm coming," she reassured her friend. Millie had already broken in her new school shoes and was anxious to get to the Five-n-Dime to spend their money on fashion accessories.

"Okay," Essie said breathlessly as she caught up to Millie outside the store. Together the two girls walked in, holding their heads high and refusing to succumb to giggles like children. The aisles were full of practical necessities, but Essie tugged her friend towards the cosmetics and hair decorations. "This way," Essie said pulling Millie's arm to the hair accessories. The girls perused the headbands, turning the rotating display case slowly, intent upon finding the perfect one. They decided to buy matching black velvet bands for the first day of high school.

"Come here," Millie said in a stage whisper. She'd meandered to the costume jewelry on the next rack.

Essie saw the shiny gold beckoning.

"Look at these gold lockets, Essie! We could have matching necklaces."

Essie's hand instinctively went to her bare throat. She was itching for a pearl necklace and hoped to get one for Christmas that year. If Daddy saw her with a different one, he might think she didn't want the pearl necklace anymore. The one she'd circled in the magazines that she'd left prominently displayed on the coffee table.

But she looked at Millie's shining eyes. Her friend was so excited. And a locket would be neat. The necklaces weren't real gold, but if they shined them every day and took care of them, they'd still look pretty. And she'd keep hers in a pocket to put on at school and take off before Daddy came in from the fields.

"Okay, Millie." With the last of her allowance, Essie splurged. The girls took their matching purchases out into the humidity of a Georgia August.

"Whew! It's hot. Do you have enough money left for a root beer float?" Millie asked. When Esther shook her head, Millie grabbed her arm. "I have enough for two. C'mon!"

The girls sat in the soda shop sipping their ice cream floats. Instead of a table with parlor style chairs, Essie chose a red vinyl booth with an aluminum-edged table.

High school would be the best days yet for her and Millie!

"Essie, look," Millie whispered conspiratorially and slid a sideways glance towards the lunch counter. Both girls were hunched over their drinks.

Essie sat up straight, expecting a celebrity of some sort to be there. Instead, two boys stood paying for Cokes. With slicked back hair and dungarees with white tee shirts tucked in them, Essie knew they were high school students. Puzzled, she looked back to her friend. "Who?" No one else was nearby.

"It's Henry Wade. You know, the football player at the high school. He's a senior and so cute," she gushed.

Essie barely refrained from an eye roll. Millie's recent obsession with boys annoyed Essie. She wanted Millie to focus on their writing future. Besides, this one just looked like a regular guy to her. Older and kind of cute, but just a guy. But she humored her boy-crazy friend. "I guess he's cute, Millie. But a senior? He's too old for you, don't you think? We're barely even freshmen."

Millie raised her head and pulled her shoulders up. "No, I don't think so. Age is just a number," she said with an air of a wiser, older woman.

"Oh brother," Essie muttered. She changed the subject. "I hope we get English class together. We've got to practice our writing so we'll be ready for our travels. Graduation sounds so far away, but these years will fly by. I'm hoping to get a spot on the school newspaper or the yearboo—" She stopped as she realized Millie wasn't listening.

Essie followed her friend's lovestruck gaze which had been pinned on Henry and his friend.

As if the boys could sense it, they looked over and smiled.

Essie looked down at the table and sucked up the last of her root beer float. "Ready to go, Millie?" she asked quickly.

But Millie had smiled back, holding eye contact, and now the boys headed their way.

"Hello, girls," Henry said. "May we join you?"

Before Millie could make room for them, Essie said, "We've just finished. Sorry. We're heading to the library." Essie had scooted out of her side of the booth. "Coming, Millie?" Essie couldn't get out of the soda shop fast enough. She was embarrassed for Millie, trying to flirt with senior boys.

Millie frowned at her. She recovered quickly though and said, "Sorry, boys. But we'll see you around school soon." Millie sidled out of the booth and gave a coquettish smile to Henry.

Then she sauntered out of the shop, hips swaying.

She looked ridiculous to Essie.

In the sunshine and heat once again, Essie feared Millie would yell at her for dismissing the boys. Millie surprised her. "That was smart of you, Essie. Boys don't want girls who seem eager. Good play."

Essie's mouth opened. But instead of correcting Millie's assumption, Essie snapped her mouth shut. Whatever got Millie off the topic of boys was good enough for Essie.

"C'mon! Let's read about all the new places we want to see." Essie linked her arm with her best friend, excited to fantasize about the future careers of the soon-to-be two best travel writers of Georgia.

•   •   •

The soda shop memory spoke with clarity to Esther's old brain. As early as the start of high school Millie longed for the traditional life— marriage and family. Why had Esther never seen that? The fixation on boys and longing to impress the older ones. The appeal of an older man that eventually cost Millie a pregnancy and their friendship. Esther had worn blinders.

In her quest to chase her own dream, she'd pulled Millie with her. And her friend hadn't the heart, or the courage, to correct Esther. And Esther, too absorbed in her own dreams, had ignored the signs.

She'd made the same mistake with Tessa. Tried to force her own ideals onto her granddaughter. Why hadn't Esther learned from her broken friendship with Millie not to push her own dreams on the ones she loved?

With the headstrong determination that once defined Esther Wilde, she decided to drive to Debra and Tessa's house and rectify the wrong. Esther pushed herself up from her chair. Her legs wobbled with the effort. But she put one foot forward intending to get her purse and keys. She felt herself teeter.

There was nothing near her to grab and Esther toppled forward, the momentum too much for her. What felt like a slow fall was an instantaneous tumble. Esther twisted her head to avoid crashing face-first. She fell on her left side, landing sideways against a bookcase, her body throbbing. Esther cried out a garbled "Help!" but it sounded weak and feeble to her ears.

She tried to wiggle herself to lie flat, but pain shot from her lower back through her left leg all the way to her ankle. She stopped moving and lay there like a turtle that had bumped into an obstacle and was immobile, wedged on its side. Esther would not be a turtle. Scooting away from the bookcase, she gritted through the jabs of pain and ended up on her back. Instead of a turtle, she was now a paralyzed cockroach. She was exhausted. Maybe this was her end.

She closed her eyes. "Art, come get me," she pled silently.

CHAPTER TWENTY-FIVE

Tessa

Once they returned from the flea market, Tessa went upstairs to shower while her mom ordered pizza.

Where did my love for old stuff come from? Tessa wondered as she dried off. *Did Lou Ann have a fascination for old things?*

"Pizza's here!" her mom called.

"Be right there!"

She towel-dried her blonde hair, or Lou Ann's blonde, and combed it. The only Wilde family traits Tessa recognized in the mirror were her eye color and hair texture. They came from Grandmother.

Tessa walked into the kitchen where her mom had just made a tossed salad. Typical Mom. Even a pizza dinner had to have a healthy vibe to it. Tomatoes, cucumbers, and carrots overloaded the lettuce.

Tessa poured soda in their Tervis cups. The insulated drinkware was a staple in their house. As familiar to Tessa as teacups were to Grandmother.

"Salad dressing is in the fridge. Can you grab it?" her mom asked as she opened the pizza box and the aroma of pepperoni wafted through the kitchen.

Tessa's mouth watered. She put the dressing on the table and sat in her usual seat across from her mom. She picked up her gooey piece, catching the melted strings of mozzarella before they hit the plate, gathering them in her mouth and filling her taste buds with a cheesy zing. This was comfort food. For a little while, Tessa would forget Lou Ann and Grandmother and even Chip. She'd concentrate on having a nice dinner with her mother.

Her mom took a few bites of her own slice. When she put it down, she wiped the grease off her fingers on a napkin and held up a finger. "Be right back," and she hurried to her desk. She returned with a photograph in her hand.

She sat back down and clearing her throat said, "I looked through my old photo albums and surprisingly, found a picture of an old beach party from New Years Eve Day, 1999. Lou Ann is in it." She stared at Tessa for a moment. "Do you want to see her?"

A wave of anxiety and excitement washed over her. Tessa wiped her hands on a napkin and placed them on either side of her plate. "Do I look like her?" she asked quietly.

Her mom handed it over. "Why don't you decide for yourself?" and placed the photo in front of Tessa.

Tessa peered closely. She recognized her mom and dad right away. Debra's curly brown hair covered her shoulders, and she sat on a beach towel next to Tessa's dad, their legs touching. Her hand rested on his thigh; muscular legs that glistened with suntan oil. His dark hair was cropped short, and his arm was behind her mom's as they sat with their legs straight out. Behind them, on the sand was a lone girl whose hand was raised as if to ward off the sun. She was petite, her shaggy blonde hair—the same color as Tessa's— caught in a breeze, covering up some of her face. She rocked a hot pink bikini.

Tessa squinted and brought the photo closer to her face. "Is that her?" She knew it was— there was no one else in the picture. The girl didn't seem bothered by the sight of Arthur and Debra snuggled together. In fact, she didn't seem to notice them. She looked over them as if she were scanning the area past them, searching for someone or something.

"It's the only one I could find," her mom admitted. "Not the best shot of her face, but it's something," she added hopefully.

"What was she like, Mom?"

"Lou Ann Parker brought excitement everywhere she went. Fun trailed her. When she showed up at a beach party, enthusiasm came with her like firecrackers chomping to go off. She was the epitome of carefree living."

She looked up at Tessa and smiled sadly. "She could have gone places. She could charm anyone."

Okay, she was fun and charismatic, somewhat like Tessa remembered her father being on his sober days.

"You have her build and her color. See how she was petite and could make a swimsuit model jealous? You can't really tell in this picture, but her hair was layered around her face in a kind of shaggy bob. Not thick like yours—that's from your grandmother."

Tessa bit her bottom lip. She tried to feel a connection with the girl in the picture. But she was a stranger.

Her mom continued. "She was feisty and spoke her mind. Maybe that's why she attracted everyone, boys and girls. Girls wanted her carefree attitude, and boys wanted her fearlessness."

"Tell me about this day," Tessa said pointing to the photo.

Her mom looked up at the ceiling as if remembering. "Lou Ann's car had broken down. At this point," she referred to the picture, "it was after lunch and most of us had been there a couple hours. I remember asking your dad if we should head back to get ready for the party at Esther's club later."

Tessa leaned over the table and put up a hand. "Wait. You went to a New Years Eve party at the Sutton Country Club? Grandmother's club?"

She wrinkled her nose in understanding. "I know. Stuffy and formal, but we'd agreed to have dinner with Esther and then go to a real party at someone's house. Anyway, we were going to pack up. Lou Ann had been there only a few minutes when she asked if anyone could help her with her car." After a pause, her mom added, "That happened a lot."

Tessa looked back at the picture. "It doesn't look like she'd been driving in that bikini."

Her mom shifted in her seat. "Well, Lou Ann wasn't known for her modest and conservative fashion. She might have had a coverup on, I don't know." She shrugged. "A girl was taking pictures with one of those little digital cameras that day. I remember her saying she'd get them developed and give some to us all. That's how I got this one."

"And did someone help Lou Ann?" Tessa prodded the story along.

"Of course. Your father did. That was also the day she told him she was pregnant," she said softly.

Tessa stared at the girl with the flat stomach and the flashy bikini. "She doesn't look pregnant."

"No. She didn't show much until spring."

Tessa continued to hold the picture and burn Lou Ann's image in her mind. "And she never wanted to be pregnant. I probably cramped her style, held her back. Maybe that's why she rejected me so easily. Used me to get money from Grandmother."

Her mother leaned across the table, and Tessa saw concern in her eyes. "She didn't 'reject' you, honey." Then inhaling deeply, she said, "Tessa, she *couldn't* care for you. Drug addicts don't choose to be irresponsible." She said quietly, "The drugs took over. Lou Ann's partying had gone farther than just having a good time. Once you were born, she had to think of more than just herself. She needed money for baby necessities, and Arthur always came through. As much as he could." She took Tessa's hand and smiled wistfully. "For almost a year we shared you. Maybe not equally. We had you more, but that's because your dad always asked Lou Ann for more time." A few beats of time passed when her mother added, "She tried, honey." Her mom sighed. "Drugs are a powerful distraction from life."

Annoyance and a lack of understanding passed through Tessa. "Mom, I don't understand you. One minute you tell me Lou Ann was a drug addict who couldn't think of anyone but herself and the next, you're defending her!" She sat back, crossing her arms. "She should've just gone to rehab or stopped the drugs."

"It's easy to judge someone when you don't walk in her shoes," her mom said softly.

"Mothers are supposed to put their children first," Tessa muttered.

"I understand you're hurt. And frustrated because you can't get the answers you're looking for. Not with Esther's dementia. But don't let your heart harden so much that you forget your blessings. You had a father who tried to raise his only child. A grandmother who wanted to help. Don't discount all that effort put forth in love."

Kendra had said something similar.

Tessa didn't want to be selfish or bitter, but her feelings were bouncing everywhere, like a pinball machine gone haywire.

"Lou Ann gave me you," her mom said brightly. "Of all the difficult decisions I've ever had to make, raising you was never one of them."

Still, Tessa struggled. "What if Grandmother hadn't had Alzheimer's? Would you ever have told me this?"

Tears shone in her mom's eyes but her voice hardened. "Maybe it was wrong, but all I ever wanted was to give you a sense of family. I didn't have any brothers or sisters. My own mother always said it was her and me against the world. I didn't want that for you. I wanted you to have people you belonged to, a sense of family, small as we were. The only way I could do that was to preserve ties that might've been cut. To keep you and me and your dad and even Esther bound together. Even after I was divorced, I struggled to make sure you had time with your dad. And, of course, your grandmother."

After a moment, she added, "Sometimes decisions have to be made that are both right and wrong."

Tessa sat still, absorbing and weeding through all her mom had said.

After a few minutes, her mom stood up and left the kitchen.

For all her intentions to move on from the past, it wasn't so easy. Old hurts still stung. She sat with her feelings bubbling inside, wondering how to find peace.

If she'd learned anything from Grandmother, it was that resentment built. Anger burns if left unresolved. And relationships wither if left unnurtured. Tessa didn't have an opportunity to have a relationship with her father. She was losing any time to repair the one she had with her grandmother, if that was possible. She did not want her relationship with her mom to sour, too.

Tessa put away the leftover pizza and salad and went to her mother's bedroom door. "Mom, can I come in?" Tessa called.

When her mom opened the door, Tessa entered and sat on the bed. "I know you love me. I think Dad did, too. But when I think of being left out of the most important information of my life, well . . . I feel stupid. Like I have toilet paper trailing my heel while everyone points and laughs."

Her mom sat next to her and said gently, "I can't undo what's been done." She picked up both of Tessa's hands. "I was thrilled to receive you as my daughter. It was horrific that Lou Ann died. Your father and I had just been married, and the most important thing to both of us was to raise you. We should have explained things as you aged. I don't have an excuse for it, I know. We should have told you when you were a child, like adopted parents do for their children." She let go of Tessa's hands and took a deep breath. "When your relationship with your father went south and things with your grandmother got sticky, I didn't want to add to the drama." She held up a hand as if to ward off any protests. "I know they both made mistakes. Your father was unreliable and your grandmother narrow-minded, but they were the only family you had, besides me. I didn't want to see you destroy the chance to have something I never could. I chose to make things as normal as I could." She looked into Tessa's eyes. "I don't want you isolated from the only family you have left."

Tessa couldn't see past one important fact. "Grandmother didn't see me as her family. She saw me as Lou Ann's daughter. That's why she never liked me."

Her mom paused a moment before saying, "Remember, you're also your father's child. When Esther saw you, she also saw him."

Tessa hadn't thought of that. And Grandmother had adored her son. Could she have loved Tessa even while hating that connection to Lou Ann? Maybe she equated Tessa's desire to be independent with a license for abandon like Lou Ann, or a pathway for addiction like Tessa's dad.

After a moment, her mom nudged Tessa's side. "How about we turn our pizza dinner into an ice cream one, huh?"

Tessa welcomed the distraction.

In the kitchen Tessa rummaged through the freezer, pulling out the green ice cream container. "Mint chocolate chip since it's almost St. Patrick's Day."

Debra chuckled. "Well, you did win the ice cream game. You found the oldest camera at the flea market." She waved the ice cream scoop in the direction of the bag on the counter. "And a great find at that," she added, setting bowls and spoons on the table. "Mint chocolate chip it is. Of course, *I* would have picked the classic Cherry Vanilla."

Tessa rolled her eyes teasingly. "You gotta let loose a little, Mom." She sounded like Kendra.

They had just dug into their ice cream when her mom's phone rang. She looked at the Caller ID and frowned.

"What?" Tessa asked after her first mouthful. A feeling of cold ran through her that had nothing to do with the ice cream.

"It's Sunset Shadows," her mother said quickly. "Hello?"

Tessa listened to the one-sided conversation, her ice cream melting slowly. She watched as her mother scrambled for paper and a pen.

"What hospital?"

No! Not yet. I'm not ready, Tessa thought, gripping the edge of the table to steady herself for bad news. "What happened?" she asked as her mother hung up.

"Esther took a bad fall and broke her hip." She looked at Tessa who had lost her appetite and pushed her ice cream bowl away.

"We need to go back tomorrow." Tessa stated what they both felt inside.

That night brought a restless sleep. Tessa wanted to see Grandmother. How ironic. She never thought *that* day would come. What she'd say to her, Tessa didn't know. Only that she had to be there.

.   .   .

Early the next morning, Tessa and her mom headed back to Florida Coastal to drop off Tessa's car before going to visit Grandmother in the hospital. As Tessa followed her mom across the state, she noted the reverse in the scenery from just two days ago. She left the palms and springy grasses of home for the dense trees and thick forests of school. Today, those forests seemed ominous and threatening.

Tessa glanced at the plain, unadorned box that sat like a blinking light on the passenger seat. The stereoscope. She thought of a reason to give it to Chip—a thank-you gift for the idea of *The Art of Words*, her information-card writing website she hoped to start soon. She and Chip had come up with a name, just not the details. Yet.

Just then her phone rang. Tapping the Bluetooth connection on her dashboard, she answered.

"Hey, Tessa. It's Chip."

Her heart leaped.

"Just wondered how your break is going." His sultry smooth voice sent tingles all the way to her toes.

Concentrate on driving. "I'm on my way back. My grandmother fell and is in the hospital. Mom and I should be there in an hour or so. I'll be at school the rest of break."

"Oh no! So sorry to hear that, Tessa," Chip said. After a pause he continued. "I know the campus cafeteria has limited hours during breaks. How about you come here for dinner one night? And your mom too."

Tessa's heart danced. "I'd love that. I'll call you after I see my grandmother and we know more about her condition."

The thrill of his invitation was tempered by guilt. Should she really be joyful while her grandmother was possibly dying in a hospital bed? Besides, Chip invited her *and* her mom, so it wasn't a date.

They pulled into the university parking lot. Together they lugged her stuff back to her room. Tessa figured she'd tell her mom about Chip after their hospital visit.

As they put Tessa's belongings back in her room, her mom said, "You know, now might be the time to say anything to your grandmother you need. Mayra said these kinds of falls sometimes accelerate things."

Tessa bit her lip. She didn't know what to say. Or what she wanted to say. Or how to handle it if Grandmother didn't know her or thought she was Lou Ann. But she didn't want to end up a resentful, bitter woman like her grandmother, so she'd try.

Tessa grabbed her charm bracelet. Like a lucky rabbit's foot or a good-luck charm, she prayed it might be a connection to Grandmother.

CHAPTER TWENTY-SIX

Esther

Esther had been dreaming of running through the pecan groves with Daddy, giggling as he huffed next to her and pretending her five-year-old legs were faster than his. A bright blue sky and Daddy's face were all young Essie saw when she looked up. Those and the tops of pecan trees, their leaves blowing in a steady breeze, and brown trunks like an obstacle course of fun.

Short blips of noise sounded like they came from the trees. And her legs grew heavy and sore. Well, one leg.

The pain and noise wakened Esther. And the beeping wasn't coming from trees but rather a machine. The odd box sat on her right next to the strange bed in which she lay. Numbers flashed on it. As she closed her eyes to figure out where she was, Esther became aware of a dull throb in her left side. Her leg hurt. She tried to move it and winced with pain.

Esther turned her head from side to side. Walls of sad blue, not the Easter egg blue sky of her dream, surrounded her. *Where in tarnation was she?* She spotted bedrails. A hospital?

She lifted her head off the pillow and looked around. A small window with a ledge underneath was on her left, and a TV mounted on the wall hung in a corner across from her. She recognized nothing. Where were her posters? Her quilt and recliner?

Her brain was blank. The pain radiating from her leg told her something bad had happened. A car accident? A fall from the ladder? Slipping on ice? She searched for answers, but they didn't come.

A door opened and a woman in a white coat strode through. She came to Esther's bedside with a tiny television contraption in her hand. "How are you feeling, Mrs. Wilde?"

Without waiting for Esther's response, she continued. "That was quite a fall you took." She consulted the square box.

Why couldn't Esther remember falling, and what in heaven's name could that box tell that woman?

White Coat looked at Esther. "I'm Dr. Brinley. I'll be taking care of you while you're here. Is your daughter-in-law coming?"

Who? The woman made no sense.

The door opened again. Two youngsters entered, both dressed in lavender uniforms. The boy spoke to White Coat. "Mrs. Wilde has some trouble communicating, but I've found she can handle nods and shakes."

Esther frowned. How dare that boy with his head full of braids refer to her as a simpleton. She opened her mouth to refute his claim. Grunts and nonsense followed. Esther gasped and covered her mouth. Then she cleared her throat and tried again. "Can com—comya—muna." She snapped her mouth shut, embarrassed.

Esther looked at the small bedside table, seeking her bracelet, her escape into comfort and solace. It wasn't there.

"Bra—Brace—brace," she stuttered. *This was humiliating.*

The young girl, who had been smoothing bed covers, straightened up. She tossed her long ponytail over one shoulder and joined the other two standing next to Esther.

Esther tried again. "Char—brace."

The three huddled over the screen-thingy again, looking between it and Esther.

"There's no mention of a brace here," Braided Boy said, his black braids swaying like wind chimes.

"Is her daughter-in-law's name Charlotte?" Ponytail guessed.

When White Coat shook her head, all three looked at Esther.

She felt their pity. *Don't you pity me!* Esther wanted to say. What came out was "Daw pi, daw pi—"

Ponytail patted Esther's legs, which were tucked under a white sheet and blanket. "Mrs. Wilde, we'll take good care of you. Soon, your daughter-in-law will arrive. We'll explain your condition to her and your treatment plan, too."

What condition?

What treatment plan?

What daughter-in-law?

Oh, where was her bracelet? She tried to ask again. Like last time, the words were jumbled. Ponytail, Braided Boy, and White Coat just stood there, staring at her.

Esther felt like a cartoon character clinging to the breaking branch. Helpless.

She shook her head and balled her hands. She hit the bed with her fists, furious to be trapped inside her failing mind. When Esther turned slightly to reach for someone and compel them to understand, pain shot up her leg. She shrieked.

White Coat addressed Ponytail. "I'm authorizing an increase in the pain meds, Indira. Let's get her on a drip." Then she tapped the screen of her mini television and placed a cover over it.

It reminded Esther of the Trapper Keeper organizer Junior used for school.

"I'll return when your daughter-in-law arrives, Mrs. Wilde," White Coat said. She addressed Braided Boy. "Follow me and let's get Mrs. Wilde some pain meds." She turned on her heel, footsteps clicking like the high-heeled sounds Esther remembered from the country club. Braided Boy trailed White Coat.

Ponytail remained. She reminded Esther of someone, but she didn't know who. She watched as the girl's hair swished. Thick, long, blonde hair. When Ponytail pushed some knobs and buttons on the bedrails, Esther could feel the bed move slowly and her back rise to a sitting position. Her leg ached. She heard music faintly. Ponytail hummed a jaunty, happy tune.

"Song?" Esther asked, hoping the word came out clearly and relieved when it did.

Ponytail stopped her fiddling and looked at her with surprise. "Oh, I got this song stuck in my head. I wasn't even aware I was humming it. It's called 'Rain on Me' by Ariana Grande and Lady Gaga. Ever heard of them? Great song about powering through trauma." Without waiting for Esther's response, the girl continued. "Maybe I should play it for you. The song might help you get through your recovery and rehabilitation. We women have to build each other up, am I right?"

Yes, this girl definitely reminded Esther of someone. And now she remembered: her independent-minded Tessa. A quality Esther spent too much time trying to suppress. Why didn't Esther urge Tessa to reach for her own dreams? Why had she never listened to Tessa's aspirations like Millie listened to Esther's so many years ago?

Esther snapped out of her musings when the blonde girl gently sat Esther forward to resettle the pillows behind her head. "Well, Mrs. Wilde, I gotta go check on some other patients. But I'll be back." She consulted a big, square watch on her wrist. "Romeo will be here shortly with your pain meds. Hang tight!" She sauntered out humming.

Romeo?

Esther laid her head back to rest. The next thing she knew, someone was gently shaking her shoulder, prodding her to wake up. Braided Boy. "Hey, Mrs. Wilde. You need to take these now. Doctor Brinley says it's important to stay on top of the pain, so it doesn't get unbearable. You avoided surgery for that hairline hip fracture, but you'll be uncomfortable a while. We're getting a drip in here shortly, so I won't have to wake you just to take medicine."

He shook his head disapprovingly. "Seems like waking them up only reminds patients they're in pain."

While he talked, he pulled over a table on wheels. It rested in front of Esther. On it sat a clear plastic cup of water. And Braided Boy offered her a little, white paper cup.

That Esther recognized. From somewhere. She swallowed the pills automatically, not really caring what they were. She laid her head back and closed her eyes.

Esther didn't know how long she lay there reliving childhood memories. *Swinging in the old tire. Retrieving pecans and peaches that fell from trees. Lying in the soft grass as clouds raced above.* Millie's face floated in front of her. Esther saw her smile. Oh, how that warmed her heart. Where was Millie now?

Voices drew Esther from her thoughts. She lifted her head to see a woman and a teenager nearing her bed. Both wore worried expressions—creased brows, downturned mouths. Bells of familiarity rang in Esther's head.

The women stopped at her bedside. The older one picked up Esther's hand. "Esther, it's Debra and Tessa. How are you?" The words were soft and laced with warmth.

Debra. Tessa. The ringing grew louder.

After a moment the woman added, "Junior's wife and daughter."

Esther's brain pinged with answers. She grasped Debra's wrist and asked, "Junior? Here?" She looked beyond them towards the door, hoping her son would enter.

Debra shook her head and bit her lip.

The young girl stepped forward.

Esther gasped. *Tessa!* She released her grip on Debra and extended her arm towards her beloved granddaughter.

Tessa held out her hand.

Esther clasped Tessa's hand in her own. Now was the time to share her revelations with Tessa. "Be. Dreams. Go," Esther croaked. Words in between vaporized without sound.

Tessa cocked her head and drew her brows in.

Esther cleared her throat. "Your life. No boys." She squeezed Tessa's hand.

Tessa tilted her head to the side. "Are you telling me not to date anyone?"

Esther had gotten the message across. She smiled and nodded as satisfaction coursed through her.

Tessa, however, didn't look so satisfied. She stepped back a little, but kept her hand tucked in Esther's. "Grandmother, you sure do confuse me. I thought that was all you ever wanted. For me to find a husband and have children." She shook her head at Esther, and Esther could feel her granddaughter's bewilderment in her voice. "I don't know what you want from me."

Esther's smile faded. How could she express that she wanted Tessa to pick her future, not to let a boy do it for her. She clasped her granddaughter's hand firmer. "No. No." Tessa simply had to understand.

Tessa untangled their hands. She paced.

Esther watched as Tessa inhaled and exhaled, the signs of someone gathering thoughts, energy, or courage. Tessa approached Esther's bed again. "You know," she said, "you can have both."

Esther knew it was impossible. Something had to give. A woman must either put her career aside to raise her children or never allow those dreams to materialize in the first place. Like Esther did. "Can't do," she said.

Tessa closed her eyes and clamped her lips together. After a moment, she said, "Women today can balance a family and a fulfilling career, too. It's a different world from when you were young. Times have changed, Grandmother."

Too many words. Esther couldn't follow them all, but she could read Tessa's eyes. They shone with excitement and anticipation. *Had Tessa met a boy?* Esther's heart raced. She didn't want Tessa to throw away her hopes or convince herself they were foolish dreams in the first place, all for the sake of a boy. Unless . . .

"Ricardo." Esther could only say the name of the one who might have shown her how to make the most of life. Could Tessa have met her own Ricardo?

Tessa's brows creased, and she turned to address Debra. "Who's Ricardo?"

When Debra shrugged, Tessa turned back to Esther. She seemed to hesitate, opening then closing her mouth. "I—I—might have met someone. And if he ever became my boyfriend, I'd never give up my career. I'd have both."

Esther heard Debra pipe in. "What?"

Tessa cut a quick glance to Debra and offered a half-smile. She leaned closer to Esther. When she did, her wrist banged against the bedrail, metal clanging against metal.

Esther saw something silver. A charm bracelet. She pointed to it and then her own empty wrist. "Brace—" she said.

Tessa looked at the bracelet. "This is the one you gave me, Grandmother." Tessa held up her wrist. "It has the graduation charm. From high school. Thank you for this. I understand why charms can be mementos of important events." Tessa added quietly, "I wish I knew what your charms represent, Grandmother."

Esther heard wistfulness in her granddaughter's voice. Esther's brain captured the word *charms*.

Where was her own bracelet?

Debra cocked her head. "I wonder if Esther wants hers." She addressed Esther. "Do you want your bracelet?" Debra asked.

Esther simply looked between the two of them. "Brace—" she repeated.

"I'll call Sunset Shadows and see about getting it." Debra left the room.

Esther pressed Tessa again. "No boy."

Tessa pulled a chair over and sat, leaning close. "Grandmother, I wish we could find common ground. I understand you came from a different world than me. I even sort of understand why you kept the knowledge about Lou Ann from me. I wish you could explain it, but I'm choosing to accept that I'll never know. But I'm going to make my own choices. And if I want to date Chip—" Tessa stopped talking. She sighed and gripped the bedrails with both hands. Her head was bowed.

Most of what Tessa said sounded foreign or nonsensical, but Esther caught a name. *Who's Chip?* She stared dumbly at Tessa, willing the words to come to her.

Tessa released the bedrails and stared silently at her lap, toying with her bracelet. "I'm sorry I never understood you," she whispered. "We might have more in common than I'd ever imagined."

Esther wanted to hug her granddaughter and start over. A do-over for that part of her life. But mostly, Esther wanted to speak. The mistakes she regretted and wanted to make amends for stayed locked in her head, an inaccessible vault.

Debra reentered and addressed Esther. "I reached Mayra. She's going to bring your bracelet over later today." Debra looked between the two of them. "Everything all right?"

Tessa looked up and blinked a few times, as if clearing her eyes.

Just then Ponytail walked in. "Hello, I'm Indira. Ms. Esther seemed to enjoy my singing earlier, so I thought I'd put some music on. Well, humming, not singing, but she seemed to like it." She picked up a small, black rectangular object and pointed it at the television in the corner. The one hanging on the wall. "Do you know what kind of music she likes?" She smiled at Debra and Tessa.

Esther saw the television screen light up. The picture showed landscapes. As Esther watched, the pretty landscapes changed. She saw a prairie, then a beach.

Ponytail continued to talk. "We've got a lot of music channels on this service. Country, Top 40, classical, hip-hop."

Esther didn't understand Ponytail's words, but she liked the cheerfulness she brought into the room. The air around her felt springy and fresh. Like Mother's sheets hanging in the May sunshine.

Tessa, meanwhile, had stood up from the chair and walked to the window, her back to Esther.

Esther heard Tessa sniffling and could see Tessa bring her hands to her face. Then she wiped her hands on her pants and turned to face them all.

Debra, meanwhile, stood quietly next to Esther's bedside, watching Tessa and biting her lower lip.

"Do you know my grandmother?" Tessa asked Ponytail.

"Not her specifically, just some understanding of Alzheimer's," Ponytail said as she fiddled with the black thing.

Esther didn't know that word. Alzee—? But she kept her mouth closed, fearful of what might come out if she tried to speak. She closed her eyes, trying to find comfort in the bed. But the sheets were stiff, the pillow scratchy, and the mattress crinkly. Being uncomfortable was exhausting.

Her eyes popped open when music filled the room. She lifted her head from the pillow. Andy William's smooth voice sang as *Love Story* scenes flashed in front of her. Esther opened her mouth and sang a few bars of the movie's theme alongside Mr. Williams. Her voice wavered and gravelly sounds escaped but they formed the lyrics she once loved. She could see the faces of Ali MacGraw and Ryan O'Neal. *Oliver taking Jenny's hand. Jenny lying in a bed dying.*

When the song ended Esther smiled, Debra and Tessa stared open-mouthed, and Ponytail grinned. "Easy listening it is," she exclaimed, putting the black thingy down. "Sometimes memories unlock words."

Esther traveled back to the times she watched movies with young Tessa. Specifically *Love Story*. She wanted to ask Tessa if she remembered the storyline. And tell her she was sorry. Unlike Jenny, Esther realized love *does* mean saying you're sorry. She tried, despite her fears, to speak. When only mixed-up pieces of thoughts came out, everyone looked at her with compassion. Or pity.

Esther turned away, tears leaking from her eyes. She was lost to that tight vault. The one that refused to give words to her tongue. And her leg hurt. If only she could wish the pain away. Wish herself away. How had life turned so upside down and inside out?

Sometime later she awoke. She was alone and her world was all wrong. Strangers surrounded her. She lay in a bed wracking her brain for recognition. Nothing came. A small window on a dingy blue wall gave her a view of a gloomy, gray sky outside. Outside of wherever she was.

A woman in white—a nurse?—clicked buttons on a machine next to the bed in which Esther lay. The woman manipulated tubes and a bag that hung by the floor.

The word *hospital* came to Esther. But why would she be in a hospital?

A boy hovered near the doorway. A boy with braids.

Esther fought panic. *Who were these strangers?* She blew out small breaths, willing herself to control her fear.

The woman in white smiled at Esther. "You're awake? I was just adjusting your pain meds drip. Can you give me a number between 1 and 10 to indicate your pain level?"

What was she going on about? Esther just stared.

"Sorry, Mrs. Wilde." The woman tapped her chin a few times. "Let me try again." Then she moved Esther's leg slightly.

Esther winced.

"I figured you had pain," the lady said knowingly.

Esther always had pain. In her leg. In her joints. In her heart.

The woman fiddled with a machine and bent over a tube that ran somewhere by the side of Esther's bed. Then she offered a quick smile and strode toward the door, leaving Esther even more confused and fearful.

The boy with the swinging braids approached. She calmed a bit in his smiling presence. Braided Boy carried a tray. "Hi, Mrs. Wilde. Time for dinner." He pulled over a brown table attached to a pole that could rest in front of Esther, all while balancing the pink tray with the covered dish on top. "I'm going to raise your bed a little," he said as he set the pink tray on the brown table.

Esther heard a soft drone and felt her back lift to a seated position. She tried to shift her weight forward, but pain coursed through her left leg. With a yelp, she laid her head back and cried.

"Oh, Mrs. Wilde. I'm sorry that hurt." The bed moved slowly, and Braided Boy supported her back. He propped pillows behind her. "Is that better?"

It was. Sort of. The unfamiliarity of Esther's world closed in on her. She wanted out. She wanted Art. She scratched at the bed covers and tried to stand. Pain again.

"Whoa, Mrs. Wilde. Slow down there." His baritone voice reminded her of Ricardo. Esther turned to the voice expecting a tuxedo-vested Puerto Rican. She saw instead the same boy with the braids. He lifted the pink lid.

Esther peered hopefully. Her bracelet? She was dismayed to find food. She wasn't hungry.

Before she could tell him that, a woman strode through the door. Esther felt the comfort of familiarity as the lady's face registered in Esther's mind. Not-Sally!

"Well, you took quite a fall, Ms. Esther," she said.

Esther didn't know what Not-Sally was talking about, but her voice was soothing.

"Hello. I'm Mayra from Sunset Shadows." Not-Sally addressed Braided Boy.

"Romeo," he said in reply, shaking her hand.

Not-Sally chuckled. "Is that right?" Laugh lines appeared around the corners of Not-Sally's eyes.

Oh, how Esther felt Not-Sally's warmth. It filled her, making her a little less frightened. She watched them talk, a chuckle here, a shake of the head there. Esther didn't understand what they said, but she sensed a camaraderie between them.

Not-Sally reached into a bag hanging on her shoulder and brought out Esther's bracelet.

Esther gave a shriek of delight and held out her hand. Once she had it, Esther clasped the memory-holder close to her heart. The world righted itself. She saw Not-Sally grin.

"I wish I could tap into your memories and find the ones that bring you such joy, Ms. Esther."

Braided Boy smiled at Not-Sally, as if the two shared a secret.

No matter that Esther was left out of that secret. Esther had the charms; they were all she needed. While Braided Boy and Not-Sally chatted, Esther grasped the petals of the Lotus flower charm. A purchase she had made on a whim after Art had died.

Junior had grieved for his father alone. He'd isolated himself in his room when he was home or spent God knows where with his teenage friends. She didn't want to nag him, but she'd been worried about him. And she was so lonely. Fighting despondency, Esther had meandered the aisles of a farmer's market one Saturday morning and spotted the beautiful flower charm. The petals seemed layered, almost holding each other up. Like a family should be. Instead, her already small family of three had shrunk to two.

When she'd bought the Lotus flower, she'd had high hopes that Junior would one day marry and rebuild their tiny family unit. If only she'd known . . .

•   •   •

Esther was fifty-five years old, and she was restless. She'd heard that Ricardo had moved away, and Junior had a new job and had just begun dating someone new. Thank God he'd dumped that Lou Ann girl. She was not of their kind. But Esther found herself alone. A lot.

One evening she sat in her living room chair watching television. She'd taken to having a cup of tea and watching a movie in the evenings. She'd found Grease on one of the television channels. And she needed the antics of Danny and Sandy to pull her out of her depressing funk.

Junior came through the door, head down, shoulders sagging. His normally relaxed face was full of worry and frown lines. It was much too hardened for a twenty-year-old young man.

"Dear, whatever is wrong?" Esther asked.

Junior didn't answer immediately. He plopped down on the sofa and ran his fingers through his wavy, brown hair.

Stretching his legs and leaning his head on the back of the couch, Junior reminded Esther so much of his father she had to stifle a gasp.

He sat up straighter and cleared his throat. "Lou Ann's pregnant, Ma."

She closed her eyes and felt the air leave her lungs. There was only one reason why Junior would tell her that.

"Yours?" she asked, unable to stop the disdain from slipping out.

When he nodded, Esther turned off the television. How ironic—Rizzo was singing about how there were worse things than being pregnant.

"Are you sure it's yours?" That girl had a reputation. Esther could imagine her finagling the best boy in town to be the father, whether it was true or not.

"Yeah. It is. She just didn't tell me for a while, but the kid will be born in a few more months." He inhaled deeply and pulled himself up straight. "I'm going to do the right thing, Ma. I'll marry her."

Esther snapped to attention. "You'll do no such thing, Arthur Junior." Her voice steeled with determination. He would not ruin his life with a marriage for the sake of legitimacy. For God's sake, it was not the 1950s. "Does she want to keep it?"

"Yeah," he admitted.

This threw off all Esther's plans. Junior was supposed to marry a nice girl and fill his home with children. Not get some floozy pregnant out of wedlock.

What's done is done, Essie. *Her mother's words rang through her head. Mother had always focused on moving forward and not pining for what was long gone.*

Junior could still find a nice girl. His girlfriend now—Debra—seemed lovely. That Lou Ann girl was a piece of work. Dressed provocatively when Esther saw her around town. It was only through gossip that she had even known Junior had been seeing her. He'd never brought her around. And now—good Lord. The girl would be entwined in Esther's life forever. Still. . . she had a grandchild coming!

Esther took a deep breath and pulled her shoulders back. "Tell that girl you'll help raise it. I'll help raise it."

Esther would do for her son what she didn't do for Millie—she'd support him and help him become a father. But Junior didn't need to be that girl's husband. She'd bleed him dry.

More gently she insisted, "We can do it together, son. No sense ruining the best years of your life with a loveless marriage."

Her son looked at her warily. "You don't want me to marry her?"

Oh, Lord no! she wanted to scream. But she didn't. Keeping her lips sealed was a smarter move.

Junior said, "Well, that's a surprise. And a relief," he added, slouching into the sofa. "I figured you'd be concerned with your reputation. And want me to marry her." To his credit, he looked ashamed and added, "I'm sorry."

She was disappointed and angry with his irresponsibility. And yes, she was embarrassed. They'd be talked about at the club, but . . . Esther would rather have an illegitimate grandchild than give Lou Ann her last name.

Junior scooted to the edge of the couch and leaned forward, putting his elbows on his knees. He addressed Esther with an impassioned promise. "I'm going to slow down on my drinking and be there for this guy . . . or girl."

Esther's hopes rose. The baby would bring stability to Junior's life. If he cut down or cut out the alcohol, Junior would be a stronger man. "We'll take care of that baby together." She walked over and gave Junior a hug.

Junior smiled and nodded, relief seeming to waft off him.

In spite of her disappointment in Junior, Esther felt a small thrill. Although a child was coming earlier than Esther had expected, she would pour her love into him or her.

She carried her teacup and saucer to the kitchen. At the kitchen sink, she looked out on the starry sky. Oh, how she hoped Lou Ann would prove pliable and amenable to Esther's good intentions.

Lou Ann was a tougher sell than Esther had thought. The girl demanded payment for her doctor's visits in order for Junior to get joint custody. But he agreed. Unfortunately, his partying habits didn't abate.

But since he was in for a big life change soon, Esther let it go. He needed a release. But once the baby was born Esther was sure he'd put away the flask.

As Lou Ann grew bigger, so did Esther's hopes and dreams for her unborn grandchild. Once they found out it was a girl, Esther decorated a baby room. She fantasized about a granddaughter with whom she'd share secrets, hobbies, and love. Esther could hardly wait.

After Tessa's birth, Lou Ann's behavior became even more reckless. Junior had a serious girlfriend in Debra, and he married her. She was a good stepmother to Tessa, and Esther hoped Lou Ann would give Tessa to them. Instead she demanded more money. Esther refused. When she heard Lou Ann had crashed her car and died, Esther was shocked. She knew the girl was reckless, but she didn't know she was a drug user. Esther felt badly for the girl who'd lost her life so violently, but she had to admit she was a little relieved that Lou Ann couldn't endanger sweet Tessa with her wild ways. And that she couldn't mess up Junior's life anymore. Debra was just what Junior needed—she was mature and grounded. Esther assumed Junior would stop drinking and they'd raise little Tessa together, with Esther's guidance and support. A perfect family.

•　　•　　•

Esther held the charm, sadness and regret filling her. The large family she'd wanted never blossomed. Not for herself and not for Junior. And more importantly, the plans she'd had for Tessa went awry. Instead of creating an unbreakable bond between them, Esther had built a crevice. Pushing her own agenda onto Tessa had backfired. Instead of taking Tessa's dreams and helping her realize them, she'd ignored them. And worse, she'd tried to force her beloved granddaughter on Esther's life track. She moaned with the reality of regret. It might be too late to right those wrongs.

CHAPTER TWENTY-SEVEN

Tessa

When they left the hospital, her mom seized on Chip's name. "I thought there was nothing there," she said.

Tessa heard the hurt in her voice. "*Maybe* there's something growing between Chip and me. Or maybe it's a crush. Either way, I'm not getting involved with someone. I just wanted Grandmother to know that *if* I wanted to, I would. But I wouldn't give up my dreams just for a guy."

Her mom looked over at her, puzzled. "Why not date Chip? He seemed like a nice guy."

"I need to concentrate on my future," she insisted.

"What does your future have to do with dating—or not dating?"

Tessa stared over while her mom focused on the road in front of them. "Mom. I need to think about my career. Focus on getting my degree and finding a job. A boyfriend would interfere with that."

"How?" her mother's voice sounded genuinely incredulous.

Tessa smacked her thigh. "Because it would be a distraction. A possible loss of independence. I'm not changing my life for a guy. Not like Grandmother did." She crossed her arms.

"Your stubbornness and narrow-mindedness remind me of someone we just saw," her mom said.

Tessa's jaw dropped. "I'm not narrow-minded!"

"Well, you won't acknowledge that life is a series of balancing acts. And if you want to have a career, you don't have to tip the scales away from a relationship, too. There's room in anyone's life for both." She said softly, "The expectations for women were different in Esther's times. She had no one in her life who had balanced the scales. Therefore, she'd assumed she had to either follow the wife track or be alone."

"You're one to talk," Tessa shot back. "You didn't become a designer until I was almost done with high school. You sacrificed what you wanted because a husband and child got in the way."

Her mom pulled into the parking lot of school and parked. She cut off the engine. "I didn't sacrifice anything. I had no ambition to be a home designer when you were little. I only wanted to raise you, spend time with you, and provide for you." She turned in her seat to Tessa. "You can't dictate what comes around the bend on life's journey. And if you want to be an art restorer, having a boyfriend will only interfere if YOU let it." She shook her head. "Love doesn't have to be an either/or choice."

Before Tessa could argue or ask questions or consider her mom's words, her phone rang.

"Hey, Chip." She turned toward the window as her mom fiddled to open the car door, probably to give Tessa some privacy.

"Did you make it back? Are you at campus or the hospital?" he asked.

Tessa could feel her mother's intentional nonchalance as she waited outside the car.

"We just left the hospital and are back at school."

"How's your grandmother?"

"She seems okay. She broke her hip, but they aren't doing surgery."

"Do you and your mom want to come here for dinner tomorrow?"

Tessa's heart began the dance of infatuation she'd come to associate with him. Even through the phone. She tried to sound neutral and friendly. Emotionally cool. "Sounds great. Let me check with my mom."

Tessa got out of the car and relayed Chip's invitation.

Her mother smiled but shook her head. "Tell Chip thank you, but I'll go home tomorrow morning since Esther seems stable. If I need to return later in the week, I will."

Tessa nodded. She tried to keep her voice light and casual even as her pulse raced. "Mom is leaving later." She took a breath of courage. "I'm free, if that works."

"Absolutely," he said. "Looking forward to it."

A polite statement or a real expression of emotion? "What can I bring?" she asked.

Chip told her he had dinner covered and that he'd text her his address. They disconnected. Tessa peeked over at her mom to see a smile growing on her face.

"He's just being nice," Tessa insisted as they walked into her dorm.

"Sure," her mother said, but her smile said something different.

That night, Tessa lay awake. She'd given her mother her bed and lay on the floor in a sleeping bag. Her grandmother's words played through her mind. *No boy.* What happened to landing a boyfriend, the mission she'd always set in front of Tessa? What was Grandmother trying to say now?

Tessa groaned and put a pillow over her head. And who was Ricardo? A boy Grandmother wanted to introduce to Tessa? Or was it a slip into an old memory—someone her grandmother secretly loved. Possible, but not probable. Grandmother was nothing if not consistent with her advice that Tessa find a boy like her grandfather, Art Wilde.

Tessa bunched and punched the pillow, silently commanding it to inspire sleep. Perhaps she'd solve the puzzle in a dream. *Dream.* There was another word Grandmother used. And when she said *Go* after *Dream*, Tessa got the impression her grandmother wanted her to live her own dreams. But that would mean a 180 degree turn in attitude. Grandmother had never encouraged Tessa to be independent or follow her heart.

She stifled her frustration. Even riddled with Alzheimer's, Grandmother still exasperated Tessa.

•   •   •

The next evening Tessa stared at her little closet again. She had a . . . something . . . with Chip. She couldn't call it a date because it felt like a mercy dinner. Offering her food because she was unexpectedly back at school. But she chose her outfit carefully—white jeans and a black tee shirt imprinted with the name of one of her favorite bands. She added a denim jacket and grabbed her retro canvas bag with the John Lennon glasses stitched on it. She maneuvered the hair straightener to form the big waves Kendra had managed. That was all of Kendra she channeled. This was Tessa's night to succeed or fail on her own.

With a quick look in her full-length mirror, she took note of her empty wrist. Instinctively, Tessa reached for her multitude of silver bracelets. She hesitated, sliding her eyes to the charm bracelet that lay on her dresser. If this bracelet was all about keeping track of memories, like Grandmother had said, Tessa hoped to make some good ones tonight. Before her mom left this afternoon, she reiterated to Tessa not to turn away from love. Or whatever this was between her and Chip. And reminded her that life could be short, and she had to follow her heart, not just her dreams for her future.

She clasped the bracelet to her wrist. It dangled, heavier than what she usually chose. But it was growing on her.

Chip's apartment complex was about a fifteen-minute drive, and she pulled into the lot. A sandpaper-colored, cement exterior gave the building little appeal and no character. Her mom would hate it. Tessa leaned over to the passenger seat and retrieved a big bag. In it, she had the plain box containing the stereoscope. She'd also brought a container of chocolate chip cookies. She walked towards the building, her canvas bag on one shoulder, the bag of goodies hanging from the other. It was early evening, but the sun was already almost gone. The sky lit up with muted shades of purple and rose, sprinkled with a few early stars.

On the outside wall was a plexiglass box advertising collegiate events—concerts, exhibitions, and plays. Above it was an intercom with a list of apartment numbers and call buttons next to each. The building held sixteen apartments, pretty small for college standards. But it was an old building. And it was known for housing recent grads and graduate students. Tessa pushed the button for Apartment 303 and waited.

Chip's voice floated through the box with a jaunty welcome. "Hark, who goes there through yonder . . . um . . . intercom?"

Tessa groaned. Shakespeare never sounded so bad. "Sorry, not Juliet," she answered. "And I think you made Will roll over in his grave," she added.

She could practically hear Chip's grin as well as the buzz that opened the building door and granted her entry. She waited for the elevator, using deep breaths to steady her nerves. Once it arrived, it moved slowly to the third floor, creaking and groaning like this was its last ride. Her jumpy nerves urged it to move faster.

Chip opened his apartment door before she even rang the bell. "Hi. I promise not to terrorize you with more Shakespeare." He grinned and opened the door wider for her to enter. Standing in perfectly pressed khakis with a black collared shirt and loafers, he was stunning. His hair was secured in a ponytail and a musky, woodsy cologne wafted off him.

She suddenly understood the meaning of "swoon."

"More like 'butchered' Shakespeare me thinks," she joked, trying to regain some balance.

His apartment met Tessa's expectations—minimalistic with only a few pieces of furniture. Second-hand but tasteful, the simple pieces fit the small space. Pictures of Florida's nature preserves and unpopulated coastlines filled the room. Tessa could almost hear the palm fronds rustle and the seagulls squawk.

She put both bags on the living room coffee table. As Chip wandered into the kitchen, she reached in and retrieved the tub of cookies.

"I brought dessert," she said, setting them on the bar that separated the tiny galley kitchen from the dining area. "Homemade chocolate chip cookies if you count slicing and baking as 'homemade.'"

"Slice-and-bake are my favorite. And I hope you like fajitas," Chip added as he stood at the stove.

Tessa pulled out a bar stool, sat down, and peered over the counter. Onions and peppers, cut and mixed, lay in a shallow bowl next to the stovetop. Thin slices of chicken marinated in a separate bowl. Several soft tortillas were lined up on a baking sheet.

"One of the few dishes I excel at," he said as he tossed the vegetables into a frying pan. He put the flavored chicken pieces in a second pan. A sizzle hit the air. A steaming pot of rice sat next to it all and black beans simmered nearby.

"Fajitas with rice and black beans," he announced. Rubber scraper in his hand, he pointed to her cookies. "Those will make the perfect dessert," he grinned. His smile caused all kinds of aerobics in her stomach.

For a few moments neither spoke as Chip tended to his dinner and she inhaled the smell of spices and citrus. Her mouth watered. Then she found her manners and jumped from her stool. "What can I do?"

Following his directions, she poured salsa into a bowl, grated cheese into another, and found the sour cream in the refrigerator. She carried everything to the table as Chip placed tortillas in an oven and scooped the spicy-smelling vegetables and citrusy chicken into a large bowl.

"Pitcher of iced tea in the fridge," he called over his shoulder as he bent down to retrieve the warm tortillas.

She moved in tandem with Chip's actions, opening the refrigerator door, squeezing past him, and bringing drinks to the table. There was an air of ease between them.

Once the food was out, Tessa took a seat. Chip brought a candle over, placed it in the middle of the table, and lit it. Her heart skipped.

"The chicken makes the apartment smell like Mexican. A candle helps with the odor." He placed the lighter to the side and sat down.

A wave of disappointment rushed over Tessa, her romantic notions squashed, but before she could respond, Chip added, "And I think it's a nice ambiance for tonight."

Not so squashed then.

Tessa bit into her fajita, pleased with the blending of flavors. Chip was right. He was a great fajita maker. She told him so.

"Thanks, I'm not good at a lot of dishes, but this one I got down."

He grinned and Tessa's heart melted a little. "What do you want to do with your photography?" she asked, hoping to generate conversation to mask her attraction.

Between bites, he explained his plans. "I really want to travel and photograph nature. Some of my dream spots are the Amazon River and the Galapagos Islands."

Tessa listened intently, loving his passion as he shared his dreams. Her plans weren't as specific, but she still shared them. "I hope that one day I can unearth artifacts and antiques and restore their beauty. There's nothing like seeing an old, rusty canister shine with polish to take its rightful place in someone's hutch or buffet table."

Before she knew it, they'd finished dinner. "Do you have time to hang out?" Chip asked when they'd cleaned all the dishes.

"Sure," she answered with nonchalance that belied her quivering heart.

Chip took the cookies into the living room and put them on the coffee table, moving the bag containing the stereoscope aside. Tessa picked it up and sat on the couch with it on her lap.

"I almost forgot." She felt the heat creep into her face and fumbled for the words to explain this gift. She took out the box, placing the bag on the table. "This is for you."

Chip sat next to her. He opened the box and took out the stereoscope. "Wow, thank you. But why?"

"Do you know what that is?" Tessa asked, avoiding the question.

"I do. A stereoscope. I learned about them in one of my first photography classes. But how do *you* know about them?"

Tessa explained the game she and her mom had played at flea markets. She skipped the part about it being her idea to find an old camera on their last one. She fudged a little, saying that what the vendor told them made her think of Chip.

He grinned, a smile spreading from his mouth to his eyes. "Thank you. This is really thoughtful."

Tessa's heart filled. "Oh—and there're slides in there, too." She pointed to the gift bag and then tucked her hands under her legs, feeling a little shy about his gratitude. "I wanted to thank you for all your help with the website."

"It's my pleasure," he said as his eyes sought hers.

Did she imagine the flash of desire?

"Here, let's try one," he said. The moment had passed.

He placed a slide in the holder at the end of the instrument and scooted closer to her. Their shoulders touched, and Tessa felt electricity spark between them. Chip offered her the stereoscope, and she willed her hands to remain steady. She peered through the lenses. The picture featured a couple looking in the distance. One of the man's hands rested on the woman's shoulder, his other pointing to a faraway spot. The woman leaned into him as she looked where he gestured. The tall grasses seemed to sway at their ankles, and the picture felt so alive Tessa could sense the breeze and almost see the woman's skirt billow in the wind. Self-conscious of both the couple in the picture's tenderness and Chip's proximity, she handed the stereoscope over wordlessly.

As he looked through it, Tessa became aware of their thighs touching, her body tingling. She thought about moving to add space between their legs and ease the emotional dizziness. But she didn't.

Chip said casually, "Looks like a happy couple, huh?"

"Mm-hmm," Tessa answered, not trusting herself with actual words.

Chip put down the stereoscope and turned towards her. "Thank you again, really." He extended his arms to give her a hug.

She leaned into them and breathed in the scent of springtime rain. Even his shampoo was nature fresh. As he released his hold, he lingered.

Chip's eyes sought hers, and before she knew it, he tilted his head and kissed her.

His soft lips captured her heart. His arms encircled her, bringing her closer. Her scalp tingled. Butterflies fluttered wildly in her stomach. It felt like magic.

Chip pulled away slowly but held her in his gaze, searing her heart. "Did I violate a graduate student/undergraduate rule or anything?"

Tessa swallowed, finding her breath. "I think that's only for professors. And if there is such a rule, we'll just ignore it." This time she leaned in. If kisses could set off sparks, there'd be a four-alarm fire raging. Some things *were* just as good as the first time.

Tessa broke away reluctantly. Chip sank into the couch cushion, holding her hand in his. He leaned his head back and exhaled. "Wow. Tessa, you're—" He brought his head up and searched her eyes. "a very unique person," he finished. "I haven't met someone like you in a long, long time."

Was that a good thing?

Then he sat up, still holding her hand, and turned to her. "Would you be interested in going to the Ocala National Forest with me tomorrow? I need some photos for a contest I'm entering. I'll take you kayaking," he offered.

As if Tessa needed convincing.

"That sounds fantastic. I've only been to Crystal River springs, never to the forest," she admitted, trying to focus on words, not the tingling sensation her lips still held.

Chip cleared his throat. She hoped he needed to shake the sensation, too.

"Great. Leave it to me. I'll pack us lunch. Come over about 9 am. We'll leave your car in the parking lot and take my truck."

Was that a date?

She nodded again, unable to trust her voice. The kiss took their friendship to a new level.

Chip let go of her hand and grabbed the cookies, offering her one. The sugary middle and rich chocolate topped a perfect night.

"Do you want to work on your website?"

"I do," she said. Tessa moved the stereoscope off the coffee table as Chip brought over his laptop. For the next hour, they worked. The camaraderie between them settled any nerves Tessa might have had at the start of the evening, and any lingering awkwardness of the kiss. Kisses.

The Art of Words was becoming real. A business to help artists capture the beauty of their visuals with words. This might be just the right niche for Tessa to break into the art world. And she would start with Chip's photos first. Their relationship felt comfortable now. He'd bump her shoulder and joke about something on the screen. They'd lean towards the laptop, faces practically touching at times. When they'd worked through the minutiae of setting up the site, he turned to her. "You're good to go. We can make it 'live' right now." He raised his eyebrows for her approval.

Was she ready to make this website active? Her knee-jerk reaction was to put the brakes on, wait for . . . anything . . . and delay action. But Tessa needed to act. Be the lead singer instead of harmonizing in the background. "Let's do it."

Once he set the wheels in motion, they grinned at each other like schoolkids embarking on an adventure.

This had been a perfect night. Tessa was in business. More importantly, Chip seemed to reciprocate her feelings. Possibilities filled her heart with joy. They had a . . . date. She'd call it that. Enough tiptoeing around.

CHAPTER TWENTY-EIGHT

Esther

Esther felt itchy. Not physically. She wanted to get out of the bed in that strange room and return home to Junior. He hadn't visited yet and she didn't know why.

Names flashed in her head. Junior. Tessa. Art. Mother. Daddy. The words toggled back and forth, and she struggled to hold on to any of them. Images of Tessa floated in front of her. An older, teenage girl with lovely blonde hair standing next to her. A bracelet that matched Esther's own. It could have been a dream.

Esther eyed a plate of food sitting on a metal tray. Untouched. She had no appetite. Not for food and not for life. She'd lived all she'd needed to at that point. She was ready to go.

"Good morning, Mrs. Wilde," a bubbly blonde said, sauntering over to her. "Today we are going to try a shower. I know I always feel grungy after a couple of days without one, and you've been here for three days." Bubbly Blonde began to hum.

Been where? It was happening more and more. Esther couldn't follow conversations, sentences, or phrases. But she followed the girl's humming. A Carole King song. Esther closed her eyes, traveling backwards. "You're So Far Away" spoke to Esther. She missed Art. And where was Junior? She had a fleeting image of a funeral. Junior in a casket. No, that couldn't be right! She must be hallucinating. Or dreaming. But she was awake.

And the heartache felt real. It grew more pronounced. Pressing into her until she found it hard to breathe. Crushing her lungs until Esther gasped.

Tessa's face flashed before her again. An eager three-year-old. A cautious ten-year-old. A dismissive fourteen-year-old. A flippant seventeen-year-old.

Esther drew in deep breaths, but her lungs had holes in them. The air left her as soon as she inhaled. Pinpricks of black clouded her vision, but she saw a person standing at the end of her bed. Art gazed at her with a half-smile on his face.

"Art!" she called.

He didn't respond; he just observed her lovingly.

Hadn't she spoken aloud?

Esther strained to get the words out, her mouth unmoving but her mind racing with words that needed speaking. *I loved you. You were the perfect partner; you stood by my side. At awkward dinners you covered my silence. I'd retreat to my thoughts; you'd draw me out. You loved me more than I loved myself.*

What she heard were pieces of words, garbled, nonsensical, childish sounds of effort. Tears leaked out, gaining speed until they were rivulets covering her face.

Art's body began to vaporize from the edges, shrinking within itself.

"Wait!" she called out. She couldn't hear her own voice.

Art's eyes locked on hers, his smile strong and steady, but he remained silent. The edges of his body faded inward until he became shapeless. He seemed to blend into the air, fading away even as Esther squinted to keep him in sight.

"Stop, stop!" she yelled.

Were the words only in her mind?

She longed to reach out, grab his hand, and follow him. But she couldn't move. Her muscles felt glued down, her body tethered in place.

"Take me," she whispered.

Art's eyes were the last to disappear, full of compassion and love.

All of him evaporated and she was left staring at nothingness.

Esther was suffocating. Cinder blocks on her chest pressed her into the bed. When she inhaled, sharp pain radiated from her chest down her arm.

The humming girl bustled around her, not humming anymore. She was a blur of blonde as she leaned over Esther and wiped Esther's cheeks with a tissue. "I know it hurts, Mrs. Wilde. A doctor is coming right now. Hang on."

So the tears were real. Art must have been, too. Why did he leave her again? Why didn't anyone stop him?

The door burst open, and several white-coated people rushed in. Someone shined a flashlight in her eyes, another lifted her arm and attached a soft vise. Still another fiddled with the bed. The next thing Esther knew, she was moving, still in bed, out the door and into a brightly lit hallway. She turned her head, searching for Art. Only strangers with concerned expressions looked back. The pressure in her chest was intense. Esther wanted to succumb to the pain and join Art.

Where was he?

She silently pleaded for him to take her home and finish the life they'd started so long ago. The air stirred as Esther was whisked through some doors. Stark white walls and bright lights surrounded her. Maybe this was Heaven's waiting room.

Someone placed a large, clear mask over her face. Esther closed her eyes. She was ready.

CHAPTER TWENTY-NINE

Tessa

Chip lifted his paddle and cut through the calm waters of the Ocala National Forest, making the kayak move smoothly onward.

Tessa watched from behind in her own kayak, attempting to mimic his style. She managed to drip water on her shorts and imitate a paddlewheel moving through molasses.

She concentrated on her strokes but still struggled. In her kayak, she carried a waterproof bag with her cellphone and paper products for their picnic. Chip's kayak carried a similar bag with his camera and his own cell phone. And lunch in an insulated cooler. The thought of picnicking somewhere in this beautiful place with Chip encouraged her to keep paddling, uncoordinated and jerky as it was.

"Lift your oar and place the blade in the water about halfway the length of the paddle itself. Don't stab the water; cut it like you're parting the Red Sea," Chip instructed as he glanced back to see her floundering.

"Sure, I'm Moses," she muttered. Still, she tried. And still she splashed herself. She was several kayak lengths behind him. With all this effort, Tessa wasn't enjoying the peaceful scenery Chip loved. But she did appreciate it. Thick shrubs on either side of them created a canal-type path that they followed. Palmetto and palm fronds provided a mini canopy, and the dense, live oaks gave a lagoon effect. Tessa felt like she was in the rainforest coves she'd only read about. She stopped paddling and inhaled, smelling the slight musk of mangroves, a hint of salt, and damp leaves. Her whole being relaxed. She searched for otters that were supposed to frolic along the shoreline, but she didn't see any. She did, however, see lots of Florida scrub jays. Along with hawks. Egrets and herons lined the shores, seemingly oblivious when she drifted by. They looked at her lazily, lifting one leg then the other casually to move on, as if Tessa were part of their scenery.

"Going to pull up there," Chip called over his shoulder and pointing with his oar towards a sandy island.

"Okay." Tessa set her paddle back in the water and concentrated on Chip's last set of instructions. Soon, she was gliding instead of lurching through the shallow water.

Now, I get the appeal of kayaking.

Pulling her kayak alongside Chip's, she climbed out and set her feet on the shore, relieved to be out of that small boat and onto shady, firm ground.

Chip began to unpack their lunch on the picnic bench. Tessa didn't realize how hungry she was until she saw the thick sandwiches on the tabletop. Turkey lined with Swiss cheese, crunchy lettuce, and ripe, red tomatoes made her mouth water. She dug in, not caring if she appeared ravenous.

"Once we finish eating, we can paddle through some of my favorite spots for photos. "We'll probably see some gopher tortoises," Chip said between bites. "Maybe some otters if we're really lucky. Capturing them in their natural habitat makes the best photos."

"Sounds great," Tessa said. She loved hearing Chip talk about photography. His eyes lit up with excitement.

After they'd eaten, she pulled out her own waterproof bag and peeked at her phone for the first time. She had nowhere to be and no one demanding her time, but she planned to see Grandmother before visiting hours ended.

Tessa gasped when she saw seven missed calls from her mom. "Chip, I have to call my mom back," she said, tamping down panic. "She's never called me seven times before. Something must be wrong." Her mind conjured up the worst-case scenario.

Chip was gathering their trash into a plastic bag. He stopped and looked at her with caution. "Oh geez, I really hope you have service here." He glanced around their desolate spot.

She checked her bars. No service.

Tessa jumped up from the bench. "I need to go. It might be about my grandmother. You get those pictures you want. I'll head back and return my kayak—" she stopped mid-sentence.

They had ridden together in his truck; how would she get to the hospital, if there was an emergency with Grandmother? *Think, Tessa, think*. She could call Uber.

"Tessa." Chip broke through her thoughts. "We'll go together." He placed their belongings in the kayaks.

"No, you stay here," she insisted as she checked her phone one last time. Still no service. "What if I'm making a big deal out of nothing?" She hated to think she'd ruin this day for him for nothing. She walked to her kayak still insistent. "I'll go alone." She was certain she'd have a phone signal back at the kayak rental office.

Chip ignored her offer, stepping into his kayak.

"Honestly, Chip. I'd feel terrible if this were a false alarm." And guilty and foolish.

He furrowed his brows and said gently, "Let me ask you this, Tessa. How do you get to the kayak rental spot?"

Tessa looked in the distance hoping to see it. She saw nothing but canals and mangroves and scrub brush.

When she couldn't answer, Chip raised his eyebrows. "Do you really think I'd let you kayak by yourself, alone and unguided? What kind of a guy do you think I am?"

"A good one, but what if I'm overreacting?"

"And what if you're not. We have to find out. The Ocala National Forest will be here another day." His arms swept the area, encompassing all the beauty before them. "Besides, I want to be with *you*, not my camera." He sat down and raised his paddle to push off.

Tessa felt the heat rise to her cheeks. Despite her fears about the missed calls, her mind focused on Chip's words. He wanted to be with her. "Thank you," was all she could say. Then she climbed in the kayak before he could see her feelings all over her face.

The route back didn't look at all familiar. "Are you sure this is the way?" she called up to him. "Nothing looks the same."

"Remember, you're approaching it from another angle," he said, over his shoulder. "Your perspective is different each way. This is right. I promise," he added.

She concentrated on her strokes, coasting this time, gliding through the water like a seasoned kayaker. A quick learner. She would've patted herself on the back if she dared to stop concentrating. As they rounded a marshy inlet, Tessa spotted the aluminum roof of the rental building. And more kayakers. Chip was right. Without his help, she wouldn't have found it this quickly. Or maybe even at all.

Chip called out to the attendant as they pulled onto shore. "Sorry, man. We're in a hurry. My girlfriend has a family emergency. Can we just leave these here?"

Girlfriend?

Tessa jerked her head Chip's way, but he was pulling their kayaks to higher ground.

She tucked the word inside her heart.

Chip handed off their kayaks, fished his keys from the backpack, and they hurried to the parking lot. Once they were on the road, Tessa called her mother.

"Tessa, I'm so glad you called."

Tessa could hear relief in her mother's shaky voice. "Mom, what's going on?"

"I'm driving to the hospital. Honey, your grandmother had a heart attack. She's alive but the doctors said her heart isn't strong. She's in and out of consciousness." The words came out in a rush.

Tessa put her hand up to her mouth. She knew Grandmother might die, would die eventually, but Tessa wasn't ready. She didn't want her grandmother to die with contention hanging between them. It was time to forgive. For herself.

"I'm with Chip. We were kayaking and I didn't get any of your calls. I'll get my car and head over to the hospital as soon as I can."

"Save the minutes it will take to get your car," Chip said to her. Then more loudly, so that her mother could hear he added, "I'll drive her, Ms. Wilde. We're not that far."

"Please thank Chip for me. I'm about an hour away. I'll see you there, honey."

They both hung up and Tessa filled Chip in.

He listened without comment and gave her hand a quick squeeze.

Tessa never imagined she'd feel this distraught about Grandmother's death. *If* she died. But things had changed between them. She understood Grandmother had lived through different times and circumstances. The lens with which her grandmother saw Tessa's life was distorted by her own experiences. If Grandmother made a full recovery, Tessa vowed to spend time unraveling the experiences that had sculpted Esther Wilde. And share her own life-shaping experiences. And she wanted to tell her about Chip.

Chip must have sensed her need for quiet time because he drove silently, occasionally glancing her way. "Tessa, I can drop you off," he said as they pulled into the hospital parking lot, "—and park the car. I'll wait for you in the main lobby."

No more waiting anywhere. "Why don't you come up? I'd like to introduce you. That is, if Grandmother is allowed visitors."

Chip nodded. "I'd like to meet her, Tessa."

After they parked, Tessa checked at the main desk. Grandmother was stable but weak. And she was allowed visitors, a two-person maximum, and family only. Chip quickly became a cousin.

In the elevator, Chip transferred his backpack from one shoulder to the other. "It's a habit to bring my photography stuff." He looked sheepish and embarrassed.

She put her hand on his arm. "Don't be embarrassed for being yourself." Tessa believed that with all her heart. If she got the opportunity, she'd tell that to Grandmother, too.

The elevator doors opened, and Tessa took a deep breath. She paused to take out the charm bracelet she'd stuffed in an interior pocket of her backpack the other day. She clasped it on and hoped it would temper Grandmother's reaction to meeting her. . . boyfriend.

CHAPTER THIRTY

Esther

Esther opened her eyes. Art's name rested on her heart. She turned her head from side to side, but he wasn't there. She lifted her head from the pillow. It was so heavy that she plopped it back down.

"Mrs. Wilde." A man in a white coat approached her bedside. "I'm Doctor Henderson. You're probably feeling tired and weak. That's normal."

Gobbledygook was what Esther heard. The strange man's coal black eyes reminded Esther of Ricardo. The soothing tone of his words sounded like Art. She closed her eyes and Ricardo became Art, then Art became Ricardo. A blended vision.

"Mrs. Wilde. Mrs. Wilde." Ricardo/Art called to her. "Can you open your eyes, please?"

A cool touch on her hand made her jump. When she opened her eyes, the man smiled. With a skinny flashlight in one hand, he shined it on her face.

Esther wanted to swat his hand away, but she had not the strength or motivation. Exhaustion overtook her and she felt her eyes close as if the Sandman himself shuttered them. Snippets of her life made up a movie reel that she watched from afar. Twelve-year-old Essie sitting attentively in the classroom, learning about history, and planning her future travels. Seventeen-year-old Essie watching life's complicated events change those plans.

Journalism aspirations evaporated. Esther watched as they literally drifted away, like a cloud moving on the horizon.

Esther felt a pang in her heart. A jab. Not strong enough to make her cry out but it left an ache that seemed to press relentlessly. As if someone had placed a set of encyclopedias on her chest.

The movie reel continued. Essie waddling around the house, eight months pregnant, restless, anxious to make an impact as a mother if not a journalist.

And then Essie became Esther, hardened against the bitterness of unfulfilled dreams, her husband gone and her son floundering.

Compression, like a cuff squeezing her chest, took her breath away. Pain shot down her arm. She gasped, inhaling as much oxygen as she could. None seemed to reach her lungs. As the pain intensified, someone placed a bite-sized piece of chalk in her mouth which melted, leaving the bitter taste of aspirin behind. Within a few moments, some of the chest pressure eased and Esther's breathing regulated.

As she relaxed, her life movie resumed. Adult Esther saw herself alone—Art was gone; Junior was gone; Tessa was never around. Esther only had Sally, a housekeeper-turned-friend.

You have time to fix what can be fixed.

It sounded like Art. Whispering from above her.

Esther's eyes flew open, and she expected Art to hover over her bedside. He wasn't there but bright lights were, making her squint. She put her hands over her eyes. All she wanted was to go back to her movie. Go back to Art's voice.

Instead of his soothing, rich voice, another one rang out. A voice tinged with fear and urging. *Tessa.*

Turning her head towards the sound, Esther saw her beloved Tessa. Her heart reacted, fluttering and thumping unevenly. She ignored it. Esther extended her arm toward Tessa. "Tessa," she whispered. A raspy, rattling sound that formed in her heart, moved through her lungs, and exited her mouth.

Tears pooled in her granddaughter's eyes. And something Esther recognized from so many years ago. Love.

Tessa grasped Esther's hand, entwining their fingers.

Esther struggled with words, her mouth unable to form all she wanted to say. She tried to declare her love through her eyes.

Tessa spoke, but Esther couldn't understand the words. They were only syllables and sounds, nothing definitive, nothing recognizable. Still, just being in her granddaughter's presence made Esther feel at peace.

With her free hand, Esther covered their entwined ones and squeezed. A gesture of apology and acceptance.

Movement behind her granddaughter caught Esther's attention. As she looked past Tessa, she saw a boy—man—a young man. He stood in the background respectfully but was completely focused on her granddaughter.

Esther scrutinized him. *A little older than Tessa.* He wore shorts and a tee shirt with a backpack slung over his shoulder. Some kind of sandal adorned his feet. And his hair! Good heavens, it was pulled back in a ponytail! Like a girl. But he was a quiet and unobtrusive presence. Who was he and why was he here? She took one hand off hers and Tessa's linked ones and pointed.

Tessa turned toward the boy. Then she untangled hers and Esther's fingers and gripped the bed rail. She said something that caused the boy to come over.

"Grandmother, this is Chip. He's—" Tessa paused.

Esther saw Tessa bite her lip in thought and tap her fingers on the bed rails. "My boyfriend," she added.

Although Esther missed a lot of words, she heard that one. Boyfriend? *NO!* she wanted to shout. *Live your life. Don't abandon your dreams like I did.* Esther wanted to tell Tessa to be herself, make her mark in this world, and choose her path. When she spoke, though, only random sounds and puzzle pieces of words escaped. Like she placed her thoughts in a blender, mixed them together, and poured them out.

"No—boy—dre—life—dre—." She scowled at the young man.

But neither one cowered from Esther's hard stare.

In fact, Tessa linked an arm through the young man's. In union. Solidarity. And she picked up Esther's hand again, clasping it to hers. Chip connected on one side, Esther on the other.

"Grandmother, Chip is a good person." Tessa looked at the boy and smiled. Then she turned back to Esther. "He might be like Grandfather, I don't know, but he's good for me."

Esther saw Tessa's mouth move and knew she continued to speak, but there were gaps. Some of Tessa's words pierced Esther's brain, others sounded like radio static. But there was no denying the smile when Tessa looked at that boy. Or the light in her eyes. As for the boy, he grinned as she talked.

"I know you want the best for me even though we disagree on what that is. I have dreams I want to go after."

Esther couldn't follow all the words, but she understood the urgency in Tessa's voice.

The pain in Esther's chest returned. A nagging sensation like the time she had spicy chili and ate Tums for an hour.

Then she spied the silver charm bracelet on Tessa's arm. The arm linked with the boy's. Her heart leaped inside her chest as if desperate to escape. But it also filled with joy. The bracelet was Tessa's link to Esther.

Satisfaction and peace surrounded her like a long-lost friend.

Tessa had stopped talking. She disengaged from the boy and held up her wrist, showing Esther the charm bracelet. "Just like yours, Grandmother. I think I know why you love your charm bracelet so much."

Tessa unclasped their hands and walked around Esther's bed to the side table. She returned with Esther's beloved charm bracelet in her hand.

Holding it up, she said, "I get how this can be a memory keeper, a way of reminiscing over the important events of your life. I'm going to do the same." Then she placed it in Esther's hand. "I wish you could tell me what each one of these charms means. I wish I knew more about your life, Grandmother."

Esther saw tears shine in Tessa's eyes as her granddaughter said, "The past has passed, Grandmother. I hope you can accept that I'm going to take my own path regardless of your approval. And I do love you."

Esther understood the tone of her granddaughter's words—steely with determination. And she heard "love you." Her heart warmed a thousand degrees, burning with love.

Esther clutched her bracelet. Like a child's security object, the charm bracelet had pacified her on lonely days and lifted her up during tough times. It also reminded her of the choices she'd made. She might have made mistakes pushing Tessa to become a version of Esther, but now she believed Tessa understood she'd only done so out of love. Her heart felt like it was bursting from her chest. Full of love and relief. She and Tessa had finally connected.

Tessa turned to the boy and said something. He unzipped the backpack slung on his shoulder and took out a small television-like contraption. She held it up for Esther to see.

Esther saw her granddaughter's smiling face on the screen. She didn't recognize any of the words printed there or the words Tessa said while pointing to it.

Tessa talked. The boy watched. Tessa gestured between herself and the boy.

All Esther could figure was the boy helped her with whatever the television picture was. It didn't matter what Tessa said. Esther saw the affection between the two of them. She smiled inwardly. Tessa had found her Ricardo and Art.

Her heart ached. And beat erratically. Like a jackhammer tearing it to pieces. But Esther ignored it. She had one more connection to make.

Esther placed her hand on the bed rail, palm up, with her bracelet resting in it. She wiggled her fingers and nodded toward her hand, trying to get Tessa to place her free hand in Esther's. When Tessa did, Esther gestured for the boy to put his hand on top of theirs. It was the only notion of acceptance she could think of.

For a moment, the three of them looked at their stacked hands. Like a team declaring its unity.

Esther was tired. With a final look at her hands entwined with Tessa's, she closed her eyes and saw Art. This time he smiled lovingly at Tessa and the boy. Then he summoned Esther with the crook of his finger.

CHAPTER THIRTY-ONE

Tessa

It was a beautiful day for a burial. Puffy white clouds sped overhead in an ocean blue sky. Tessa stood between her mother and Chip. The two most supportive people in her life. The two who understood her mixed reactions to Grandmother's passing.

When her father had died, Tessa was angry. Angry at a man who Tessa thought didn't love her enough to clean himself up. With her grandmother's death, the anger was different. And it wasn't anger so much as regret. She wished she'd had the chance to know who her grandmother was. She wanted the stories that lived in the charms, the events that made up Esther Wilde. But it wasn't to be. Instead, she had to take those regrets as lessons for life: don't let too much time escape without smoothing bumpy relationships and clearing up misunderstandings.

She looked at Chip and squeezed his hand. He'd become her best friend as well as her boyfriend. He squeezed back, their solidarity firm. For now, anyway.

Chip had handled the details of the funeral and the luncheon that would happen after. She leaned on him, and he propped her up and pushed her forward.

Mayra came. She had seen Grandmother as Esther Wilde, the woman, not just a grandmother or mother-in-law. Tessa saw Mayra dab her eyes with a tissue. Her grief was genuine, and Tessa appreciated it. Mayra was probably the only one who looked past the disease called Alzheimer's and embraced the human within. She saw Grandmother's sassy, spirited side, and Tessa was glad her grandmother had had someone who did.

In Mayra's other hand, she held one of the tribute cards Tessa had written. Tessa didn't have anecdotes of memories to share, intimate details of a close relationship, but she'd tried to paint a word picture of what she'd learned. Grandmother had lived her convictions and wanted what she thought was a good life for her only granddaughter.

On the back of each card was Tessa's website in bold.

Tessa had decided that Grandmother would be proud of her determination and drive. That summer she'd move off campus to an apartment she'd share with Kendra. She would continue her business, helping other artists maximize their potential as best she could, as well as continue with her art history major.

The graveside service ended and Tessa turned away, closing her eyes to the lowering of the casket. She preferred to remember her grandmother through the old charm bracelet. Today, she wore Grandmother's on her right arm, her own on her left.

Chip tugged her hand toward the parking lot while her mom lingered to say a few words to Mayra.

A burst of bright purple caught Tessa's eye as Kendra sidled over, her hair the color of royalty. "I'll meet you at the restaurant, roomie. Gotta say a few words to a cute guy." Kendra cocked her head towards the funeral director's apprentice.

He looked Kendra's way and grinned. Kendra, in turn, waved. Tessa couldn't help but roll her eyes, but with a big smile on her face. "Live for the moment, Kendra," Tessa said.

Kendra nudged Tessa's side. "Listen to you, Miss I'm-All-About-Living-Life-Fully." Then she addressed Chip. "All kidding aside, don't let this girl forget to have fun. She's so intent on pursuing that business and that degree I don't want her to forget to live."

"No worries, Kendra. Later tonight we're going to see *Jaws*. No time to appreciate life than when you're defying death by a shark, right?"

Tessa laughed.

As she climbed into Chip's truck to head to the Celebration of Life luncheon, Tessa said, "You've made a tough moment bearable and not so lonely. Thank you."

He paused and looked almost shyly at her. "I got something for you." He reached into his pocket and pulled out a small box, offering it to her. "Open it."

She did and took a little charm out of the box. The charm consisted of two clasped hands. One wrinkled and one smooth. Each hand featured a wrist on which a tiny charm bracelet rested.

Tessa studied the intricate details of this charm of charm bracelets. It was personal and perfect.

"Chip." She whispered his name.

He leaned over and cupped her face with his hands. "It's how you remember your grandmother best."

"I love you, Chip Foster," Tessa responded and gave him a deep, heartfelt kiss.

Another memory in the making.

THE END

ACKNOWLEDGMENTS

What If?—a question that launched this story.

As a child, I played with my mother's charm bracelet, much as little Tessa played with Esther's, and as I aged, I asked my mom about the charms that filled it. While she didn't suffer from Alzheimer's or dementia, Mom did capture events of her life through those charms. And shared the memories with me. And as an adult, an idea sparked: Could a charm bracelet be a conduit to repairing a relationship? *Voila!*

The Memory Bracelet was born.

But it didn't come to life on its own.

Thank you to my phenomenal Women's Fiction Writers Association critique partners, Nanette Littlestone and Joanne Lehman. Their honesty and insight proved invaluable. A special shout-out to another early reader, Michelle Allen. A writer herself, she was also a caretaker for her Alzheimer's-afflicted mother, becoming both a sounding board and source of research for Esther's struggles.

Without Black Rose Writing, you wouldn't be reading this. Thank you to Reagan Rothe and his team for giving this story a home. His dedication to publishing puts writers in capable and comfortable hands.

While the writing needs critiquing, editing, and publishing, it would be nothing without early readers whose suggestions and observations gave me much to ponder (and to fix!). Thank you, Nancy Scott, Brenda Hargroves, and Joanne Tailele (God rest her soul). And finally, a special thank you to my mentor and writing coach, Celeste Davidson, co-founder of the Bardsy writing community. Her honesty made this story so much better.

And how could writers even muddle through from beginning to end without some emotional support? My best friend and husband for 35 + years, John listens to my rantings about plot holes and narrative arcs, even if he has no idea what I'm talking about. And when I need a break, my grandsons Connor and Mason provide lots of pretend games that allow me to put my mind in new directions and stoke my imagination.

Finally, the biggest thank-you goes to you, the readers. For reading my words and hopefully enjoying the story. I'd love to connect with you (you don't even have to own a charm bracelet!). Please drop me a line at my website pamelaraleigh.bardsy.com.

ABOUT THE AUTHOR

Once a middle school English teacher, Pamela Raleigh turned her love for teaching stories into penning them. Laced with hopefulness, her writing tackles the struggles of relationships of all kinds. Raised in the Blue Ridge Mountains but living most of her life in the sunshine state, Pamela now travels between the two, always picking up new ideas for more stories. She loves the sun and the ocean and walking the trails in North Carolina.

Pamela's happy place is the library. Her favorite food is French Fries, and she's never met a carb she didn't like. She loves meeting new people—some of them ending up in her books. If she's not writing, she's playing the role of Gigi to her young grandsons. Learn more at pamelaraleigh.bardsy.com.

NOTE FROM PAMELA RALEIGH

Word-of-mouth is crucial for any author to succeed. If you enjoyed *The Memory Bracelet*, please leave a review online—anywhere you are able. Even if it's just a sentence or two. It would make all the difference and would be very much appreciated.

Thanks!
Pamela Raleigh

We hope you enjoyed reading this title from:

www.blackrosewriting.com

Subscribe to our mailing list – *The Rosevine* – and receive **FREE** books, daily
deals, and stay current with news about upcoming
releases and our hottest authors.
Scan the QR code below to sign up.

Already a subscriber? Please accept a sincere thank you for being a fan of
Black Rose Writing authors.

View other Black Rose Writing titles at
www.blackrosewriting.com/books and use promo code
PRINT to receive a **20% discount** when purchasing.